AN
Italian
SECRET

BOOKS BY ELLA CAREY

ELLA CAREY

AN *Italian* SECRET

bookouture

Published by Bookouture in 2023

An imprint of Storyfire Ltd.
Carmelite House
50 Victoria Embankment
London EC4Y 0DZ

www.bookouture.com

ISBN: 978-1-83790-030-5
eBook ISBN: 978-1-83790-029-9

For Kelli

CHAPTER 1

CALIFORNIA, PRESENT DAY

ANNIE

Annie yearned for the words she had heard this morning to be swallowed up by the treacherous sea that swirled below the coastal road. It was all she could do not to stop the car, climb out, take in great lungsful of fresh, salty air, and lean against the guard rail that was the only thing between her and the angry ocean while letting the tears that burned her eyes fall.

She increased the speed of her car and reached for the cardboard cup of coffee that she had bought in Monterey. It was her third of the morning, and her hand shook as she brought it to her lips. But she had been working well past midnight last night, catering for a party in one of San Francisco's famous painted ladies' houses. The client had wanted a French theme for a birthday celebration, so Annie had made colorful macaroons that matched the light pink color of the house, tiny chocolate eclairs, and perfect miniature tartes Tatin.

Annie stopped at the ornate gates that led into the private community where her father still lived near Carmel-by-the-Sea, swiping her entry card, her fingers tapping impatiently on the steering wheel while she waited throughout the achingly slow seconds for the gates to slide open and let her in. As soon as there was enough gap for her car to fit, she wound her way up the private road until she came to her father's beautiful home. There were no gates to his property; instead, there was a view of the white-painted wooden house that stood tall and strong on the clifftop where Annie had grown up. She swiped a stray tear across her cheeks.

Bringing the car to a stop, she turned off the engine and closed her eyes. It had been the phone call she had dreaded.

"Annie prepare yourself. Papa has suffered a stroke. Can you cancel everything and come down quickly?"

Annie's older brother, Paul, had said it was time for Annie to come home and say goodbye.

She had asked frantically what hospital her father was in, had leapt out of bed, grabbed her keys, phone, handbag, pulled on a pair of old jeans, and put her long blond hair up into a messy ponytail, frowning at the dark circles beneath her blue eyes.

"He's at home. The doctor said there was no point moving him now..."

At home, where he had suffered with his illness for nearly a year, refusing to be admitted to hospital. Instead, he had hired a private nurse, and spent most of his days looking out at the sea, lost in his own thoughts and increasingly distant from his family. Annie had traveled down to his house at Carmel-by-the-Sea every day that she was not working, running errands, sorting out food shopping, cooking enough meals to last several days and storing them in Papa's freezer, and dealing with the phone calls from friends.

She had done everything she could to try to tempt him back into life, bringing him coffee-table books on architecture to inspire him. He wasn't a great reader of novels and had always loved to look at pictures of houses and gardens. But lately,

Annie had noticed how even his passion for these had waned. Her father had become lost somewhere, perhaps in the past.

The books had lain untouched, and even though Annie had known something had shifted, she had continued to believe he would recover, and was unable to imagine a world without him.

Annie reached for the car door, opened it, and stepped outside onto the raked gravel drive. She rushed to her older sister, Monica, in the doorway.

Immediately, Monica swished toward her, and enveloped her in one of her motherly hugs, but Monica's perfectly styled, short, dark hair, her beautifully made-up face, and her stylish blue summer dress did nothing to quell Annie's apprehension and fear.

"It's okay," Monica whispered. "It's okay, honey."

How can it be okay? Annie did not bother to check the tears that flowed freely down her cheeks.

She tucked her arm through Monica's and allowed herself to be led inside.

Annie lifted her chin bravely at the familiar sight of the photograph of Papa and her late mother, Valerie, on a side table in the vast entrance hall, next to the telephone underneath the staircase that curved elegantly to the upper floors. It was a photograph that had sat in the same place for as long as Annie could remember. Papa and Mom were standing arm in arm out in the garden of this wonderful house. She had lost her mother, and now her father was ailing too.

As she walked with Monica into the living room, Annie dreaded every step. The blue sea spread out marvelously beyond the floor-to-ceiling windows. There was no sign of the swirling undercurrent that beat against the cliffs below. From here, the sun glittered on the water, and a yacht was sailing past. Annie could see legs dangling off the boat, people out to enjoy the day.

She gasped when she saw her father propped up in the

hospital bed that he had bought so that he could stay at home. The nurse was right next to him, and in the window, Paul was standing with his hands on his hips, staring out at the ocean. He had said this morning that the doctor had been here for two hours and was returning after morning surgery.

At the sound of Annie and Monica's footsteps, Paul turned, his brow furrowed with worry, and his dark eyebrows drawn together in a frown.

"He's holding out to say goodbye to you, Annie," Paul muttered. He took in a ragged breath and his eyes searched her face.

Unlike Monica, Paul was making no pretense that this was manageable. While Monica had mothered Papa during the last months, Paul had gone into an unashamed tailspin. Annie couldn't remember how many frantic late-night phone calls she had answered from her brother. He worried about Papa insisting that he stay home, what they were going to do with the house, whether they should move Oscar into an aged care facility, why he was refusing to be in hospital. Paul raged against their father's acceptance of his fate, his lack of fight. Once, he had told Annie, his voice breaking, that he could not cope with the fact that their father had given up.

Paul had urged Papa to try every alternative medicine there was. He had brought faith healers to the house, and eventually it had been Papa who had laid an old hand on his son's shoulder and told him that what was happening was natural. That he was not going to fight the end of his life. Papa knew that he was going. He had said that his body was looking for a way to die.

Annie had tried to come to terms with Papa's philosophical approach and had busied herself doing what she did best—helping him and cooking—but now reality was right in front of her, and she knew that it would only be hours until it was time to say goodbye.

"Annie."

Annie sobbed again, and she rushed toward the dear sound of Papa's voice. "I'm here," she managed, grief already lacing itself like a corset around her insides.

His eyes were closed, and his papery skin was pale. He had lost so much weight in the last few months that he was barely recognizable.

"I'm about to give him some morphine," the nurse murmured. "Once I do that, he will lose consciousness. He wanted to wait until you were here, Annie."

Annie acknowledged the nurse, but leaned forward and clasped her father's still hand. "Papa?" she whispered. "I love you," she said. *What else was there to say?*

"I love you too," Papa murmured. His words were slightly slurred, but they were clear enough to Annie.

"I don't want to say goodbye," she whispered. And she felt the unmistakable weight of his hand on hers. They had sat like that, the two of them, a few months ago when the diagnosis seemed grim.

As her mind spun into turmoil, panicking about a life without her darling papa, wanting him back, wanting more time, knowing there were so many things still left to say, he began mumbling in a low, uneven voice. Annie struggled to make any sense of it.

Monica came and knelt on his other side. "What is it, Papa?" she asked.

"A letter," he managed. But his voice was strained with effort. "It is in my desk. In my study. For Annie."

What was in it? Why now? Surely, if it was anything important, he would have given it to her before now? Opposite her, she sensed the nurse getting out the medicine.

"It's time," the nurse said gently.

"I love you," Oscar whispered. "Annie. My beloved child."

"Goodbye, Papa, I love you too. Always," Annie managed.

Monica still clutched Papa's other hand. Paul came and

stood, stroking their father's tired gray head. "My darlings," Papa murmured.

"Are you ready?" the nurse asked.

Of course she wasn't ready. She never would be. All she wanted to do was carry on holding his hand. Somewhere in the distance, she heard her siblings mutter their assent. And she closed her eyes and swallowed. She would never see him again. He had always felt like home for her. She would always remember his joy and passion for designing houses, the way he welcomed his clients and friends. His books, his beloved rituals... Coffee in the mornings in his favorite chair overlooking the sea while classical music played on the radio, the glass of red wine in the evenings in the same chair while he watched the sun go down. The way he had been hopeless at cooking, leaving Annie to take over and discover her own passion for creating beautiful food.

"You are happy to have morphine? Mr. Reynolds?" the nurse asked.

An unbearable rock formed in Annie's stomach and she stared at the floor.

"Annie?" her father whispered.

She squeezed his hand.

"I love you more than words could ever say. Remember that no matter what happens, darling." And, as if with one great last dignified effort, Papa looked to the nurse and nodded.

"Papa?" she asked as she had always asked, knowing that he would give her the answers she sought.

But the nurse administered the morphine through the drip, and he rested his head back and slowly, his eyes closed.

He would rest until he drew his final breath.

He had no more words left.

Annie buried her head on her sister's shoulder.

.   .   .

The following morning, Annie stood in front of her father's rolltop desk. There was a small key tied with a pale blue ribbon to the locked drawer underneath. She had always been fascinated by this as a child and had begged and begged Papa to let her see what was inside. It had become a game. He never told her. But he had allowed her to create fanciful stories about what might be in there. Letters from witches, secret potions to make magical gardens, and long after her mother had died, Annie had imagined that there was something special from Valerie in there. Something her mother had only wanted their father to see.

Monica's voice filtered through from the living room. The nurse had left, and the undertakers were here to remove Papa's body. Annie had not been able to face this. She, Monica, and Paul had sat with him all night, until he had taken his last breath this morning, just as the dawn had risen over the sea.

The sun now shone in a glimmering arc across the water, and the sound of the waves beating against the cliffs below the house was a low accompaniment to Monica's voice. They had both slipped into their usual roles, Monica and Paul. Monica had offered to deal with the undertaker, and Paul had gone downstairs to the kitchen to make phone calls. Annie could imagine him now, pacing around the room, his mobile glued to his ear, talking in that urgent way he had.

Annie had been amazed at how her older brother and sister had been able to move into organizational mode so quickly. Gone was the panic that had enveloped Paul in the past months. Maybe this was because finally he could do something. The entire situation was not slithering beyond his control. The attorney in him had taken over. And Monica's profession as a realtor had come to the fore when she had started talking to the undertaker about the best way to access the house.

But Annie had stood at the window after Papa had died, her arms wrapped around her body, the devastating loss washing over her. This was going to change her life forever. Papa had been her one constant.

Now, she managed a watery smile at the thought of the little girl she had once been, so keen to find out what was in this locked drawer. She hesitated to open it. Because doing so seemed to make the fact that Papa was no longer here seem more real. Taking a breath, she turned the key in the lock and slid the wooden drawer open, her hand moving with surprising smoothness, for there was just a single envelope inside. Nothing else. Annie frowned as she pulled it out, and her eyes grazed the handwriting. It was addressed to her.

Annie.

She held it close for a moment, reluctant to open it, still reluctant to acknowledge what opening it meant. Finally, after a few moments, she moved across to stand in front of the vast picture window and looked out at the sea. It was the only way she could cope right now. The sea had always been her lifeblood. And she knew that the water ran deep in her father's soul too. They had been for so many walks along the local beaches together, combing for shells after her mother had died, and then taking long quiet walks together as Annie had grown older. He had listened intently while she had discussed the difficulties of her career.

She had always told him everything. And she felt that trust had always been returned. Was there something he hadn't told her?

The envelope was unsealed. There was no need for a paperknife and Annie slipped her fingers underneath the lip and pulled out a single sheet of paper and two brass keys, a small one and a large one. The paper was thin, and Papa's sloped handwriting filled the page.

Annie sank into Papa's wingback chair by the window, wrapped one arm tightly around her waist, and began to read.

CHAPTER 2

TUSCANY, ITALY—EARLY SUMMER, 1944

CARA

Cara stopped at the entrance to the magical gardens of the Villa Rosa and looked up toward the old house's peach-and-rose-colored façade. The Villa Rosa shimmered in the early-morning sun, and the soft hills in the distance looked as if they had been shaped by the palms of gentle giants. The scent of Contessa Evelina Messina's roses and geraniums was so intoxicating that it was easy to imagine there was no war if Cara closed her eyes and pretended the Villa Rosa was all there was. But gentleness had left the world in the past five years, and Cara had become used to staring out of the windows of the striking villa where she worked as the Contessa's secretary, thinking that Italy had been forgotten.

The world seemed focused on the imminent French landings and on the American air raids on Japan. By contrast, Tuscany had been left to suffer under German Field Marshal Albert Kesselring's forces in the mountains north of Florence, where Italian laborers had been forced to dig a dense network of fortifications called the Gothic Line. None of them knew how long the Nazi occupation of Tuscany was going to last.

Cara's beloved valley where she had lived her entire life with Papa in the small pensione, the hotel that he had always run in the village below the hill, was cloaked in fear. The pensione had been closed by the Nazis, and gunfire ricocheted through the hills on a regular basis, and the sound of terrified citizens screaming at the hands of the local Nazis who had stormed the area when the Germans invaded last year was torture. In the evenings, Papa sat with his head buried in his hands.

Cara paused and frowned over the valley, with its familiar view of two castles sitting proudly on the distant hills, as they had done since the thirteenth century. The same farmhouses that had dotted the valley for centuries were all there, war or no war, their terracotta roofs shimmering against the soft green of the olive groves and cypress trees, but the tiny village where Cara lived sat as if in a terrified huddle below the Villa Rosa. Coming up here felt like walking into a different world, allowing her to leave all the horrors below, if only for a short while.

The Contessa Evelina Messina had taken over the management of her late husband's villa and his forty-seven farms in the beautiful valley after he had died in 1935, working without fatigue to ensure that the farming system that had been in place in Tuscany for seven centuries did not change with the death of the head of the Messina family. The Contessa had managed the family's relationships with their tenant farmers as if she had been born to do the job, continuing the traditional system whereby the landowner contributed half of the costs toward farming while the tenant contributed half and they both shared the profits equally.

Contessa Evelina Messina had become respected and admired by the local tenants in the last few years and Cara had jumped at the opportunity to work as her secretary. Cara had only worked as the general runaround, bookkeeper, secretary, and solver of problems at her father's pensione, and thought she would be the last person whom the glamorous Evelina Messina would consider worthy of a position at the Villa Rosa. But the Contessa had looked at her hard during the interview and declared that Cara was perfect.

And Papa had encouraged her. He had thought that the Contessa might be a wonderful role model for her.

Cara shook her head at her darling papa's kindly intentions as she let herself into the front door of the villa using the key that Evelina Messina had given her recently. Like so many locals, she had never locked a door in her life until the Nazi occupation began.

Cara stood in the grand entrance hall, bathed in sunshine from the fanlight that sat like a peacock's tail over the front door.

"Cara?" Evelina Messina's voice rang out from her charming office to the right of the entrance hall.

"Si, good morning, Contessa." Cara whipped into action, making her way toward the Contessa's office.

The Contessa arrived in the doorway. Evelina Messina always *arrived*, she never just came in. Now, she stood in a rose silk dress that Cara knew her employer had owned since 1939, with a white carnation pinned to the front, and her blond hair brushed back from her forehead in soft golden waves that fell to her shoulders. Evelina was in her forties, but she had the complexion of a girl of twenty-one, and her beautiful green eyes curved downwards in a perpetual whimsical look, just like her youngest son, Rafaeli.

Rafaeli.

No. Raf would not enter Cara's thoughts today.

She straightened her simple blue cotton dress, aware, as usual, that she could never compare to her employer's elegance, nor her understated sophistication and patrician bearing. She drew her hand up to smooth her hair in its long, dark ponytail.

The Contessa was pale, and dark circles from lack of sleep bloomed beneath her eyes. She glanced about the room as if she were expecting someone to climb in the window of her late husband's office and attack them. The idea was not so far-fetched these days.

But the Contessa had gone to great lengths to ensure that the Villa Rosa would not be the subject of the Nazis' anger or pillaging. Other landowners in the valley had rallied to provide food and supplies to the growing bands of local partisans who were hiding out in the forests, and some of the Contessa's neighbors were taking in Allied soldiers who had escaped from prisoner-of-war camps, but Evelina had informed the staff that it was too much of a risk for her to defy the Nazis, because she had forty-seven farms under her care. *What would happen to all her tenants*, she reasoned, *were she to take the risk of helping the partisans, and the Nazis retaliated?*

Privately, Cara knew that Evelina Messina's hesitation to commit to the cause of the Italian resistance, and the local partisans, was because she was an Italian aristocrat, and everyone knew that the upper classes in Italy all expected Mussolini to rise again and put everything right.

"Cara, sit down. Please." The Contessa indicated toward the Louis XV chairs covered in pale-blue silk that sat either side of the fireplace, which was surrounded by built-in bookshelves.

Cara glanced quickly at her employer. It was unlike her not to jump straight into her instructions for the day.

The Contessa moved to the fireplace and pressed her hands into the wooden mantelpiece, closing her eyes, and bowing her head, until finally she lifted her gaze to meet the photograph of her late husband, Arturo, that hung in pride of place. Evelina Messina murmured a small prayer out loud.

Cara sat up in her seat, beginning to feel worried. "Please? What is it, Contessa?"

The Contessa had only ever opened up to Cara once when Cara had witnessed her employer break down after her eldest son, Nicolas, had abandoned the Villa Rosa in the summer of 1940. Mother and son had fought bitterly about Italy's involvement in Hitler's war; the last thing Nicolas wanted was to be a soldier, and Cara had heard him shouting at his mother that he was a businessman, not a fighter. In the end, the Contessa had let him go, but she had left everything in his bedroom, just as it had always been when he had been home. The Contessa clearly hoped that her beloved eldest son would return one day. When he had marched out of the house with his manservant and a retinue of exquisite Italian luggage, the Contessa had retreated into a dignified silence.

Evelina turned around in a slow semicircle until she faced Cara. The older woman's fists were clenched such that her knuckles had turned white.

Cara's mind went back to that day. *Had something happened to Nicolas?* Evelina would grieve terribly if her eldest son had come to harm, and she could not be there to help.

And then Cara blanched. It couldn't be Raf. It simply could not.

Cara had sworn not to think of him, even though they could be nothing more to each other than mother's secretary and son of the house. She half rose from her seat, only to have Evelina Messina raise a hand and indicate that she sit back down.

"You must prepare yourself."

Cara gasped. The impulse that had risen within her at the thought of anything happening to Raf intensified tenfold. "What is wrong, Contessa?" she said, her nose starting to tickle uncontrollably, and tears wanting to well behind her eyelids. "Please—"

"I am afraid there is no easy way to tell you this." The

Contessa folded her arms, her eyes searching Cara's face. "There has been an incident. Your father was involved."

"Papa?" Papa had gone out to visit with one of his old farmer friends in the valley for the weekend. He was worried about his friend's ailing health and was going to ensure that the man's wife and daughter were managing, so had stayed with them overnight and was due home this morning.

"I have just had an urgent call that your father has been shot."

Cara stood up. She went to stand behind her chair so that there was some barrier between her and the Contessa's words. It couldn't be true. It wasn't true.

Not Papa. Not Papa who had survived the death of his own wife, Cara's mother, and had stoically raised Cara on his own. He had welcomed everyone wholeheartedly into his simple *pensione* until the government had cracked down, and his British expatriate guests who had refused to leave their beloved Tuscany were declared enemy aliens and eventually thrown into detention. This had been a situation that had left Papa heartbroken. He had tried to reason with the authorities to no avail.

A bird started singing in the garden, and the sun threw pale lemon light on the small golden clock that sat on the marble coffee table between the two silken chairs.

"Where is he? Please. Is he still out on the farm?"

The Contessa nodded.

"Please. I will need to go to the farm immediately, Contessa. I will make up for any lost time. A bicycle? Do you have a bicycle I could borrow?" Cara fluttered about with her hands. "Do you know what happened?"

"It is not good," the Contessa whispered. A troubled expression passed across her face. "Apparently a pair of Nazis came and tried to demand that the ailing farmer hand over the last of his livestock to them. Your father stood up to them, and one of them tried to rape the farmer's daughter. Again, your father intervened. My understanding is the second Nazi shot him. Word was sent to the villa just now. One of the farmer's neighbors rode all the way here and appeared at the kitchen door, quite distressed."

Cara stared at the older woman in disbelief.

"I am sorry," the Contessa murmured. "It was a terrible incident."

Just then, the Contessa's gardener, Alphonso, appeared with his hat in his hand at the door. "Signorina, I wanted to pay my respects, and to say that I am sorry. Your father is a good man."

"Please, I need to go to him," Cara said, and her body burned, and then froze, and all she could see was her papa.

"Alphonso will drive you to the farm," Evelina said. "Take my late husband's car. It has more fuel left than mine."

"Of course, Contessa," Cara heard Alphonso say.

Cara knew she was pale as a new bridal dress, knew she was shaking, but she sent the gentle gardener a brave smile and clenched her hands by her sides. She hardly knew what she said to the Contessa, and she followed Alphonso out through the entrance hall and into the morning sunshine. For once, she was only thankful that the Nazis had allowed the Contessa to keep her cars due to her loyalty to Mussolini.

Soon, in a blur, she was sitting beside Alphonso in the late Arturo Messina's estate car, the windows open to the warm breeze outside. The car purred down the neatly raked driveway, and Cara stared straight ahead. Her eyes alighted on a figure coming through the Villa Rosa's wrought-iron gates. Cara leaned forward in her seat, her heart beating wildly.

And she sensed Alphonso flicking his gaze toward her. "Rafaeli," he murmured as he slowed the great car down.

Cara took in a sharp breath. "Alphonso, we cannot stop."

"But, signorina..."

Raf shaded his eyes against the morning sun, and Cara's hand flew to her mouth when they drew closer, and she saw that Raf's arm was in a sling. "He is injured..." she said, closing her eyes. She could not be distracted by this. She must not be distracted.

But Raf placed his good hand on the edge of the window as they drew up, and his eyes scoured Cara's face. "*Mia Bella*," he whispered.

Alphonso cleared his throat.

"We have to go," Cara said to Alphonso.

But Raf's gaze raked over her tearstained face, and his eyes crinkled in worry. He was as handsome as ever, tall, skin the color of local honey, and there were those eyes that mirrored his mother's. Cara wrapped her arms around her aching insides. He had broadened out since she last saw him. Now, he looked more like a man than the youth who had gone away to war.

"Signorina Cara's father is in trouble. He has had an altercation with the Nazis down at one of the farms and he's injured," Alphonso said.

Cara tipped her head back against the seat—thank goodness Alphonso was here. That he could manage to string a sentence together without his voice breaking, along with his heart.

"I should come with you."

Cara heard Alphonso's sharp intake of breath. She could not let the Contessa's employee think that there had ever been anything untoward going on between her and Raf. It had been more than enough when she had overheard the Contessa telling Raf that if there was anything between him and Cara, he could kiss the Villa Rosa goodbye. They had been spending time together, but Cara had ended the relationship after that. She could not live with herself if Raf was cut off from his family and the home he loved. And it went without saying that she could not afford to lose her job. Since that day, the Contessa had retreated into silence and had not said a thing to Cara. It was as if she did not matter... except as a secretary. She had to remember her place.

"No." Her voice came out firm. "We must go now."

Alphonso nodded, and Cara knew that Raf was searching her face. But she shook her head resolutely.

"Please, Alphonso..." Her words came out as a whisper.

The chauffeur drove on.

If Papa was injured seriously, it would be impossible to know how to go on.

CHAPTER 3

ANNIE

My dear Annie,

I know this letter is going to come as a shock. Indeed, it is one of the most difficult letters I have ever had to write in my life.

When you read it, you may think of me as a coward. I would not blame you, and yet, I am still going to beg you to forgive both of us. Valerie and me.

My darling girl, there is no straightforward way to tell you this.

When you came into our lives, a perfect baby, with pearly fingernails, and feet as soft as butter, when you gave us both your first toothless smiles, and when your little eyes lit up, and your chubby legs started jigging in delight at the sight of us, when you uttered your first word, Mumma, this moment meant as much to Valerie as any natural birth mother would feel.

Valerie did not give birth to you, but you have always been our daughter.

I know, at this point, you are reading this in horror. I only wish I were there to encircle you in my arms, and to tell you that everything was okay. I understand that what I am about to tell you is going to break your heart, but, please, read on, and don't give up on me.

You, my darling, are a child of Italy. We adopted you from a charming woman who comes from an enchanted place under the Tuscan sun. There is a villa overlooking a valley full of olive groves, where tall, strong cypress trees stand like sentinels.

I want you to go back there. I want you to discover who you truly are, to meet your other family, the family of your birth and to learn of your past and your present.

Now, I come to the most momentous news. You are the owner of an exquisite villa in Tuscany. The Villa Rosa stands tall, proud, and beautiful, just like you.

Please, go and visit the notary in the village at the bottom of the hill below the villa. He will tell you everything.

With all my love,

Your loving father, who views you more dearly than anyone could imagine, and just as dearly as you have always known.

Papa

Annie sank back in the chair. A breeze had gathered outside, and sea air was flowing through the open window of his study, as if Papa was saying goodbye to her.

His letter rustled in her hand.

Soft voices came from the room next door. The undertakers were departing with Papa's body.

Annie waited until she heard the front door closing, and

then she moved slowly toward Monica and Paul. She stood in the doorway and simply held the letter out toward them.

She turned away to look at the sea. If only she could reach out to Papa, but he wasn't here anymore.

Paul took it and read, his back to her, facing the window with his head bent.

"Paul? Did you have any idea?" She might even have been born with a different name.

Paul swung around to her, his face expressionless and blank. He had stepped into the domain in which he was comfortable. The legal man. "Of course not." He sounded brisk.

He sent a worried glance toward Monica and handed the letter to her.

"I need to check the veracity of this. Where is this Villa Rosa? How on earth can you own it, Annie? And if these people have left you a legacy in Tuscany, why did they not tell you themselves?" Paul was talking in that low, clipped, professional voice that she had heard him use with Papa when they were discussing business matters.

And suddenly something reared up in Annie. A swell of hot fire. The real question was why had Papa kept such a secret from her? Why had *he* not told her? Had she been judged too young, too immature, too darned incapable of knowing who she really was? Did she not deserve to know? Have a right to know before she was thirty-three years old?

Monica finished reading the letter and held it by her side. "I'm speechless."

"Come and sit in the living room." Paul frowned intently. He held out his arm, and his brown eyes were serious, and full of concern.

Clearly Monica and Paul had not known who she was either. Why was she a secret? With so much for her to get her head around, Annie took his arm in a daze and let him lead the way. Monica followed behind them.

Papa's empty hospital bed sat in the living room; the sheets pulled back. The room that had always felt so filled with love and family seemed strange and still. The space where she had had a family was gone.

Annie slumped down in one of the chairs that overlooked the sea. Monica handed her a glass of water, and Annie cradled it in her palms.

Paul opened his mouth to speak, and Monica turned expectantly toward him.

"The first thing I need to do is ring the notary," Paul said. "We need to get to the bottom of this as soon as possible. The whole thing sounds ridiculous."

But Annie held up her hand, her words coming out in a clear, distinctive voice that surprised even herself. "No."

Her elder brother and sister turned toward her.

But she held firm. "Thank you. But I will handle it."

A deep indentation formed between Paul's eyes.

"I'm going to go to Tuscany."

Annie held Monica and Paul's gaze. Papa's empty bed sat, impersonal, white, the life in it gone. The life she had always thought she knew had gone with him. And she needed to figure out who she really was.

CHAPTER 4

Annie stood in the kitchen of her apartment in San Francisco. Monica had suggested she buy it because of its postcard view of the bay. Paul had said it was a sound investment, something she could hold on to even when she met someone and decided to start a family of her own, moving out into the suburbs, far from her little piece of paradise here.

The tiles beneath her feet in the kitchen were made of terracotta. She had been drawn not to their practicality, but to their warmth, to something in the way they had aged, so that they held a rich patina, with underlying pale colors hinting through the faded foreground.

She grew herbs on the balcony that were traditionally used in Italian cooking. Oregano, rosemary, vivid green basil. In a larger pot, there was a lemon tree. And after long evenings spent catering, or weekend afternoons cooking for weddings or anniversaries, Annie loved nothing more than to come home and fix herself a meal consisting of no more than three ingredients. The first one was always pasta, and the second often crisp, fried, unsmoked Italian pancetta, cooked in plenty of olive oil. Then, she would add arugula—the wild rocket that she bought from her favorite Italian stallholder at the local markets where she always shopped.

If she were honest with herself, she had long dreamed of going to Italy someday. She had felt a connection to the country and she had just thought it was the food. But was it something else? Something deeper?

She had stood at Papa's funeral, her grief feeling like a lead weight in her heart. Saying goodbye to him felt even more heart-breaking when she had so many unanswered questions about her own life.

Monica had been quietly supportive since Papa had died, and Paul had sat with her while she spoke with Papa's attorney here in San Francisco about the strange and shocking news she had been given on the day that Papa died. And now, her suit-cases were packed by the front door, ready for the trip she was about to take to Tuscany.

"You can be sure we will take care of everything," Lucy said.

Annie turned and smiled at the young woman whom she had never regretted employing since the first day they had met.

Lucy held Annie's cat, Portia, snuggling her soft face against her cheek. "Lauren and I can manage and, honestly, the chance to live in your apartment for a while? It will be a godsend. I love my parents, but some things are beginning to grate."

"Thank you," Annie said, meaning it. One of the hardest hurdles she'd had to face was who to leave Portia with while she went away. She was devoted to the cat, and who knew how long this was going to take? Monica had come to feed Portia if Annie had ever gone away for a weekend here or there, but she lived a long drive away.

Annie's weekends away were usually work-related, as she hated to turn down clients who might want her out at their country homes to cater for family or major social events. And Portia was an apartment cat. Once, Annie had tried to leave her with a friend. But Portia had spent the entire time wedged under the kitchen table, hissing at anyone who came by, and refusing to eat a bite of food.

Annie reached out and stroked her furry friend. Portia was good company at home. While Annie was contented living by herself, it was comforting to know that her little cat was waiting for her no matter what. And she loved the way Portia wound herself around her legs, and mewed in a way that she never did for anyone else. It was going to be difficult to leave Portia for so long, but she was grateful for Lucy.

Annie started to go through a mental checklist. "You will have plenty of backup with the team. And I'll be on the end of my phone should you need me at any time. I'll check in every morning, and—"

Lucy held up a hand. "Annie, how you've got through this last month is beyond me." She lowered her gaze to the floor, her sandy eyelashes grazing her cheeks, and her strawberry blond bob falling around her face. "I'm sorry I mentioned my parents." She shaped her head. "It was insensitive of me."

Annie reached out and placed a reassuring hand on her employee's arm. "Not at all."

She sighed. She had not told a soul beyond Monica and Paul of her extraordinary discovery. It still seemed fantastic that tomorrow she was about to board a plane and fly to Tuscany. And yet, when she thought about it now, she felt, somewhere deep inside, that she was going home.

CHAPTER 5

CARA

Alphonso was not driving slowly, but the journey in the great estate car to the farm where Papa had been shot seemed achingly slow. The fields spreading out either side of the road felt endless, and the cypress trees that had been planted in honor of the fallen locals in the Great War threw slim pencil shades across the car as they passed out of the road from Cortona.

Cara looked over at the Contessa's loyal employee. Small streaks of gray had begun to thread like wisps of molten silver through Alphonso's dark hair.

"My father has just risked his life to help his friends." Cara bowed her head and shook it. She curled her lip. She could trust Alphonso. "And I am doing nothing. Alphonso, I cannot go on like this."

Alphonso turned his round, honest face toward her, his eyes full of sympathy, but stayed quiet. The gentle purr of the engine was the only sound to break the silence.

"If Papa is really hurt, if..." Her words were shaky, and she swallowed hard. "Anyway. I can't go on doing nothing and playing it safe. Not after this."

"The Contessa is making decisions that will protect her farmers."

Cara started at the way he knew exactly what she was talking about. "But I am not the Contessa. It is time for me to make up my own mind."

The Contessa was dismissive of the partisans, as she felt they were a disorganized rabble who would do Italy more harm than good. Indeed, back in March, a group of partisans had thrown a bomb at an SS unit in Rome, and in retaliation, the Nazis had slaughtered three hundred and thirty-five innocent Italians. But in the valley, the local partisans were carrying out random attacks on individual Nazis, while trying to destroy the German communication lines and munitions storage facilities. It was said that up to half of the Allied soldiers who had been detained in Italy had escaped their prisoner-of-war camps and were helping the partisans.

"If you take risks, you risk her, signorina. She trusts you."

"Yes. But she is protecting herself."

Alphonso lifted one of his hands from the steering wheel a moment, and then placed it back down. "Signorina Cara, please. You are so closely associated with her."

Cara sighed loudly.

"But if you want to talk about doing more, then we can do that when we get back home."

Cara hardly moved in her seat. She had suspected it. Had suspected that Alphonso was helping the partisans in some way. She also thought that the Contessa's cook, Bettina, might be in on something. Sometimes, when Cara came into the kitchen, Alphonso and Bettina would stop what they were talking about and change the topic too quickly.

"And," Alphonso went on quietly, "perhaps you might speak with Rafaeli."

Cara stared out the window, taken aback. Where did Raf fit in with the resistance? He always seemed so obedient, following his mother's directive, and wanting to be a good son to her. It was impossible to imagine him joining the partisans.

Alphonso slowed the car and was turning into the farmyard. He brought the car to a standstill, and the black hood shimmered in the burning sun through the gleaming windscreen. Alphonso began to open his door, planning, no doubt, to come around and hold her door open for her, but before his foot touched the ground she was out.

"Thank you, Alphonso," she called, remembering her manners. But she flew through the courtyard toward the simple wooden green front door of the farmhouse, pushing it open, and muttering a quiet curse that the farmer was still too trusting, not locking it up.

"Papa?" she called, her voice close to breaking.

The kitchen was empty, the polished brick floor swept clean, and everything mercifully looking as if it was in place. But a strange silence hung over the house.

And then she heard it. Footsteps on the stairs. At the same time, Alphonso came in through the open kitchen door behind her, turning it and locking it securely.

"*Buongiorno*, Cara," the farmer said as he appeared at the bottom of the narrow staircase. His face was ashen, his breath labored, and a question formed on Cara's lips about how he was coping with his infected lung, but he beckoned her upstairs. "Come. Your father is in my bed."

Cara moved toward the simple stone staircase, the soles of her shoes clattering noisily. "How is your daughter? How is my papa?" Her words came out as a sob, and she could hear Alphonso's steady tread on the staircase behind her.

Cara reached for the simple cross that hung around her neck and murmured a small prayer. *Please let Papa survive.*

Don't take him away, don't let him die in such awful circumstances.

"My wife is looking after our daughter in her bedroom. She is deeply distressed. She is only twelve..."

So young. Cara nodded dumbly.

The farmer said no more, making way for her as soon as they reached the door to his bedroom on the small landing upstairs. She stumbled into the bedroom, shock shooting through her at the sight of Papa, laid flat out on the bed, his eyes closed, and a great red stain spreading across his stomach.

Cara let out an involuntary cry. She dropped to her knees at his side and grasped Papa's pale waxy hand. "Please," she whispered. "We need a doctor!" She turned around wildly to the farmer.

But the farmer clasped his hands in front of him and looked down at the ground. Next to him, dear Alphonso stood with his hat in his hands, and silently he shook his head.

"The *dottore* has just left," the farmer said. "I am afraid there is no hope, and all we can do is wait."

"No!" Cara's shout burst through the air in the quiet room. But then she felt the gentle squeeze of Papa's hand on hers.

"*Bambina?*" Papa whispered, addressing her in the way he used to when she was a small girl.

Tears fell silently down her cheeks, and she swallowed, but her throat stuck. "Please, Papa, don't leave me," she said helplessly. She knew she was being selfish, could see the extent of the wound.

"*Bambina.*" Papa's voice was faint. "These are terrible times; awful things are happening." He whispered the words, but his grip on her hand was firm. "Cara, *tesoro,* please. Go on and continue the fight. Stand up for your friends and neighbors. Help them... And live a life of which you can be proud. It is all we can do. I love you Cara, be brave." And Papa squeezed her hand one last time, and then, he closed his eyes.

"Papa, I promise... But please, don't leave us," she whispered.

Cara buried her head in his hand, and after a while, his grip grew slack. He was her family, and she had lost him. He was the bravest, most loving man she had ever known, and he could never be replaced.

CHAPTER 6

ANNIE

"There are complications."

Annie frowned at the young notary sitting opposite her. Outside, the air shimmered with heat. The sky was cerulean blue, and a tall line of cypresses ran along the road that led out of the Tuscan village like pretty telegraph poles. The bus driver had told everyone on the way here that the cypresses had been planted to commemorate local inhabitants who had fallen during the First World War.

The two brass keys, one large, one small, that had accompanied Papa's letter sat on the notary's desk.

"There is no documentation."

There were no title deeds, nothing for her to sign, nothing for her to look at so that she could understand why she had inherited the villa in the first place.

"The Villa Rosa has been empty for decades. That is all I know, signora."

Annie wiped her hand across her perspiring forehead. They

were going around in circles. "I see. But could you clarify what you mean about complications?"

"After the Contessa died, we know nothing of what happened to her descendants."

Annie eyed the young notary. Sweat was beading on his upper lip too. "Are you saying that the ownership might be contested?"

The notary scrolled through documents on his computer, his eyes tracking back and forth whip-fast. "My only instructions are to allow you to enter the property and take possession. There is an email from your lawyer in San Francisco..."

"Would there be someone in the village who might know what happened to the remaining members of the Messina family, someone who knows the history around here, who might be able to help?"

The notary looked uncomfortable. Two indentations appeared between his eyebrows, and he shook his head in small, precise movements. "I do not know anything. The villa is a mystery. Most of the people around here see it as a haunted house. Is that how you say it?"

Annie wanted to rest her head in her hands. *Yes, but, you see, this is my family, potentially. This is who I am. Someone must know something.*

"Is the villa inhabitable?"

The young man shrugged. "I do not know." He looked at his watch. "I am sorry, signorina bella."

Annie raised a brow. "You are not familiar with the Villa Rosa?"

The young notary paused and then moved on to a different tack. "My father used to attend to these matters. I contacted him after I heard from your attorney in the United States. My parents are traveling for several months. They left for an extended holiday, a vacation once he retired. I am only stepping in until someone more permanent wants to take over the role of notary. Normally, I live in Rome, and I don't work here. I see no problems with this situation. If the Messina family descendants contact me, I will let you know. I have not been to the villa myself, but my father says it is exceptionally beautiful, if a little... decrepit. I wish you the absolute best of luck, Signorina Reynolds."

Annie closed her eyes and nodded. Exhaustion was starting to pound through her system once again. The long flight to Rome, the train connection to Florence, and then the bus journey out to Cortona where she was staying, then the ride to this tiny village beneath the Villa Rosa to see the notary. She had been too fatigued to begin to comprehend the breathtaking beauty that had greeted her when she had stepped off the bus yesterday. When she had arrived, the valley had been cloaked in a green stillness, and now she wished she could have bottled it.

The sky had been pale blue, with proper fat white fluffy clouds, and she had found a charming trattoria run by an elderly husband and wife who had cooked for her: crostini Toscani—chicken liver pâté served on thin pieces of toasted bread—panzanella—a salad made of crisp bread, tomatoes, onion, basil, olive oil and balsamic vinegar all tossed together, and then Bistecca alla Fiorentina served simply seasoned with rosemary and sage. Then, they had carefully brought out a torta di ceci—a sweet chickpea flour pancake—followed by biscotti di Prato—the local sweet biscuits made of flour, sugar and nuts— along with a glass of local vin santo.

She took the keys back. "Thank you for your help," she said. "Please let me know when the documentation arrives."

Paul would be appalled. He would insist that she not even take the keys to the villa before she had perused and understood the documentation.

But Paul was thousands of miles away. He had offered to come with her when she decided to travel to Italy, as he had said that she would need someone here to take care of things. Perhaps he was right... Or maybe, he was wrong.

There had been nothing on the Internet, no photographs, no mention of the Messina family. There were no answers, only questions. It was, in a strange way, exciting to have no idea what lay ahead.

The notary stood up. Annie shook his hand.

It was time.

CHAPTER 7

The gates to the Villa Rosa were made of rusty wrought iron. A deep red patina was layered over the original black and a series of flowers were embedded in the design, formed delicately out of intricate iron lacework. There were tulips, daffodils, pansies, and winsome irises. Annie traced her finger over the rough surface. Someone had once loved this place. These details were not only timeless, but still charming today. She had walked up the hill from the notary's office in the village to the villa, out through the old village gates, following the steep road that afforded a stunning vista of the green valley below.

She frowned, looking for some evidence that the keys that she had tucked away in her handbag were going to be of use. But the gate was already slightly open. Annie placed the larger key into the keyhole, and it fit perfectly, but because the gate was ajar, she reached for the rusted handle and pushed it with her hand. The gate gave way with a loud creak, and she was in.

Annie stood at the base of the steep hill. The garden had been arranged into a series of terraces. The bottom terrace held olive trees, their leaves silvery and soft against the eggshell blue sky. Small, hard buds of ripening fruit sat on the branches, and on the next terrace, there was a wide orchard. Annie placed her hands on her hips and looked up at apricots, apples, and cherry trees. How wonderful. Were she to stay here, she would bottle them.

She shook her head. She must not think in that way.

Drystone walls, tangled with ivy, separated one level of the terraced hillside from the next, and above the orchard, she peered up at a huge stone pagoda, covered by tiny climbing roses.

And then there was the villa. Annie shaded her eyes against the pale rays of sunlight that beamed onto the pink and apricot façade of the gorgeous old building. There were four sets of French doors on the first floor and faded green shutters, and then this pattern was repeated on the second floor. The windows, even from here, were clearly aged and dusty, and yet they still turned their smiling faces toward the sun.

Was this really all hers? The villa was like something out of a fairy tale. There had to be a good reason for this stunning house to have been left alone for so long.

Annie walked toward the drystone wall. There must be a set of stone steps that would take her up. Steps where, once upon a time, women in slippers had placed their delicate feet, and where dashing gentlemen had accompanied them, with their smooth, unworked hands.

The thought that these people had been her ancestors was unbelievable and strange. At home, Papa had been wealthy, but this was another world, an extraordinary lineage.

The olive trees rustled gently beside her in the breeze. She stopped and took a deep breath for a moment. Centered herself. A bird called from the orchard above, and flitted off, disappearing into the yellow and blue of the sky.

Annie searched up and down along the length of the drystone wall, looking for a place where it would be safe to try to clamber up to the next level, but the wall was higher than her

head, clearly designed to provide adequate terracing for the
steep hillside on which the Villa Rosa had been built.

"*Ciao?*"

Annie whipped her head up.

A man stood on the top level, framed by the ancient, strag-
gling rose-covered pergola, with his hands on his hips. He
looked down at her. From where she was standing, she could
make out a tall, tanned profile, blond hair. He was wearing a
pair of navy-blue shorts and a green T-shirt.

"Are you here to help with the well?" He spoke English
with a British accent.

Annie shook her head. She crinkled her nose. "The well?"
If she was the owner of the Villa Rosa, did people have the right
to dig wells on her property? The notary had said nothing of
anyone working here. She shook her head. "No. I'm not here
about the water."

He swiftly came down to the orchard level, and Annie was
able to see where the small staircase was hidden. She still
looked about for a way to get up to where the staircase started.
She wanted to be standing on an equal footing with her new
companion. It felt strange standing down here looking up
at him.

An odd expression passed across the man's face. "Are American tourists booking solo visits to the abandoned villa? What's
going on, *signorina bella?*"

A smile played around her lips. With every man in this
country addressing her this way, her ego would be inflated to
the size of a balloon before the end of the week.

The man crouched down. He was framed by the fruit trees
and beady-eyed birds. "Here. Come on up and have a look at
the view. It's majestic. Stunning." He reached out a hand. His
skin was golden, and the hairs on his arms were bleached blond
by the sun. "I'm Luca, by the way."

Annie stepped closer toward the wall, and her shoe landed

on a tiny patch of herbs. The smell of lemon balm and rosemary filtered up into the air. She closed her eyes a moment. "I'm Annie. Pleased to meet you. But—"

"Amazing, isn't it. The whole place?"

Annie nodded. "It's magical," she breathed.

"Come and have a look at the view from the terrace and the formal garden above the rose arbor," Luca said. "I don't mind the odd tourist. In fact, it will give me a break from searching for this well that is supposedly hidden away somewhere."

Annie reached up and took his hand.

"Okay. Put your foot in that little gap there." He pointed down to what had clearly become a foothold in the rock in recent times. Her palm still in his, she found a footing, and a secure place for her other hand, and then, "Give me both your hands," he said.

She placed her hands in his, and he hauled her up over the edge of the terrace, until she was lying flat on her stomach and staring at bundles of rotten fruit. She coughed, and sat up, brushing down her dress.

"Sorry, it was much more elegant in my head," he said, and they both laughed.

The man reached out a hand again, and she took it, and allowed him to help her up. She gazed out at the valley, where shafts of sunlight beamed down on the trees, and the villages and the houses. "I honestly don't know whether I have ever seen anything so gorgeous in my life."

"I know."

She turned to him. "But who has asked you to search for a well on the property?"

"The Villa Rosa's owner."

CHAPTER 8

CARA

Cara stood in the cemetery on the outskirts of the village. The simple black dress that the Contessa's cook Bettina had loaned her hung too loose on her frame, and when she had fastened her long dark hair back into a bun this morning, her face had looked back at her, her cheeks hollow, and her brown eyes round, huge, shocked.

Bettina stood next to her now with Alphonso on her other side. It was incredibly moving to see Papa's oldest friends, standing in a semicircle with their hats in their hands, acknowledging her loss. And as the pall bearers lowered the simple wooden box that Alphonso had made for a coffin into the grave, Cara turned away. The priest intoned words that washed through her, and she was startlingly aware of Raf and the Contessa standing at a little distance behind the gathering on the side of the hill.

She risked a glance upward and felt Raf's eyes burning into hers. They stood out, he in an expensive black suit with a silk handkerchief in his pocket, and his dark hair smoothed back so that his warm eyes were highlighted like rich golden honey, his arm held in a white sling, and the Contessa, her own blond hair pulled back into a chignon, the black silk skirt and blouse she wore only embellished with a string of pearls.

Cara turned back to Papa's coffin, resting now underground. She stared at it one last time, her stomach hollow, with something that she knew would never be replaced. The light that Papa had been in her life was permanently gone.

The priest handed her a single white rose to place on his coffin, and Cara took it, staring at it, unable to move. Bettina reached out and squeezed Cara's hand. She turned for a moment to the curly-headed cook who had taken over when the Contessa's personal chef left for the war. This morning, Bettina had arrived at Papa's pensione, holding the dress, a soft white loaf of bread that she had baked this morning, and a bowl of strawberries that she had picked from the kitchen garden. Cara had stared at the food and had forced herself to eat something in the face of her friend's kindness.

Cara smiled bravely at Bettina now, and then turned to Alphonso and rested her hand on his arm a moment. His eyes said it all. He had respected her papa too, and in the early days of the war, had made a special effort to send spare herbs down from the Contessa's garden to the pensione, along with fresh eggs from the hens that he tended for the Contessa.

Cara accepted the white rose and held it a moment. Placing it on the coffin would feel like the end. It was all gone. Papa's morning chatter with the guests at the pensione, the way he greeted each guest with complete delight as if it were a miracle when they walked down the stairs to breakfast, as if each time they appeared, it was for the first time all over again. Last night, Cara had sat out in the courtyard behind the pensione, tears falling down her cheeks as she stared at Papa's beloved pots of tomatoes. Only last week, he had said that the crop this summer was turning out to be wonderful. Just a few days ago, Papa had said how lucky they were the Nazis had not stolen them all. And she had thought it was probably because the Contessa was refusing to help the partisans, so the whole village was being given special treatment.

Cara stood, staring at the wooden box, her hand frozen in place, and her fingers clasping the thin stem of the white rose. There was a murmur among the villagers who had gathered here, but she stood paralyzed: throwing this rose over the dirt that was piled over Papa's body felt too final.

She shook her head. She could not let the rose go.

When she sensed Raf standing next to her, she closed her eyes. She felt the presence of him as keenly as she always had, the surety of him, the comfort of him, but the fire that breathed between them had destroyed them in the end.

She had known that Papa had liked Raf.

But the Contessa was not only Cara's employer, she also owned Papa's pensione; he had only been paying her rent and running the business on his own.

The Contessa's and Raf's world was so different from hers, and there was no way that she would ever fit in with their lives.

It was Papa who had always been watching out for her, supporting her in her decisions, gently talking things through with her and making suggestions. He had always been there.

Cara took in a ragged breath and lifted her head as a realization dawned over her.

That was it.

The body that was buried beneath the earth was not Papa.

The Nazis may have taken away Papa's body, they may have slain him, hurt him, caused him so much pain that it was time for him to go to the gentle arms of God in heaven, but the truth was, she was not staring at Papa down there.

He would always be with her. That certainty, she knew would never change. Death could not take love away.

And in that moment, she felt him, everywhere, in the breeze

in the linden tree that looked over this sacred place. In the sky that spread over the valley where he had raised her, and most of all, deep in her heart, where he would always be. Those we loved would always be with us. She could sense it, and she could imagine him telling her he was right here.

Cara released the rose.

It had been several days since her father's funeral, and Cara walked down the curving stone steps through the terraced gardens of the Villa Rosa. She came to a stop among the old, gnarled olive trees on the lower terrace. The indigo night that always fell over Tuscany late in the summer evenings had been broken with shafts of moonlight that threw lemon streaks into the magical grove.

Cara stood stock-still. The sounds of Raf's footsteps following her bled into the inky silence, and she waited for him, even though every instinct within her told her to go home.

He stood opposite her in the moonlight, his eyes full of genuine concern. His dark hair was clipped neatly short for the military, and in his white linen shirt and trousers, he looked more rugged and handsome than ever, even though his arm was in his sling while he recovered from a shrapnel wound. "How are you, Cara?"

Ever since the day of the funeral, she had sat, her hair tied back in its neat ponytail, typing out letters to the Contessa's many business contacts, to her bankers in Milano, to her financial advisers in Florence, her heart aching with pain for what Papa must have suffered. And every morning when she woke up in her bedroom in the silent pensione, without the sounds of Papa making coffee, and singing in the kitchen, her stomach hurt with a deep, dull ache.

Cara had smiled through her tears when one of her neighbors had brought over a carefully made *torte della nonna,* the dessert that Cara's mother used to make for her on Sundays. Her neighbor had used up the last of her precious flour to make this special dessert. The memory of Papa carrying on her mother's tradition had flooded back to her. He had carefully shaped the dough, pouring his delicious, rich, golden custard made with the very best brown eggs and golden butter into the shallow pastry case, before carefully placing a smooth disk of pastry on top, and pressing pine nuts in decorative circles into the dough.

Cara took in a deep breath of the moonlit air. It was scented with roses, and the soft promise of the silky green olive oil that the Messina family bottled after every harvest. From the orchard above, there was the tang of midsummer peaches, along with rosemary, and the lemon verbena that grew wild along the drystone walls.

Cara gathered herself. She had pulled her hair out of its customary ponytail, and it tumbled in dark waves down her back. Her eyes, as black as her hair, felt round and vulnerable. But the fire that burned in her belly, incentivizing her to do something to support those who were resisting the Nazis, was not something that was going to die down. And as quickly as the swell of sadness had overtaken her, that passionate determination was back again in its place.

"I am consumed with grief for Papa. What happened to him was unthinkable. I cannot focus on anything else. Except..." She searched Raf's face, and his eyes bore into hers. "Except doing something to help stop others from suffering the same fate. It is all that is keeping me going."

A muscle twitched in Raf's cheek. Her words hung between them for a moment and his eyes grew wide.

Cara glanced around. "I understand that you have contacts. Put me in touch with them. And I will get to work."

"Cara... It is too dangerous, please understand this. War is not yet here in the valley, but it is coming with every step that the Allies take north, and with every unit of reinforcements that the Nazis send down to Tuscany to protect their claim. You cannot risk yourself. I don't want to risk you..."

"My father died protecting his friend's twelve-year-old daughter from being raped by the Nazis."

Raf's expression softened. "I understand. I understand how you are feeling, and I know what you are going through."

Cara shook her head as that strong fire flared in her again. "How? How could you..."

Raf bowed his head.

Cara closed her eyes. "I'm sorry." He had lost his own father suddenly. The whole valley had been rocked by it. And yet, the focus had been on the Contessa, on her courage and resilience in the face of her husband's death. But two boys had also been left behind.

Raf had always lived his life in the shadow of his mother's shining sun. And the Contessa's light burned brightly. Cara knew that Raf had obeyed his mother's wishes that he fight with Mussolini, on Hitler's side. She knew that it meant a lot to Raf to honor family, and to reassure the Contessa that he would always be there for her, especially after Nicolas had abandoned her. But she also knew that Raf could never tell his mother that he was a partisan. The only way he could be himself was to go behind his mother's back. *Secrets and lies...*

Cara understood this, but understanding was not enough. There was something she could do, and the situation demanded that she do so. This valley was as much a part of her own lifeblood as his.

The still, moonlit evening was broken only by the sound of the Messinas' fountains trickling down from one terrace to another. They were operated by a pump at the top of the garden. It had been Raf who had told her that the Villa Rosa sat on a deep spring that had been discovered by the Etruscans, and that there was an elaborate network of water pipes and channels set deep underneath the ground. He loved to help Alphonso tend to the fountains, and Cara knew that, when Raf had returned home, joy had sprung in Alphonso's heart. Alphonso had always had a special fondness for the Contessa's youngest son.

Back before Raf left for the war, he had told her how every drop of water counted, and that the fountains worked in a cycle, so that nothing was wasted. But every life in Tuscany counted too.

"Did Alphonso tell you to speak to me?" Raf asked, breaking the thick silence that hung between them.

Cara whipped up her head to search his face. "You know I would never betray Alphonso's trust. He is like an uncle to me." Her voice cracked. "I want to help of my own volition. If you won't point me in the right direction, I will find someone who will."

His voice was low and rich. "I hate the idea of you risking your life." Those eyes of his pleaded with her now. "Look what happened to your father..." he whispered.

"I have nothing to lose," she said. It was true.

He nodded and stared at the ground. "I suppose you would see it that way."

Silence hung between them like a gauzy veil.

"I am going to contribute anyway. I will find a way if you won't help me."

He looked up at her, and she felt his gaze burning deep inside her. "Would your father want this, Cara?"

"I promised him." And she turned, stumbling out toward the intricate wrought-iron gates that led into the Villa Rosa.

"Cara..."

But Cara looked down toward the village that lay at the bottom of the hill. It was only a small village, but it was worth protecting. And Papa's memory was worth more than any risk. "I will wait to hear from you," she said.

Cara walked away from him, toward the empty, silent road.

CHAPTER 9

ANNIE

Annie stood outside the Villa Rosa's front door. It was painted the same soft green as the shutters, and cobwebs traced fragile patterns around its edge. There was an elegant fanlight speckled with dirt and dust above the door. Years' worth of dried leaves were gathered in mounds on the front porch.

Luca with the British accent whom she'd met on her first visit to the Villa Rosa had made it clear that he would not allow her to enter the property without the "owner's" permission. That owner was coming to the villa today, his name was Sandro Messina, and Luca had told her he was the direct descendant of the Messina line.

Annie had needed to distract herself for the few days before Sandro Messina arrived, so she had gone to Florence, and had wandered the galleries of the Uffizi. She had climbed to the Pitti Palace and stood looking out over the view of the Tuscan hills from the Boboli Gardens, eaten at charming, family-run restaurants, simple local meals that she knew her own papa would have adored.

She had come away inspired by the produce at the markets and had returned to the pensione in the village, which she had chosen because it was closer to the Villa Rosa than the hotel in Cortona, carrying armfuls of the local honeys, cheeses, and a bottle of Tuscan wine. It seemed that every family with a land-holding in Tuscany grew grapes, had a vineyard, and produced their own wine. Old vineyards trailed down one of the surrounding hills next to the Villa Rosa. If she lived here, then she, like the old family members who had lived here for centuries, would take great delight in producing her own wine and olive oil. What if she were to become a beekeeper? She could see herself with an apiary.

Her senses had come to life in these past few days, as she had wandered the streets of the world's most charming Renaissance city. She had stopped tying her long blond hair up into a ponytail and had begun wearing it free for the first time since she had attended cooking school in Paris. She had indulged herself and bought soft leather shoes in Florence, as well as a few summer dresses in jewel tones that accentuated her olive skin.

Annie felt like being more colorful than she was used to in San Francisco, where she had favored black clothes while she was working, and tended to just wear old jeans and shirts when she was not hard at work.

No matter how much she grieved for Papa, and missed Monica and Paul, traveling on her own felt like a delicious indulgence. Was Papa looking down at her, smiling at the fact that she was in a place where she felt she could embrace life? She hoped so.

"Annie?"

Annie turned. Luca stood with his hands on his hips just as he had when she had first met him.

"Thank goodness it has cooled down a bit since you were last here," he said. He sounded conversational, pleased to see her even. "I felt terrible not letting you into the villa last time we met. Forgive me?"

Annie smiled, grateful for his charming manners. "I guess I would be hesitant letting a stranger into a house I didn't own too..." There was a silence. Ownership was a topic of contention. "I had an interesting time; I've been to Florence. I loved it."

"I suppose that's only made you fall in love with Tuscany more," he said. He looked at her and grinned, his eyes twinkling.

"Who couldn't fall in love with all of this?" She spread her arms out wide to embrace the villa, the gardens, the valley, and the distant misty hills. Being in Florence had not slowed down her growing feelings for Tuscany at all, and now that she was back in the valley, she was not looking forward to meeting this other claimant to the enchanting villa.

"I know. I'm not keen to go back to England, lovely as it is. The weather, for one thing..."

"I assumed you were Italian, Luca?" Although he spoke English so perfectly with traces of a British accent.

Luca shook his head. "My grandfather was Italian, but I grew up in Hampshire, and built up my own garden design business there. When the opportunity came to head out to Italy and redesign the Villa Rosa's gardens, I jumped at it. It means a lot to me too."

Annie frowned.

Just then, the sound of a powerful engine breezed into the air, and a low-slung sports car pulled into the curve of the driveway right in front of where they stood. Annie glanced at the telltale insignia on the sophisticated car. It was a Ferrari.

She walked down to stand alongside Luca.

"Here we go," Luca said, and then, unexpectedly, Annie felt him brush his hand on her arm as he made his way down to the sleek car. "Hang in there."

She folded her arms as she wondered, *Whose side is Luca on?*

Luca leaned down and opened the driver's door, resting his arm against the car and blocking Annie's view of the man inside.

When Luca stood aside, Annie let out a wry laugh.

The driver of the car placed one foot on the gravel, which needed a particularly good rake. As he stepped out of the car, Annie had to stifle her growing smile. He was ruggedly handsome. Gorgeous, with dark curls that framed his classical features, and extraordinary, burnt-honey-colored eyes. He was wearing a pair of faded blue jeans, and a white linen shirt that was not tucked in.

The man's sunglasses were perched on his head of dark curls, and he came across to her, holding out his hand ready for her to shake. He pressed his other hand into her arm, "You must be Annie," he said. His accent held traces of that lyrical Italian that she had come to adore listening to in the last week. "Sandro Messina. To be honest, I'm a little disconcerted that you are here."

She shook his hand and had to admit that she was entirely disarmed. "You are completely different to what I imagined," she said, unable to stop herself. She had imagined a middle-aged man with a lemon-yellow sweater tied over his shoulders, and a pair of polished tan brogues. Luca had said that, due to privacy, it was best that she wait and meet the owner herself before he told her anything more.

Sandro turned to Luca. "What did you do, terrify her? Tell her that I was evil incarnate? I hate to think what you have said about me."

Annie shot a glance over toward Luca. But he was smiling down at the gravel, his hands in his pockets, his face flushed. "I'm only the messenger." He shook his head. "I've said nothing at all." He winked at Annie.

Annie shrugged back at him. and she reached up to run her hand through her own long blond hair. She had put on a dress that she knew would keep Papa close. It was the dress she had worn to the funeral, not black, but a deep navy-blue linen, and she knew that this brought out the color in her eyes. She had decided the moment that she bought it that she would not let the funeral jinx this dress; instead she would wear it to remind her that her father was always on her side.

"I am keen to talk to you," she said to Sandro. "The situation has certainly come as a surprise for me too."

"And I expect you are waiting to see inside the Villa Rosa," he said quietly.

She nodded. "I have my own key, one for the gate, one for the front door."

He looked down to the brass keys that she held in her hand.

"Indeed," he said, his voice still soft.

Behind her, Annie heard Luca clear his throat.

"Let's see if it works, shall we?" Sandro asked in that silken voice.

Annie took her key, and she walked toward the Villa Rosa's front door.

CHAPTER 10

CARA

Cara had taken a week off work at the Contessa's insistence. She had been working herself to the bone every day since the funeral to distract herself from her grief, but burying herself in letters and phone calls had done nothing to quell the ache she felt at the tragic loss of her father.

She had sat up in her bed this morning with her coffee and the silence outside in the village unnerved her. Only ten months ago, the cobbled laneways outside Papa's pensione had resounded with cheers, and the villagers had spent the night dancing in the piazza. Mussolini had been voted out of power by his own Grand Council, and everyone had thought that decades of fascism had finally ended. But since Hitler's tanks had rolled in; it had felt as if doomsday had come to the valley and there had been no cheering or singing in the street ever since.

While the local people had managed to survive on their own produce, rations in the cities had halved to less than one cup of milk per person per day, and the allowances for flour were meager. There had long been stories of people trading their family silver for a ham on the black markets, while the price of a leg of lamb was equivalent to hundreds of thousands of lire, and fruit and vegetables were almost non-existent, so the Nazis often raided nearby villages of what little they had.

Any disagreements among Cara's neighbors seemed to have magnified with the despair they were all living under now. Last night, she had listened to the sound of her neighbor, Luigi Santino, yelling at his wife. And he was no better outside of his home. She hated the way he eyed her as if she were his tiramisu. Every now and then, Luigi would ask her in a smooth silky voice how the Contessa was doing. He would ask her to send his regards.

But it was the elderly whose expressions were heartbreaking. The way the old men sat around the piazza, watching and shaking their heads. Cara knew that they remembered Italy before Mussolini had come to power in 1922. They remembered the brief taste of freedom the country had enjoyed after the Great War. It all seemed so long ago, and so distant now.

Cara waited for the first streaks of light to appear around the old painted wooden shutters on her bedroom window, heralding the dawn of another day. Alphonso, bless him, would arrive every morning with a willow basket covered in a red-and-white checked cloth containing her breakfast: bread from the villa, and a jug of milk. Most mornings, he brought strawberries, bright and plump and firm, from the gardens.

The Contessa was supplying the market stallholders, but the Nazis always plundered the stalls first, taking what little produce they had, and these days, the local village market was only a fraction of the size that it was before the war.

Cara sat back in her bed. The sound of German voices under her window in the narrow-cobbled street outside the pensione broke into the otherwise quiet morning. They always patrolled at precisely seven o'clock. She had mentioned to

Alphonso what a help it was, knowing that the Nazis followed such strict routines. Alphonso had nodded grimly. He had said the partisans took great advantage of this. They operated by weaving in and around the Nazis, getting into the cracks, to break down the Nazis' walls.

Cara climbed out of her single bed once the patrolling Nazi voices died down. She pulled on her dressing gown of fine white lawn, and padded over to her window, opening the shutters wide. The air was still, and serene. And she leaned out and looked up at the blue sky.

She stood there for a while, thinking of Papa until she heard Alphonso's soft knock on her front door. She walked out of the cozy apartment in the pensione that she had shared with Papa and made her way down the wooden stairs, past the reception area with its wooden key holders.

Softly, she called out Alphonso's name.

"Si, Signorina Cara."

She opened her front door carefully out of habit, her eyes cast downwards, because she always checked for Alphonso's shoes. And there they were, well worn, the soles having been repeatedly replaced during the last few years by the local cobbler.

She raised her eyes and met Alphonso's kindly gaze.

"You look better today, signorina," he said.

She smiled at him, looking straight at his face, for he was only her height, five foot six. "Thank you, Alphonso. I must admit that I am looking forward to coming back up to work tomorrow."

Alphonso took a wary look down the tiny narrow lane. "Si," he said, "if I did not have my work"—he lowered his gaze—"and my home in the cottage on the villa's grounds, I hate to think what circumstances I would be living in. What Nazi would be sleeping in my bed!"

"Yes," Cara whispered.

"How are you, Signorina Cara?"

"Better," Cara said, meaning it. "Although, there are those who tell me that I will never get over the loss of Papa. That the pain will never lessen. Then, there are those who tell me it will go away, in time."

Alphonso nodded and sighed.

"I am not sure how I will be, in a month, in a year, in ten years." Cara bit her lip. "But what I do know is that Papa gave me the gift of life. And I must value it. I must appreciate every day. I think that is the last lesson our parents teach us, you know?" Her words caught and hitched, and she swallowed, hard.

"I think that's true," he said. He murmured a blessing. "We will look forward to seeing you back up at the villa tomorrow, signorina."

Cara smiled at him, and as he walked away she closed the door softly behind her and stood in the cool stillness of her home. She had wanted to ask him about the partisans, but she sensed that everyone wanted her to have some time to herself to grieve, and she respected that.

But now, she had rested, and it was time to act.

Cara made her way up through the terraced gardens to the villa the following morning, passing the summerhouse where the Contessa's husband had proposed to the young Evelina. She paused on the upper terrace at the rose arbor, which was covered with tiny pink blooms. The Contessa had given them away for so many local weddings, always insisting on picking the perfect little roses herself. She had told Cara she must marry when they were in season. Cara hadn't been able to quite meet her eyes.

She entered the cool entrance hall. To her right, the door to the study was closed. And to her left, the Contessa's serene music room opened straight through with an interconnecting door to the dining room.

Cara's hand was poised on the study door when she heard voices coming from upstairs. The Contessa's, soft, and another voice. Not Raf's. But a man's.

Cara slipped into the sanctity of the study and peered around the side of the door.

Footsteps clattered on the wide, curving staircase, with its wrought-iron balustrade designed by the same ironsmith who had worked the Villa Rosa gates. Cara saw the Contessa's feet coming into view in high-heeled pale blue sandals, and then the silk of her blue dress. Her face was made up with pale pink lipstick, and her eyes were crinkled in a smile.

Cara's hand froze on the door handle and her gaze arched upwards. An expensive pair of shoes and neatly pressed formal trousers followed the Contessa's light tread. A sharply cut suit jacket, and then a glimpse of his face.

Instinctively, Cara took a step backwards and disappeared out of view, but she kept her ear to the closed door of the study and listened, her heart beating wildly in her chest. The Contessa was laughing like a schoolgirl. And the man trailing down the stairs in her wake was murmuring in the soft tones that anyone could recognize. The tones of a lover. He was speaking German.

Cara slipped across the room to the desk and started fluttering about with the piles of envelopes that had accumulated while she was away.

She had spent too many hours alone in the Contessa's office reading the newspapers. She had seen the man's face emblazoned on the front pages too many times. One too many times.

Cara took in a set of staggering breaths.

The Contessa was having an affair with a high-ranking Nazi who was one of the commandants in Florence. From memory, she thought his name was Bruno Klein. *How could she...*

Cara glared down at the correspondence that had accumulated on her desk. She would have to tell Raf, so at least the partisans knew! *Now is the time to do something, even if it had to be right under this Nazi's nose.*

She slipped back and stood by the door again. The man was murmuring something and the Contessa's voice was low and seductive in response. He let out a deep chuckle and then it was quiet. He would be kissing her.

What would this mean for her, for Alphonso, for Bettina, and for Raf? Did the Contessa have no idea how much danger she had placed them all in by letting this man in?

CHAPTER 11

ANNIE

Annie's key turned easily in the old lock, and she stepped into the entrance hall of the Villa Rosa. A staircase curved to the upper floors, and the same elegant wrought iron of the gate was repeated on the banisters. But here the railings were decorated with what looked like initials, and then rosebuds worked into the metal.

Annie couldn't help it; she moved over to the staircase and took a closer look at the letters emblazoned there—E and A. They were written close together, so that they were almost united.

"Evelina and Arturo." Sandro placed his booted foot on the first stair. "My great-grandparents. Evelina and Arturo Messina." He reached out and traced a finger over the initials. "My great-grandparents adored this villa. I know that my great-grandfather Arturo, had he lived throughout the war, would have fought tooth and nail to stop the Nazis taking it over. It was unfortunate what happened here... unspeakable."

Annie stayed quiet. What did he mean? She knew nothing

of these people, their history, or how she fitted in. The cool stillness inside the Villa Rosa was unnerving, and it was as if by
stepping inside the house, she was making Papa's letter to her
seem real.

Luca had excused himself and gone back to work in the
garden. It felt strange standing here just with Sandro. She
would have quite liked Luca's presence now.

But at the same time, she was dying to climb that elegant set
of stairs. Sandro walked through the entrance hall, opening a
closed white door that led off to the right. He flicked on a light,
and they were in a study. A charming antique desk sat by the
shuttered window, and there was a fireplace, with a shrouded
painting set above it. A pair of armchairs were covered in dust
sheets, and there was a rolled-up rug in the corner of the room.
But either side of the fireplace, the walls held fully stocked
bookshelves. And in these there were hundreds of old books.
The leather spines were cracked and worn, but the gold
embossed writing on them was still clear and strong.

"My goodness," Annie whispered. She went to have a closer
look. Dante, Voltaire, Pushkin—it was incredible someone had
not looted these precious books.

"This is not even the beginning of the collection of books
that the villa once housed. My father told me that there were
hundreds of books here back when he was young. Who knows
what happened to them all."

Annie turned to Sandro, who was already moving ahead
through an interconnecting door, into the next room. It was a
sitting room, with another set of furniture, this time a sofa and
several chairs all covered in dust covers again. A chandelier
hung from the ceiling, which sprinkled patterned light all over
the dark room. The walls were painted in a deep yellow, with
an aged, almost magical patina.

But then, Annie saw something and gasped. On the far wall
that led to the next room, sections of the wall had been scraped

back, and underneath the antique yellow, there were traces of a fresco, people walking through a marketplace, and in their cloaks and robes there was the vivid blue of lapis lazuli.

"Oh my," Annie whispered.

Sandro peered closely at the old paintings. "Aren't they wonderful? They are an important part of my great-grandparents' legacy and I am going to organize the very best craftsmen to have them restored."

Annie frowned. *My heritage, my great-grandparents...*

"This suite of rooms was used by my great-grandfather as his office, until he died prematurely in the thirties from a massive heart attack when he was walking in the gardens."

"I'm sorry." Annie wanted to trace a finger over the frescoes, but she dared not.

"My great-grandmother Evelina was alerted, and went out to him, but he died in her arms. She had to take over the running of the villa entirely herself, which she did from that point and all through the war." Sandro looked down at the floor sadly. "That is where everything started to go wrong."

Sandro led her to the next room.

"This is a little antechamber of sorts," he said. "I think it was used to store all the business files." He waved his hand around the small dark space. There was built-in shelving all around the room, but someone had removed all the business papers. A bare lightbulb hung solitary and strange from the ceiling. "Back in the day, I think it was an animal stable, that has been converted into this storage space."

Annie felt unsettled. Despite the heat outside, she folded her arms around herself. There was something stark and strange about this room. "Might we get out of here?" she whispered.

Sandro lifted his head sharply and looked at her. "You are sensing something you don't like about the villa?"

"Not at all," Annie murmured. But she was glad when they were back out in the entrance hall.

Sandro looked up at the ceiling. "My plan is to knock the walls out between all those rooms. I want to create one huge living space, with a modern kitchen, and an open-plan living area. My architect is drawing up plans as we speak," he said. "I would like to knock down the back section of the house, the old kitchen, and the rooms where the servants used to sleep. I want to modernize it completely, get rid of the ghosts of the past that are haunting the old house. The past is the past, and we must let go of it. No?"

Annie narrowed her eyes. He was not even considering her claim to the villa. It was as if he was overriding the whole thing. She would not push him... Yet.

"And the left wing?" She asked the bland question as if she lived in houses with wings as a matter of course. "Does it repeat the same pattern?" The four equally spaced sets of front French doors had beguiled her when she first saw the house.

Sandro nodded. "My plan for the other half of the house is to have it as a formal entertainment zone."

"A zone? What a modern word to use for such a delightful old house." Her mind raced. How was she supposed to get around this guy? Go back and see the notary? But he clearly knew nothing.

Sandro only smiled. "Again, I want to knock all the walls out on this side of the house and create one huge space." He wandered through the corresponding door to the left wing, flinging it open, and turning on lights again. "It will be wonderful. I cannot wait to see my plans to completion."

They were standing in a music room. There was a full-sized grand piano covered in a dust cloth, its tapered walnut legs peeking out enticingly beneath its white cover, and in one corner, an old harp. The furniture, all covered with dust sheets, was arranged as if someone was expecting a recital to begin. There was even a raised platform for musicians to perform.

Annie's father had loved music. When he had been working, he would play the Italian composers—Puccini, Verdi, Vivaldi—and the house would be filled with their glorious tones.

Sandro strolled on, flicking on lights as he went. Beyond the music room, there was a dining room, complete with a table that would seat sixteen, and a sideboard still holding dusty decanters and silverware.

"Again, I'm staggered that nobody has looted the property," Annie said.

Sandro sighed. "Everyone lives with their doors unlocked."

He moved into a billiards room, the soft green felt table taking up most of the space. There was another sideboard, along with glass cabinets displaying crystal tumblers for whiskey, vodka, and gin. Sandro leaned against the sideboard. "I'm sorry, Annie. But this is my home. It's my legacy. There is no question that it belongs to anyone else."

Annie stayed silent. But she held his gaze until his jaw tightened, and he stared down at the floor.

"I'm happy to show you through the rest of the property, but after that, you need to respect the fact that this is not yours."

Annie narrowed her eyes at him. He started moving again, and she followed him through what he called the back wing, a huge country kitchen, a servants' wing, and then behind the study and the sitting room, there was a long hallway with several guest bedrooms overlooking a courtyard garden protected by a high wall.

"Don't you worry about pulling out foundation walls?" Annie asked. All through the house, there were chestnut beams set across the ceilings, but were they strong enough to withhold the removal of several foundation walls?

"I have had an architect give his approval. And my business partner is sorting out the finances."

Annie's heart began to beat in a strange pattern as she followed Sandro up the gracious stairs. At the top, there was a large landing, and off this, doors led to the left and the right, just as downstairs. She followed Sandro through rooms that were linked by another set of interconnecting doors. Clearly, the early inhabitants of Villa Rosa did not have privacy.

Annie stopped in the main bedroom, running her eyes over a large old wooden bed with a four-poster canopy overhead and faded silk drapes in pale blue. Was this Evelina Messina's bedroom? There was a dressing table, strangely, not covered by dust sheets. Dust hung in filaments from the mirror and coated the silver-backed brushes and combs.

But Annie's gaze moved toward the dressing table and stuck. There was a faded sepia photograph of a beautiful woman, her blond hair brushed back from her forehead, and her lips curved in an enigmatic Grace Kelly smile. Annie moved over to take a closer look at the photograph. "This is Evelina?"

"She was lovely, I acknowledge that." Sandro's expression was hard to read. "Let's keep moving, shall we?"

Annie frowned at him. What had the Contessa done?

Next, there was a dressing room, an entire room devoted to sets of built-in armoires. Annie ached to open one, and to see if Evelina Messina's dresses and coats and elegant trouser suits still hung inside. The room led into a charming sitting room, and then an old bathroom. The tiling was exquisite, hand-painted birds and flowers decorated the entire wall around the bath. The ceiling soared over fourteen feet above them.

"May I?" Annie's fingers rested on the shutters.

Sandro nodded at her, and she threw them wide. Sunlight flooded into the bathroom, and there was a patio still containing old stone pots filled with dirt overlooking the glorious view of the valley beyond.

"It's gorgeous," she whispered. And as she looked out over the valley, she couldn't help but sense Papa whispering to her, *"Don't let him ruin it all, Annie."*

I won't. Don't you worry.

On the other side of the house, the interconnecting doors gave out to a room that had clearly been occupied by a young man. The bed was still made up with a navy-blue counterpane, and on the dust-coated walnut chest of drawers, there were leather-backed brushes, and a silver cigarette case, along with a hand mirror, pockmarked with the black marks of age.

"My grandfather, Nicolas's bedroom," Sandro said. He glanced around the room once, grimaced, and moved through into another room, which had been stripped bare. Nothing was left. The walls were painted the same soft yellow as the sitting room downstairs, and a couple of tiny, stray bits of paper had lodged between the wooden floorboards in a corner of the room. Annie felt goosebumps rising on her arms and she shivered, only too glad to follow Sandro out of this empty space.

Tacked onto the back of the house on this side was a bathroom, swirling with dust.

Annie started to cough.

"Obviously, this funny little extension will have to go," Sandro said.

Annie followed him back through the bedrooms, this time, focusing on the future—she would have white-painted walls, the chestnut beams gently polished and oiled. Deep in her heart, she yearned to bring the villa back to life, but not as some extravagant monstrosity. It was too precious and dear for that, with its old roses, and silvery olive trees. It could be a perfect family home, or if that didn't happen, a cooking school... Imagine that.

When they were back outside in the searing heat, Luca looked up from where he had been pulling ivy away from the top drystone wall, still trying to find his source of water. He raised a brow, as if in question to Annie, and she sent him the most reassuring smile she could in return.

"Have you been to the market in the village at the bottom of the hill yet?" Sandro asked suddenly.

Annie stared at him. The owner of the pensione had mentioned a market in the piazza, and she was planning to go in the morning; she would not be distracted. "Sandro, my father told me that I was the owner of the Villa Rosa. Let's focus on that, shall we?"

But Sandro folded his arms. He glanced across at Luca, but the gardener had resumed his work. "I want to show you how much it all means to me. The villa, the village. Let me take you around the markets and show you that this is my home."

"But it appears it is mine, too."

An expression of genuine sadness passed across Sandro's face. "I am sorry, Miss Reynolds, but you won't fit in here. You never will. There are things I need to tell you so that you will understand, and it will all become perfectly clear." A shadow fell across his face.

"Listen here—" Irritation bit at her nerves.

But he held up his hand. "Please. I'll meet you in the village piazza at eight thirty tomorrow. We'll have breakfast, and I will introduce you to all my friends in the village marketplace. Every Saturday, it fills with local produce, wines, cheeses, honey. Tuscany is in these people's blood, just as it is in mine. By midday tomorrow, I'm certain I will have convinced you this is my home, and that I am the true heir to the Villa Rosa. I'm afraid there is no argument to the contrary."

We'll see about that.

CHAPTER 12

CARA

Cara stood by the French doors in the office and drew her cardigan around her shoulders. The day was a little chillier than usual. She toyed with the simple cross that hung on a delicate silver chain around her neck.

A lone aircraft whirred overhead, and she jumped out of her reverie. The Allies were still bombing northern Italy relentlessly.

She rushed out toward the door that led to the kitchens and the basement, only to come face to face with the Contessa.

"It is only a German plane," the Contessa said.

Cara looked up to meet the taller woman's cool gaze.

"They are delivering pamphlets over the valley. It is nothing. You can relax, Cara."

Cara still stared at her employer, wanting her to say that she was not having an affair with a Nazi. Wanting her to say that she had not brought the enemy to sleep in her bed. It was one thing to say that you were protecting the villages by avoiding resistance, but quite another to bring one of the commandants, from Florence home to the villa, as if he were an honored guest. But the Contessa simply turned and placed her manicured hand on the banister. Her polished nails glistened a deep red.

"Go out and collect the pamphlets that they will have dropped all over the garden, please. I don't want them getting wet and soggy. They will mess up my roses."

The Contessa disappeared up the stairs, and so Cara waited a moment, until the sound of the aircraft had dissipated into the blue sky.

She stepped out the front door tentatively, and indeed, several pamphlets were scattered all over the ground. She leaned down and picked one up from the immaculately swept gravel driveway.

The northern Italian people must remain loyal and steadfast toward the Fuhrer. We believe that this will be the case with most of you. However, we have been hearing alarming reports of people in this valley harboring the enemy in their homes. Let us make it perfectly clear that this will not be tolerated, and our kindness in protecting the citizens of this country must not be abused. Consider what we have done for you. Liberated your great leader Mussolini from the clutches of the insurgents, given him the northern part of your country back. Stay firm, and we will protect you. Align yourself with our enemies at your own risk.

Cara curled her lip. *Given him the northern part of your country back...* Hitler was using Mussolini as his puppet, so he could install Nazi rule in northern Italy and fight the Allies as they invaded from the south. Mussolini had no control. He was simply bowing to the power of Hitler. Cara laid the leaflets on the hall table just inside the front door. She wanted to tear them up and burn them. Put them in the fireplace where they belonged. But she needed to play her cards carefully around the Contessa.

Raf had disappeared these last few days. She had not had a chance to ask him about his mother's liaison with the high-ranking Nazi, whose name, she was still certain, was Bruno Klein.

The Contessa went out soon after lunch, and the villa seemed to take on a strange eerie silence. It felt achingly empty, and Cara worked with the office door open, trying to listen out for the sounds of Bettina and the maid carrying out their duties in the house so that she felt she had some company. But the villa was too vast, the kitchens set too far back for her to hear anything, and everything remained starkly quiet. While Cara loved the Villa Rosa, sometimes she felt a strange sense of fore-boding inside the house. At least Alphonso started working outside the office in the mid-afternoon. Cara glanced up every now and then to search for his reassuring presence. The sound of him sweeping the terrace in smooth, rhythmic strokes was somehow comforting. But when he moved away and headed off toward the vines on the nearby hill, Cara's nerves began to dance.

At five o'clock, she packed up and made her way to the front door, down the steps that led from the terrace to the orchard. But Alphonso was nowhere in sight. The late afternoon felt eerie, and the trees were throwing strange shapes on the ground. The sky was thick and bruised, waiting for a storm.

When a shadowy figure emerged from behind one of the apple trees, Cara froze. The man was dressed as a partisan. His trousers were ill-fitting, held up with an old piece of rope. His shirt hung lopsided, the buttons done up in the wrong holes. And on his head, he wore a faded gentleman's hat.

"*Buongiorno, signor,*" Cara said. But she glanced around, fearful that the Contessa's Nazi friend might be lurking, just like the partisan was.

"We need funds to purchase ammunition." The man was curt. "We require 80,000 lire, signorina. We also require your help."

"I have no money," Cara whispered. "Who sent you?" She darted a glance toward the hillside and the grapevines, but there was no sight of Alphonso, and no reassuring sounds of him working among the budding vines. Raf hadn't said anything. Had this man got the wrong person?

"Nevertheless, you must procure it. For now, I also need food. Take me to your kitchen. Please!"

Cara took in a ragged breath.

There was something about his words, the way he spoke in the imperative. He was not Italian. As much as she wanted to believe that Raf had sent a member of the Italian resistance to recruit her, and right now, she would run with them deep into the hills and hide out in whatever rudimentary form of accommodation they were living in, every instinct she possessed screamed that this was not a partisan. The Contessa was constantly saying that the partisans were corrupt and had no hope of achieving anything of worth. She described them as rough men who had no idea how to fight a war. Cara folded her arms around her body. She did not need any reminders of this. The only chance she had of doing something was to join the rogue bands of men in the forests, but now the man standing opposite her was giving her little confidence as to whom she could trust—if anyone.

Thunder rolled over the distant hills. And the man stood opposite her, blocking her path. Yellow streaks of lightning flashed far away in the sky.

The man did not move.

And then a mighty crack of thunder almost split the hill they were standing on in two.

"I am going now," Cara said. She indicated the sky by way of explanation.

Finally, the man muttered something, turned and disappeared out of the garden, running along the side of the hill.

Cara stayed where she was until he was out of view.

But as she approached the villa's gates, she stopped again. Another crack of thunder roared overhead, and the smell of rain mingled with the scent of the garden's herbs.

Somewhere down among the olive groves and the vineyards, a volley of gunshots peppered the air.

Shouts echoed against the hill. And the warnings that had been so stark in the German pamphlets burned into Cara's head. Conflict was coming closer. She could feel it in her bones.

Cara heard nothing of Raf all week. The strange encounter with the man who had appeared in the garden concerned her. Where was Raf? She needed a contact she could trust if she was going to contribute to the resistance, and she would not risk Alphonso and Bettina's safety by talking with them about their activities under the Contessa's nose.

Every morning, the Contessa's Nazi lover swept off in his car after a series of whispers and exchanges on the staircase. The Contessa had not introduced him to Cara, and Cara knew better than to ask. All she could do was keep her head down and wait for the opportunity to do something to help.

She came to dread the sight of his car. She would wrap her arms around herself as she approached the villa, unable to look at the gleaming vehicle that represented the powerful forces responsible for Papa's death.

Alphonso was subdued. Cara knew that he was endlessly loyal to the Contessa and the Messina family, but she could see it in his eyes: this was taking things too far.

With Raf nowhere in sight, she had never felt more alone in her life.

Cara was eating her lunch, a knob of bread with tomato

from the garden outside on the terrace, when the dreadful news came through on the wireless. She had left it playing in the office because she needed some form of human company. At the village of Stia, nearby, German troops had been fired upon from the window by a partisan. In retaliation, every single male citizen of the village had been shot.

Cara worked for the rest of the day with her hands shaking uncontrollably. And when the Contessa came in to speak to her, Cara could not meet her eyes.

The valley shook and rumbled the following day. The windows rattled, and smoke poured into the air in the distance. The roar of a bomber formation filled the sky. Cara looked up to see more than thirty planes coming straight toward the villa. She flew out into the entrance hall, wound her way through the passages into the kitchen, but it was empty, and Bettina was already running down the stairs to the cellar. Cara tripped down behind her friend. They cowered deep below the house while the bombers thundered overhead.

Cara sat with her head in her hands, knowing the stoical Bettina was watching her. She was still unsure what Bettina might be doing to help the partisans, and it felt too dangerous to ask, even though Bettina had stood next to her like a sister at Papa's funeral. This was the world they had been forced to live in.

"I think it's stopped," Bettina said as the sound of the bomber formation drifted away.

Cara made her way slowly back upstairs to the kitchen, lost in her thoughts. Stories about the partisans were still troubling her. Even some of the villagers were saying they were disorganized and not professional enough to be able to protect themselves from Nazi retaliation. Indeed, the tragedy she had learned of this week had proven that was sadly true.

She still had no word from Raf, and she worried that he may have fled at the sight of his mother's lover. She would not put it past him. It was his passionate nature that had drawn her in when she came to work at the villa and got to know him better. But where did that leave her? If Raf was no longer available to help her join the resistance, she needed to find someone who would.

At the end of the week, Cara knew she had to decide who to approach. The sense of restlessness and helplessness that she had not done anything yet to avenge her father felt overwhelming. She had only taken simple supplies from the villa for the weekend, just enough to survive. A heel of bread for Saturday, along with a handful of tomatoes, and a small ration of potatoes from the vegetable garden outside the empty guest wing in the villa. But still, she put off approaching anyone in the village.

Cara spent Saturday morning forming gnocchi and cooking the tomatoes down into a sauce. But she was becoming nervous, imagining the Nazis knocking on her door, demanding her food. Last night, she had awoken, drenched in sweat.

Outside, the village was quiet, people's faces turned to the ground. Shopping baskets were empty. Their children pale and strange. Mothers huddled close to their babies, terrified that they could be machine-gunned from the air. The thought of putting these people at risk by engaging with the partisans was heartbreaking, and the recent massacre by the Nazis haunted her at every turn.

At night, the valley rang with gunfire, and every now and then, a Nazi vehicle trundled through the cobbled streets. Cara slept with a knife under her pillow. Every time the house rattled, she sat up in alarm.

It was impossible to know who in the village was helping the partisans and who was not, and finding someone who was willing to open up to her and give her a role to play would be equally difficult.

On Monday morning, Cara walked up to the villa as usual, only to have Alphonso call out to her from the driveway.

"Come with me," he whispered. He indicated to her with an incline of his head.

She followed him, her nerves tight and her stomach twisting with worry.

Alphonso marched down the driveway, and turned into the garden shed that was painted green and camouflaged under a bank of trees.

Once Cara was inside, he closed the door. "Signorina, I have terrible news."

Cara froze.

Raf.

"No," she murmured.

Alphonso took off his hat and stared down at the ground.

Cara waited, her eyes raking across the gentle old man's face.

"The village of San Pancrazio has been burned to the ground. And at San Godenzo, women have been raped and a child killed."

"Santa Maria," she murmured. "God rest their souls."

Alphonso's eyes were marbled with traces of red. "Farms all over Tuscany are being plundered and burned. Göring's divisions will come to this district next. And they will not treat it any differently." He held Cara's gaze.

Cara leaned heavily against Alphonso's gardening bench. *There was no time left.* "Then tell me what to do. I spoke to Raf, but he has disappeared into smoke." Cara lowered her voice. "I suspect he is devastated by the... by his mother's... activities. Put me into contact with someone else, or give me a job to do, Alphonso."

"Please, I implore you, signorina bella. You must not risk getting arrested."

Her eyes locked with his.

"Hundreds of innocent Italians are in prison under the SS. You must protect yourself, Cara. Please, put yourself first. I know what you told me after your father was shot, and I understand how you felt but..." Alphonso went quiet. "It is not worth it. It is not worth the risk. Especially with our new... guest in the villa."

Cara moved toward the closed door of the little shed. Alphonso's jar of coffee sat on a rudimentary bench, and there was a tripod for boiling water along with his mug, and an empty jar that used to contain biscotti.

"Alphonso," she whispered. "Please. If you have something to say, and if there is any way I can help, then tell me. I am tormented by not doing anything. I can't go on like this."

Alphonso was watching her intently. A myriad of expressions seemed to pass across his face. Finally, he put a hand into his pocket and pulled out a rough piece of paper. He looked down at it. Solemnly, he shook his head. "I did not know whether to give this to you. I have had it for a few days. It is a message for you, signorina. Please... Do not do anything rash."

Cara drew in a ragged breath. She looked at the unsuspecting piece of paper in Alphonso's hands. If she took it, it would change her life, and nothing would be the same.

Alphonso stood in silence, waiting.

Cara reached out and Alphonso placed it in her hand.

CHAPTER 13

ANNIE

Annie padded across the room in her pensione. She threw open the wooden shutters and leaned on the windowsill, cradling her cup of coffee, and letting her face soak up the sun. She had been lucky to secure an apartment in the pensione, rather than just one of the hotel rooms. The proprietor had told her that this apartment had once belonged to the family who ran the pensione in the last century, and that seemed to make being here even more special.

She settled down for breakfast at the round table near the window, a plate of French toast, mascarpone, and strawberries that she had prepared in the tiny kitchen that came with her room set out in front of her, along with a pot of coffee. The day-old Italian bread was perfect for French toast, and Annie savored every bite of the crispy exterior and the soft, pillowy interior of the delicious cinnamon-flavored loaf.

Last night, she had cooked happily in the perfect kitchen, casting her worries about Sandro aside, and losing herself in balancing flavors, colors, tastes, and fragrances, using only her instincts, and the ingredients that abounded in the valley. She had listened to Puccini, in honor of Papa, while she had cooked pasta with vivid green asparagus spears and delicate curls of lemon rind, along with a dusting of Parmesan and cracked black pepper.

Annie had already planned lunch for later. She had agreed to meet Sandro at eight thirty, and, no matter what he told her, she would not let him stop her from enjoying her cooking. She would keep her eye out for the best-looking local tomatoes in the market. He might think that she did not understand Italian traditions, but in a matter of days, she had become accustomed to the fact that in Italy the fruit and vegetables were not waxed for preservation, and just as locals did, Annie was shopping for fresh produce every day. She would find some good buffalo mozzarella and a loaf of rustic local bread for lunch, and she already had a bottle of deep green, fragrant extra-virgin olive oil sitting by her stovetop.

But it was the basil that really spoke to her of Tuscany. Impulsively, Annie had bought a potted plant, and the jaunty fresh green leaves gave out a wonderful scent on the table where she ate her meals, and when she thought of going home, she knew she would miss the little plant's company.

Annie took the last bite of her French toast, sat back and stretched in her wooden chair. She moved across to the bathroom, cleaned her teeth, and regarded herself in the mirror. She would pull her long blond hair back into a no-nonsense ponytail, just for today. Annie had chosen a silky green dress that fell well below her knees and around her neck she only wore a simple silver chain. A clutch of silver bangles jingled on her arm.

She was still unsure how to handle Sandro, her... cousin, relation? She still had no idea how she fit into the Messina family, or to Tuscany. The car, the hair, the blue jeans, and expensive shoes. It all shouted privilege and ostentation. And yet, there was a sadness about him, something genuine in his manner that showed he did care about the Villa Rosa, that he did feel a connection to the property... But then there were his plans, so different to anything she had imagined, so different to the villa's regal past.

Last night, Annie's dreams had been peppered with images of the enchanting gardens restored to their former beauty. The roses tended lovingly, the trees in the orchard nurtured back to full bloom, the olives tended carefully so that they yielded plump dark fruits ready for making into olive oil and the vines pruned and fed so that the estate could produce its own delicate wine.

But while wine and olive oil were one thing, her ancestry was quite another. Yesterday after Sandro had shown her around the empty villa, she had tried and failed to navigate the Italian system for searching birth and death records. On every ancestry site, the Messina line finished with the actual family members who had been born in Italy. All she had found was Sandro's grandfather, Nicolas Messina, and a younger brother, Rafaeli. Their mother had been Evelina Messina, and her husband was Arturo Messina, just as Sandro had told her when he had shown her his grandparents' initials intertwined on the banisters of the old staircase.

It was clear that the Messina family had lived in the region for centuries, and she had no reason to doubt that Sandro was descended from the eldest son, Nicolas. She had no reason to doubt his word on this, but this was of little help. The family line had ended as far as Italian ancestry records were concerned with Nicolas and Rafaeli, and every Italian website said that it would be necessary to go to other countries to search for descendants of people not born in Italy.

The only other sources of information were the parish church or the civil registry office, but both required letters to be written to them requesting information, and both sources said that there was no guarantee of a reply from the officials.

Annie swiped pale lipstick on her lips and dusted some powder across her nose. Putting the Villa Rosa aside, Sandro was her only chance of finding out who she really was.

Sandro Messina was leaning against the fountain right in the middle of the square, exactly where he had said he would be, at half past eight. His legs were crossed, he had his face turned up to the sun, his eyes half closed, and a cigarette poised in one hand. A group of teenage girls were admiring him. Annie walked straight past them, rolling her eyes.

"*Buongiorno*, Sandro," Annie said.

Slowly, ever so slowly, Sandro opened his eyes and regarded her. He could have been a medieval troubadour, or a nineteenth-century hero in a white shirt, staring moodily out from the villa at the olive groves and vineyards below. The master of the house, with whom every girl in the valley was in love.

"*Buongiorno*," he murmured. His eyes wandered appreciatively up and down her green dress. "You look radiant this morning."

Annie folded her arms. "It's a lovely morning," she said, knowing she sounded inane and not caring.

Sandro picked up a navy jacket that was sitting beside him on the ledge, tucked his index finger into the lapel, and threw it over his shoulder. He pulled his Wayfarers down and indicated for Annie to follow him. The man was a walking designer label. He wore a pristine white T-shirt tucked into a pair of faded blue jeans. "Let me show you around the market. And then, we can have coffee and talk."

Annie focused on the market stalls. "Sure." She would have

to hear him out, but no matter how hard Sandro insisted that he was the only heir to the Villa Rosa, her father's voice was resounding somewhere deep inside her, telling her to stick to her guns.

Sandro waved her on, putting on a show of being a gracious gentleman. "Please. Let's go this way."

Annie headed for a stallholder with a selection of round wheels of cheese, the local pecorino and perfectly shaped Parmesan. She was in heaven. But out of the corner of her eye, she could see the way people were staring at Sandro, and she noticed the way he basked in the attention.

"The Pecorino around here is glorious, Annie," Sandro murmured, wandering over. "But you must refer to it as *cacio,* adapted from the Latin, not *formaggio.* It is a pure ewe's milk made between September and June. It is very important to understand these details, if you want to truly think like an Italian."

Annie ignored him and accepted the elderly stallholder's offer of a piece held out on a little fork. She allowed herself to be transported, the sweetness of the morsel of cheese tender on her tastebuds.

"Try this one, it is less picante, and my preference," the old man said. "But you can see the buttermilk tears on the cheese? This is because ewe's milk contains a very high percentage of buttermilk. The flavor varies, depending on the grass that the cows are eating. Please, enjoy."

Annie tried a slightly stronger version, and the flavor erupted straight away. This was the one to buy. She chose a small wedge for herself, ignoring the fact that Sandro was standing next to her, jacket still strewn over his shoulder, tapping his foot on the ground.

"Signor Bartucci, this is Annie Reynolds. She is visiting us from California," Sandro said to the stallholder.

The elderly gentleman held out his hand, and Annie shook

it, smiling at him.

"My family supplied the markets for centuries," Sandro went on, even though the stallholder was serving another customer now. "My great-grandparents Evelina and Arturo owned and managed many farms in the valley, and it is fresh local produce from these holdings that you are still tasting today. The farms were given back to the farmers after the war, to encourage them to stay in Italy."

"Oh, look," Annie said. Not even Sandro's lecturing could ruin her delight in the colors and the flavors all around them. A store was selling roasted pork with crisp crackling, and people were already forming a long queue. Annie wandered over to have a look.

"That is Bernardi," Sandro announced, behind her. "His farm is on the outskirts of the village, and his family were very loyal tenants of my great-grandparents."

Sandro leaned forward and patted the middle-aged farmer on the arm.

But Sandro had underestimated Annie's ability to lose herself when she was surrounded by enticing food. She took her time wandering around the fruit and vegetable stalls, choosing half a cantaloupe which she would wrap in prosciutto as a starter before dinner tonight—although, the way she was eating, a starter might be enough.

Every now and then, Sandro would chat with one of the stallholders, placing his arm around their shoulders, acting as if he had lived here all his life. But Luca had said that Sandro lived in London. If he was so fond of Italy, why had he kept away?

By the time she had bought a couple of plump ripe toma- toes, her fresh bread for the day, some perfectly formed rounds of succulent buffalo mozzarella and prosciutto, it was time to get down to business with Sandro.

Annie sat opposite him at an alfresco table outside the

busiest bar in the square. The fact that they were among all the crowds was reassuring. It was not hard to imagine the stony silence that may have hung between them had they been somewhere quieter and less populated.

Sandro sipped at his espresso, but Annie drained hers in one gulp like a true Italian, then pushed the little glass away from her.

Sandro clasped his hands and leaned forward. "Let us speak openly and honestly. Annie, you don't want my family's villa. It comes with a troubling history, and great complications. I'm afraid that it needs far more work than you could manage. And, *bella,* trust me, you have no claim."

Annie steeled herself, but Sandro continued right on.

"I watched you wandering around the market stalls this morning, acting as if you really knew what it was to be a local, but you are simply a tourist who is trying to adopt our ways. You do not understand our landscape, the green valley bathed in evening light, the red poppies dotted in the fields and the sleepy farmhouses sitting as they have done for centuries, the cut hay rolled into wheels, what it is to walk through the forests, your boots crunching on the forest floor. How exquisite wines can come out of tiny villages. The traditions that we cherish: performing nativity scenes at Christmas, every villager involved; summer concerts in the piazzas... This valley is one of the most charming, if not the most beautiful, parts of Tuscany. It is in my blood, Annie." He sounded rather sad.

"But I am told that I do belong here. That this is where I am from."

"You have not spent time here, and you do not know it—you do not love Tuscany." He waved at one of the servers and asked for another espresso. "You are not a Messina."

Annie lowered her voice. "Sandro, there were two brothers. Nicolas, your grandfather, and Rafaeli."

Sandro gazed away over the square. "Rafaeli Messina was

my grandfather's younger brother. He was estranged from my grandfather Nicolas."

"I'm sorry to hear that. Did Rafaeli have any children?"

Sandro wiped a hand across his forehead and regarded her through his Wayfarers. "Forgive me... I was not expecting to be interrogated about my home and my family, and I am surprised that you do not already know the answer to your own questions if you are truly the owner of the villa."

Annie reached for her handbag, and held on to it tight. "The notary in the village told me that I own the villa." She kept her voice firm, but her insides started to waver. The notary had also told her that he could not procure documentation, and that the ownership could be complicated, contested even. But why would Papa send her on a wild goose chase? A fierce loyalty to her father burned within her. She could not let the man sitting opposite her dismiss her out of hand.

"My father is the direct heir to the villa, and he has passed it on to me," Sandro continued. "My grandfather, Nicolas Messina, was the eldest son of Evelina and Alberto Messina. It is quite simple. I am sorry, but I love the villa and it is part of my family. It is my heritage."

"Then why," she said, "did my father leave me this?" Annie reached into her bag and pushed Papa's letter across the table.

A frown creased Sandro's strong features, as he read darling papa's words. "There can be no veracity to this claim." He handed the letter back and tented his hands.

Annie took in a deep breath. Sandro sounded like her brother, Paul. She would not let this rattle her. She had come here to sort this out, and sort this out she would.

She tucked the letter safely back in her bag. "Clearly, my father and the local notary were, and are, of the opinion that I have the greater claim."

Sandro tipped his handsome head back. "Ah, so now you admit that things are not settled? That it is not clear that you are the definite owner?"

"My father was an honest man who would never have lied to me. That letter makes it very clear that I am the owner of the villa. What's more, I have the front door key to the house."

Sandro folded his arms.

"Sandro, I am going to insist that you cease any plans to renovate the villa until this is sorted out. You can't renovate a property that you don't own when there is a dispute. And I'm afraid now we have a major dispute. The Villa Rosa is stunning. I want to turn it into the lovely family home that it deserves to be. I will live there myself and make it beautiful." She sat up, startled at her own words. There, she had said it. She was considering living in Tuscany and not going home.

"Annie, you don't understand. It is in your best interests to go back to San Francisco and forget you ever laid eyes on the Villa Rosa. Trust me."

Annie crossed her legs and sat back in her chair. "I feel at home in Tuscany. I have felt that way since I first set foot in Cortona." She glanced around the busy piazza. "All my life, I have loved cooking. You think that I know nothing about Italian food, I live and breathe cooking. I love the texture and the colors and the creativity and the darned heritage of the recipes around here. You can't turn the Villa Rosa into some conference center. It would be a travesty."

"Yes, I can. Because I own it. You do not belong in this village, in this country, or on my land. Go before this gets worse."

She lowered her voice. "How can you know that I am not the owner of the property when you have no idea who I am?"

A muscle tweaked in tiny pulses in his cheek. He picked up his empty coffee cup, only to slam it back down into a saucer. "I know exactly who you are, Miss Reynolds. And you need to get away from this village and these people now." He spoke in a soft voice. "Darn it, Annie. I have been protecting you from the truth."

Annie blanched. "What truth?" she whispered.

Sandro sighed. "I promise you; you would rather not know."

CHAPTER 14

CARA

The note that Alphonso had pressed into her hand was in Raf's handwriting, and it was written on a rough slip of paper. Cara frowned as she made her way to the meeting point in the village square that he had suggested. She remembered when the Contessa had gifted Raf with his own personal writing paper, embossed with his initials in the top center of the pages, and imprinted with his name and address in the right-hand corners like the true aristocrat he was. He had written her a dozen notes when they had been close, but she had destroyed them after overhearing the Contessa warning Raf about losing the Villa Rosa. Ever since that awful evening, she had trodden warily around the Contessa, and had ensured that she was entirely professional and kept her distance from Raf, but now, she needed to do the opposite. Raf had asked her to meet him at the fountain in the middle of the village. She had understood his message instantly. *Pigeons, 8:30.* Pigeons flocked around the fountain, attempting to steal any titbits from the people who were sampling the market's wares.

Cara entered the piazza and glanced around for him. The stallholders had set up, bravely, but with much reduced wares. Some of the tables had only a cup of olive oil or a single bunch of basil, and it was the Nazis who walked around with confidence, heckling the stall owners, attempting to bargain with them, until eventually demanding their produce for free. Some of the stallholders were too scared not to set up in case they incurred the Nazis' interrogation as to why they were not carrying on as normal under their rule.

Cara shuddered. While she, Bettina and Alphonso remained tight-lipped in the face of the Contessa's Nazi lover, protecting their jobs, the man's arrival had not deterred Bettina from providing produce to the many suffering tenant farmers who came up the hill, begging for food. Alphonso was still digging up the lettuces in the vegetable garden out the back of the villa, as well as those which had also sprung up wild in the front garden. Cara suspected that he had scattered seeds for this very purpose. The villa had enough lettuce to feed several local families from its fertile, water-fed soil.

Cara wove her way by a pair of immaculately turned-out young Nazis, their hair cropped short, cheeks flushed with health, laughing between themselves. She lowered her eyes, and walked past, not drawing any attention to herself. It was hateful to have to live this way. Keeping your mouth closed, your head down.

As she approached the fountain, the first thing Cara saw was a pair of polished shoes, pressed trousers, and then a pale blue shirt.

"*Buongiorno*," she said quietly. His arm was free of its sling, and she scanned his face. "Where have you been? How is your arm?" she whispered.

"*Buongiorno*, Cara. It's improved greatly, being back home." Raf glanced at the Nazis, stood up from where he had been leaning against the fountain, and came toward her, walking along beside her. He started talking loudly about business matters at the villa, chatting about how he had been visiting the Contessa's bank manager in Florence.

The villagers nodded respectfully toward Raf, accepting that he was instructing his mother's secretary, which was the rightful way of things.

Raf smiled and greeted the locals, shaking elderly gentlemen's hands, and placing his hand gently on the shoulders of the local elderly women. He did not rush and almost ignored Cara beside him.

Everyone adored Raf. He had been the loyal youngest son, remaining in Italy even after his older brother abandoned the Contessa. Raf was the hope for the family's future. It was not only the staff at the villa who loved him, but everyone in the valley, and at one time, Cara as well, it seemed. She had forgotten what it was like walking locally with him, had forgotten how people respected him. She swallowed down the slight lump in her throat.

Instead, she chatted with a young mother, barely older than herself, but her eyes were diverted to the sight of her grumpy fascist neighbor, who so often yelled at his wife. Luigi Santino was glaring at her from a table in the crowded café.

She ignored him. He had given her a backhanded compliment about the Contessa recently, smugly saying that it was a relief the Contessa had come to her senses and found a good man. Cara had rushed by, not engaging with him. She had heard that Luigi Santino had heckled villagers who were suspected of resistance. Another neighbor had whispered that the man had stopped scared teenagers who were terrified of enforced conscription into the army and yelled at them in the quiet village streets as they rode by on their bicycles.

Cara turned away from his stare, her lip curling, sensing the venom coming across the square. She stood by Raf, but not too close to him.

Raf kept steering them in a straight course through the market, and when they came to one of the narrow alleys that led off the square, he chose one which wound its way up the hill, switching back and forth as it had done since medieval times.

Raf stopped on one of the landings off the stone steps. He pulled a set of brass keys from his pocket and opened the curved wooden door in front of them. This was hardly surprising, as the Messina family owned several apartments in the village and rented them out. Cara was used to dealing with the tenants. They were at the bottom of the stairwell, and Cara followed him up two flights of narrow stairs to the top floor. The apartment he led her into was tiny, and the shutters were closed. If they were open, Cara knew the window would afford a breathtaking view out over the valley. Now the sun only threw striped patterns through the shutters onto the cool tiles of the floor, and the sounds of pigeons cooing on the roof was accompanied by the subdued chatter flowing up from the market in the piazza below.

The room was furnished with a table, four chairs, a rudimentary kitchen with an old stone sink, and wooden benches fronted by curtains instead of cupboard doors. The floral curtains covering the kitchen cupboards reminded her of those in the pensione, and Cara felt a twinge of sadness at the memories of cooking with her father at home.

Apart from this, there was a bed neatly made up with a white coverlet, and a simple rug lying alongside it. A pair of old chairs sat under the window.

Raf stood by the door as if listening to check that no one had followed them up the stairs.

"*Come stai?*" Raf said in soft Italian.

She turned away. "I am perfectly well. Everything is fine."

"*Bella mia?*"

But she shook her head and gripped the back of one of the chairs. The last thing she needed was him sweet-talking her.

"Are you still feeling the same way as you were last time we spoke?"

His words, softly spoken, burned into her, but she swung back around to face him, lifting her chin. "If you mean do I want to do something? Then the answer is a resounding yes."

A deep frown line appeared between Raf's eyes.

She stepped slightly closer to him, and she could smell the scent of his lemon cologne. It reminded her of the lemon balm out in the villa's garden, which grew wild along the stone walls that kept everything from tumbling down the hill. When she trod on one of the plants, the most lovely scent wafted up, and it always reminded her of Raf. It smelled like home.

When he had first left, she had yearned for him to write to her, for him to fight for her, for what she thought they had.

She allowed herself one quick memory that she had fought to bury after he left for the war. He had taken her to a restaurant in Cortona overlooking the valley. The dining tables had all been set out on the terrace, and the owner had placed votive candles on the wall that ran around the border and on the tables, so that it was as if they were surrounded by twinkling stars. They had sat together and watched the sun go down over the distant hills, and when Raf had reached out and placed his hand over hers, she had felt a new sense of contentment, and excitement. When he had held her hand, she had felt everything. But he had not fought for her when his mother had confronted him after someone saw them together. He had not contacted her once while he had been away at war.

When Papa had assured her that she would surely fall for one of the local village boys one day, she had leaned her head on her father's shoulder and had not had the heart to tell him that she did not know which boys would be coming home from the disastrous Italian campaigns, and really, there was only one she longed for.

Cara had been forced to grow up amidst this war, and one of the most poignant lessons she'd learned was that Raf would never hurt his mother by being with Cara. She was the one who didn't fit into his family, not the other way around.

"I don't want you to take the risk," he murmured, snapping her out of her reverie.

"As I said to you, I have nothing to lose any more—" She stopped abruptly. "But I have the future of our valley to fight for."

Raf walked across to the window. He did not sit down in one of the chairs, but instead leaned his hands against the back of one of them, pressing hard, and looking down. "We are planning a major attack nearby. It is going to be very close to the village."

Cara stared at his back in alarm. The outright slaughter that had taken place in other villages across Tuscany was still raw in everyone's hearts. She sank down into the chair. But this was what she'd promised her father that she'd sign up for...

It wasn't the partisans she was worried about. The kind elderly inhabitants whom she and Papa had known all their lives, the young mothers, waiting for their beloved husbands and brothers to return home from the war... The children who still ran around the marketplace. Children who lived with grim warnings not to pick up any sweets or toys that they found on the ground, for fear that they were laced with poison, because there were rumors that the Allies flying overhead were dropping poisonous sweets from the sky. This was what she was fighting for... them.

"I'm talking about the munitions storage facility that is on the outskirts of Cortona, on the side nearest the village," Raf continued.

Cara felt pale. "You must spread the word among villagers. You must warn them."

Raf turned around and came to stand next to her at the table. He spoke softly. "We don't know who we can trust, *Mia bella.*"

Of course. How could they trust that someone like Luigi Santino would not leak the partisans' plans?

She looked sharply at Raf. And what of his mother? Who, along with her Nazi friend, clearly thought that the bands of local rebels were all going to end up being blown sky high? Fascists, communists, liberals, monarchists... the Contessa said that people did not give up their political beliefs just because they took up arms. What would she think of her son being a partisan?

"There are hundreds of partisans in the area," Raf said. "I will ensure that the village is surrounded and protected at all times."

"How many?"

"Nine hundred."

Cara sagged back in her chair.

"If we don't blow up the munitions facility, we risk a bloodbath when the Allies arrive. It's important that we clear the way for them to liberate the town as freely and quickly as possible. The people are starving, but the Nazis are also turning it into an anti-aircraft base and word is that they are planning on strengthening the facility so that it is a major stronghold. It must be destroyed."

"What is your role, Raf?"

"My role, just like the other fully trained soldiers, is to ensure that the men know what they are doing."

"And the fact that the villagers trust you?" They loved him. She loved the village. She had to challenge him and ensure that he fully understood the implications of his plan.

Raf's mouth twisted. "The partisans are going to carry out

the mission anyway. With or without me. And I would rather it was with," he said. His eyes met hers and lingered a long time. "They need direction, *bella*. And they trust me to give them that." His voice held an ache that was heartbreaking.

"We are a mixed group. We do have local men involved who know the area well, but they are not trained properly. Cara—"

Cara pushed back her chair abruptly and leaned against the kitchen bench, staring at the wall. The Contessa and her family were the villagers' protectors, their friends. And yet, under their very noses, Raf's mother was sleeping with a Nazi, and her son was taking a risk that could lead to a tragedy in the village that would reverberate for generations. A reprisal like the others the Nazis had carried out could destroy the fabric of their lives.

"They are going to do it anyway?" She swung around.

He nodded. "*Sì.*"

"It is crazy," she whispered. "How are we going to forgive ourselves if the worst happens? How will you live with yourself?"

"Yes, but so is this entire situation..." Raf's words lingered in the still air, and he took a step toward her, only to stop. "Crazy," he whispered. "Sometimes, you have to make what feels like an impossible choice."

Cara leaned heavily against the bench and her insides started to quake. She was staring at him, and he at her. There was nothing to be done. War called for tough decisions, impossible choices. And just like Raf, she would rather be there and try to do everything she could to protect the people of this valley from danger.

The sound of a child calling out for their mama from the square below filtered into the room. That was what they were risking and protecting at the same time.

She knew her dark eyes were flashing, and the fire of determination inside her burned strong. "Tell me what you need me to do."

"*Bella*," Raf whispered. "What they want a woman to do is the most dangerous task of all."

His eyes pleaded with her.

But she lifted her chin. "I am ready."

CHAPTER 15

ANNIE

Annie narrowed her eyes and stared at Sandro. Was he about to say that he knew who her mother was? If he was family, why had he never contacted her? And how could some random man have known of her existence, all this time, when clearly, she had no idea who she was? She folded her arms and shook her head.

"How could you know who I am? You know nothing about me. Nothing." But something dark curled within her that she didn't like. She knew what it was. It was uncertainty. Uncertainty that she might lose the chance to live in and love the old villa. There was no denying it and no point in shying away from the fact that she had fallen for the way the gardens tumbled down the hill. The food in the valley, the simple way of life. Being away from the city. She had fallen for Italy, and she had told her colleagues at the catering company that she would have to remain here a while.

"I spoke to my father back in the States last night," Sandro said.

Annie pulled herself back to reality. "Your father lives in the States? And you live in London?"

Sandro nodded. "Family means everything to my dad. We all want to reconnect with Italy." He frowned down at the table. "I will bring him here only once the Villa Rosa is restored, and it will be an incredibly moving day for us all when he returns to his real home. He is devastated by the fact that Nicolas was cut off from the family by the Contessa. It is time to right that wrong once and for all."

Annie leaned heavily on her elbows and watched him. "Who am I, then, Sandro? Where do I fit into the Messinas' story?"

"I don't want to be the person who brings you bad news."

Annie simply rolled her eyes. "I think we are beyond that, Sandro."

Sandro lowered his voice. "You really want to know? Because I don't recommend it. Trust me, you are better off not knowing and going home."

"Come on."

Sandro leaned forward and clasped his hands on the table. "My great-grandmother Evelina Messina did not just send my poor grandfather Nicolas away." He paused.

"I see."

"Annie, prepare yourself."

"Fully prepared, Sandro."

"She had an affair with a Nazi during the war, and a child was produced from the liaison. It is something my family struggle with. We are deeply ashamed of this connection."

"A Nazi?" Annie asked. She attempted to sound as derisive as Sandro, but her heart had begun to beat an unsteady course.

Sandro was firm. "This is why the Villa Rosa has remained empty for so long and it is why I want to turn it into something completely new. I'm afraid your heritage is so tainted that the best thing you could do is walk away from it and go home. Don't seek this history out, it will only break your heart."

A Nazi? Annie wound her fingers around the strap of her handbag. Was this her heritage?

She knew that in Italy, even today, the subject of the war was sensitive. The Second World War had been a disaster for the Italians, who had been forced into a situation that none of them wanted. Thanks to the pact between Hitler and Mussolini, their young men had been wiped out in battle after battle, only to suffer further great casualties and losses under the Allies' relentless air raids. Then, when the Germans invaded, after Italy had switched sides and made peace with the Allies, the northern Italians had to live under German occupation, while the Allies invaded from the south. After the war, so many migrated, and families were torn apart. But this was all the result of government decisions, not personal ones. And now to learn this of Evelina Messina? Who was potentially her grandmother? Annie stared at Sandro, speechless, but her insides roiled and she struggled to force her breathing to steady.

"Evelina Messina's affair with a Nazi brought shame and ruin on the Messina family for decades after the war, and people avoided associating with them or the villa because of it. It is only now, decades later, that the real Messinas feel that we can be back here in Italy again."

"What are you saying about me?" Annie sat back in her seat, a flush rising through her cheeks, her eyes stinging with angry, unshed tears. How dare he? How dare he accuse her of being the product of some reprehensible liaison? Was that what he was doing? Her mind clouded. What did he know of her ancestry?

"I think we both know."

"But who was my mother?"

"The child born of the Nazi."

Annie barked out a laugh. "And who was she? Where is

she? Why was this her fault?" Before Sandro had a chance to answer, she went on. "And tell me one thing: why did your line of the family abandon the villa entirely and leave it to get into such a state? If you care about it so much?"

Sandro sighed and stared into the piazza.

"Clearly, your family left the Villa Rosa to rot," Annie went on. "It has been neglected. And that needs to change. Someone needs to step in and restore it. With great care. Not turn it into a soulless conference center for people to walk in and out of. The garden needs someone who loves it, the kitchen needs to be filled with the scent of Tuscan cooking, and the French doors thrown open to the courtyard, which needs to be filled with herbs and homegrown vegetables for a family." She eyed him. "What you are planning on doing, pulling out the strong foundation walls, is going to cause the entire building to tumble down the hill." She could feel Papa cheering her on. She was not the daughter of an architect for nothing. "If you don't want to live in the Villa Rosa, then why bother with it at all? Why are you here?" She checked herself. She was getting angry, but he had ambushed her with the story of a Nazi without any proof.

Sandro pulled his Wayfarers up and rested them on his shoulder-length wavy hair. "It was your... ancestor who ruined the entire family's reputation. Forgive me, Miss Reynolds, but what have you to do with my family home? You are the product of a curse that forced my family to abandon the villa and allow it to get into such a state. We are all finally trying to move on. Annie, we hoped you'd never come here."

Annie pushed her empty glass a little across the table. "But why has my father told me that I own the villa? You can't walk all over that, Sandro." *With your ridiculous hair.* She did not add the words. But she thought of them, and she bit back a smile.

"Why did he hide the truth of your birth from you if he was not ashamed of it too?"

The words hung in the air and locked in Annie's heart. Why indeed had Papa not told her the truth of her lineage until after his death? Had he been ashamed of her? Of himself? Was he her father at all?

"Why only leave you a letter telling you that you were born under the Tuscan sun after he died? No, Annie, we both know he was hiding the truth from you. The truth about your birth that was too hard for him to deal with. Your father would have been protecting his own reputation until he died. Nobody wants to be descended from the Nazi who brought you into the world. By association, your past is tainted with a stain."

She closed her eyes.

Sandro went on, "You don't want to face the hard truth about your ancestry. I know who I am. I have a good family. And that family has centuries of connection and ownership of the Villa Rosa."

Annie pushed her chair back and stood up. "Before we take this any further, I want to see the documentation that proves you own the villa."

Sandro sat back. "But you have no documentation, no?"

Annie tossed her head, wishing for one moment she had left her blond hair flowing down her back. The ponytail did not hold the necessary cachet. "I do not give my permission for you to touch the villa, nor its contents. The garden, too, must be left exactly as it is. Your employee—"

"Luca."

"Luca may continue to search for the water source, as that is in the best interests of the garden, which has suffered severe neglect under your family. However, in the face of our dispute, nothing else is to be touched until this is resolved." She lifted her chin and looked down at him. "Do I make myself clear, Mr. Messina?"

"Don't break your own heart, Annie. Let it go."

Annie picked up her bag and left.

CHAPTER 16

CARA

Raf went over to the rudimentary kitchen in the tiny studio apartment and pulled out an old map. "Here is where the Nazis are storing munitions, on the outskirts of Cortona, in an old barn." He pointed to another field outside the town. "This is where intelligence knows they are planning on building an anti-aircraft artillery nearby, as well as setting up heavily fortified bunkers armed with tanks to stop the Allies from entering Cortona. Once completed, it will be very difficult for the Allies to liberate our valley. Many more soldiers and villagers will die. It is vital that we stop them."

The barn was only ten minutes from the village. Cara frowned at the map.

"The facility is, of course, heavily guarded, but every three hours, there is a change of guard."

"Hardly enough of a diversion."

"But it must be."

Cara stood up. She circled the room, and came to stand by the shuttered window, looking at him. "What is it that you want me to do?" She enunciated her words clearly enough, but even as she uttered them, they seemed unbelievable, unreal to her.

"Bella, have you heard of the *staffette?*"

Cara held his gaze. The *staffette* operated as couriers for the resistance, carrying documents and important messages for the partisans. But sometimes, on the most dangerous of occasions, they also carried weapons. Raf's meaning became clear. He was not asking her to transport letters, maps, or documents. And given the proximity of the barn, she doubted that he was going to ask her to sit on the relative anonymity of a train.

"You want me to transport the ammunition. The explosives. And you need me to do that on a bike or on foot, don't you."

"That is what we need a *staffetta* to do. Because they won't suspect a woman."

Cara lowered her voice. "I work for your mother. She is a good fascist. They will *never* suspect me."

"If I had my way, you would be safely in the villa with her."

"The villa is not safe," Cara whispered. "Raf, if the Contessa carries on in the way she is," she went on in a low, urgent voice, "the partisans will attack the Villa Rosa. You will not be able to stop them. We both know they are targeting members of the upper classes who are staying loyal to the fascists. And your mother is sleeping with a Nazi."

Raf ground out the words. "Bruno Klein. He is working for the commandant in Florence."

"Yes. Heaven help her," Cara whispered.

Raf buried his head in his hands.

"I'm sorry." Cara moved over to him, until there was only a hair's breadth between them. She reached out and squeezed Raf's hand. An electric jolt of attraction seared through her, even though he didn't raise his head. He had lost his father. His mother was behaving reprehensibly, and making choices that may haunt the family for years. His brother Nicolas had left. ... All of this could leave him with no close family. Just like her.

"I cannot control what my mother does." Raf pulled his hand away. "I can't be held responsible for her."

"Of course," Cara whispered.

"But I worry that her actions will implicate you," he said, raising his head, his eyes raking over her face. "I worry they already have."

She stood stock-still. *Of course, they have, and this will always hang between us. What might have been...*

Cara gathered herself, folded her arms. "Tell me what you want me to do."

Half an hour later, Cara understood everything. She sat, poring over the map with Raf. "So, the explosives are currently stored in a building in Cortona. I am to ride my bike there next Saturday morning, collect them, place the box containing the dynamite in a shopping bag in my basket, and then bring it back here until the day of the mission."

Raf eyed her. "Not to the village. It is too risky. If the explosives are uncovered, the Nazis will murder everyone in the town." His gaze only wavered slightly. "I want you to store the explosives in the summerhouse at the villa before they are transported to the site," he said. "And no, I don't want you to take your bicycle. I want you to take my mother's bicycle."

"What?"

But Raf held up a hand. "If anyone stops you, you can tell them that you are picking up a gift for the Contessa in Cortona, some of her favorite *cocci*. The *cocci* will be a gift from me. Along with the gift, there will be a letter to her, explaining that I am well and safe. The letter will be full of love."

"Of course," she said. "You will give me the collection address in Cortona?"

"Remember it, and destroy it," he said. "This week, be sure to tell my mother that you bumped into me at the market in

Cortona while you were on leave, and that I wish to send her a letter. Along with a small gift. You can tell her that I am working in Cortona with the... authorities. You can tell her that you don't know where I am living in the town if she asks... that you would not expect her son to divulge his address to you."

The secretary. The girl who would be utterly inappropriate as a daughter-in-law at the Villa Rosa... The Contessa's words spoken so many years ago after their magical first date, hung in the air.

Cara stood up. Raf stood up too, and ever so gently, he placed his forefinger under her chin. Her eyes searched his, back and forth.

"My only fear is for our friends in the village."

He had reassured her over and over that the partisans would be stationed here and were instructed to shoot any Nazis they suspected of harming the villagers. It was hardly comforting.

"Darling Cara," he whispered. "I know how much you care about everyone here. This valley. Tuscany. The future. This is why I..." And he leaned down, and he was so close to her, but she pulled away.

The Contessa was a ruthless and powerful woman. If Cara were to step out of line, the Contessa could destroy Cara's repu-tation and even her safety with one phone call. The fact was, she did not trust her employer. She did not trust Raf's mother.

"I will pick up the ammunition." She pulled away from him and moved toward the door.

CHAPTER 17

ANNIE

Annie sat in the office in the Villa Rosa, papers spread all around her on the floor. Luca had allowed her access to the stately old house behind Sandro's back, and she had begun what she hoped was going to be a fruitful search. But so far, she had found everything, and nothing. There were only farming records and business documents kept and filed meticulously in the office. However, they ran from 1947 to 1990, the year of Annie's birth—which was also the year the old Contessa had died.

The records appeared to have been kept and overseen meticulously. Every letter, every document was signed by the Contessa. One telling detail was that there was no mention of Sandro's grandfather Nicolas Messina. Clearly, his arguments about primogeniture rang a little false.

The only thing that seemed certain was that the Contessa had never involved her oldest son Nicolas in the villa's business affairs.

That fitted in with what Sandro had told her; however, it

did not explain Annie's link to the villa. Was she really the Contessa's grandchild? She was trying to block out Sandro's insinuation that she was descended from some Nazi, and there was nothing in the papers she'd found in the office to suggest this was true.

Luca came into the study at lunchtime. Annie had thrown the French doors open to the garden, and it had been companionable working in here while she could hear Luca outside. He, like her, was carrying out his own search, for the well that would allow the water to flow again through the lovely gardens.

"Any luck?" Luca stood framed in the bright sunlight that beamed through the French doors. The golden Tuscan light threw a halo around his blond head.

Annie looked up at him, and almost had to shade her eyes.

"The Contessa Evelina was very precise in her recordkeeping, but extremely obscure when it comes to what I'm looking for."

"Want to tell me more?" Luca asked. His voice was gentle.

Annie took in a shaking breath. "Sandro says that the Contessa Evelina had an affair with a Nazi during the war. He told me I was descended from that liaison." The documents on the floor started to swim in front of her eyes.

"How on earth can he prove such a thing?" Luca's voice filtered through the quiet room. "You've floored me with that."

Annie shook her head. "I know."

Luca came around to crouch down beside her, carefully picking up one of the neat stacks of papers she had arranged on the floor. "Are you okay?"

Annie shrugged. "I don't believe him. And yet, there is no other explanation at this point." She turned to face him, her eyes huge. "Unfortunately, all the pieces are falling into place. As Sandro pointed out, it would explain why my father could not face telling me who I was. And it would explain why the villa was abandoned, why no one wanted to associate with it after the Contessa died along with her shameful past. All these things make an awful lot of sense." Annie buried her head in her hands. "What a horrible legacy."

She felt Luca's hand resting softly on her back. "It might not be the truth," he said hopelessly.

"I don't want it to be. I actually just want to go home."

"Okay, but let's not give up yet. All the war records are missing?"

Annie nodded. "And the storage room at the end of this wing, which, according to Sandro, used to be an animal stable, is empty of any files. Someone has cleared it out. It gave me the creeps to be honest."

Luca ran a hand over his chin. "It does seem strange that everything has been kept since 1947, but nothing before that point. Someone must have been hiding something."

"That's what worries me." Annie stood up and arched her back from the hours spent sitting on the floor. She should have sat at the desk, but it felt as if she was imposing, setting herself at the place where this woman who had held the reins of the Messina family had sat for so many years. *The traitor who might be my grandmother.*

It still felt as if the Contessa was lingering here at the villa, even though all evidence of the war years had been cleared out. Annie had been back to revisit the old black-and-white photograph of the woman with beautifully styled blond hair in a strapless evening gown; she was smiling, yes, but her eyes held traces of steel. On an impulse, Annie had photographed the picture with her phone.

"You need a break. Would you like some lunch?" Luca's voice pierced into her thoughts.

"I was going to go down to the village to grab a panini and another espresso," she said. She smiled at him. "I owe you a thank you for allowing me into the villa. Would you care to join me?" Sandro had not expressly forbidden her to enter the villa, but it went unspoken that he would hardly be pleased...

Luca's blue-eyed gaze was level. "Your father left you a key, not me."

"Right," she chuckled.

"I am only the gardener," Luca said. He spread out his hands, and his face lit up into a handsome smile.

"Exactly." Annie laughed. "Although, we shouldn't risk having lunch together in the village if Sandro is on the prowl. He was not particularly happy last time I saw him."

"There is my cottage," Luca suggested. "If you are willing to brave it."

"Has it been abandoned for decades as well? Is it full of meticulous records that give away nothing at all?"

Luca grinned. "Not that I know of. Not that I've been snooping."

Annie smiled back at him and bit on her lip.

"Sandro renovated it for me. Had the walls whitewashed, the kitchen and bathroom scrubbed clean, and a modern refrigerator and oven installed. I even have a dishwasher!"

Annie tilted her head to one side.

"Come on," he said. "Let me cook for you."

Just then, a tiny bird flew into the study through the open doors. It landed on the Contessa's desk, eyeing them, its head switching back and forth from one of them to the other.

Annie dared not move. She hardly dared to breathe.

"The villa needs to come back to life. We need to open her doors," Luca whispered.

As if in approval, the little bird stared at him a moment, then flew right out again, freeing itself into the blue, blue open skies of Tuscany.

CHAPTER 18

CARA

Cara and Alphonso pored over the newspapers each day. All they could hope was that the Germans would beat a hasty retreat north and that the valley would be spared from the worst of their wrath as the Allies advanced. However, there was no guarantee of this, and a leaden atmosphere hung over the village. Every morning, a different group of forlorn refugees huddled by the back door of the Villa Rosa. Cara started getting to work well before dawn to help Bettina bake enough rolls to feed them.

Cara stood with Bettina outside the kitchen door, handing out fresh bread to the orderly line who had gathered at the villa this morning. So many of the children were too weak to walk on their heartbreakingly stick-like legs, their bellies distended with famine. Their faces were grimy with dirt, and Cara had set up a tub filled with warm water so that they could wash out in the warm courtyard behind the Villa Rosa's back door. Every morning, Cara picked what fruit she could from the orchard, and sliced it up on platters, heartbroken at the subdued, patient way the refugees accepted their food. They never begged for beds inside the house, not like the Nazis who were the second lot of visitors to constantly appear on the villa's grounds. This week, Cara had deflected a request from the local commandant in the village to take over the entire villa as a hospital for wounded German soldiers being transported up from the south. As the Contessa was away in Florence with Bruno Klein, and Raf was not here, Cara had simply said she did not have the authority to allow this, and the commandant, miraculously respecting the need for an authoritarian figure to make the decision, had departed, scowling, but nodding his head. However, that afternoon a German Red Cross truck had been parked right outside the villa's front door, as if to warn the partisans whose side the Villa Rosa was on. So far, the Germans were tolerating the villa feeding the refugees.

Cara reached out and placed her hand under the bony chin of a little boy. She picked a fat slice of peach and popped it in his mouth.

"*Grazie,*" his mother whispered. Her eyes were hollow, sitting in deep bruised sockets, and her cheeks were pale and gaunt.

"God bless you," Cara whispered.

The woman turned, her head down, and took her child to sit in a quiet spot to eat his bread.

As well as the refugees, there were the partisans coming for food. In the evenings, a reliable teenager named Giuseppe, who was avoiding conscription because he would be forced to fight for the Germans, would appear, a shadowy figure lurking around the outhouses behind the villa. Cara would go out to him with a basket of food for the group of young men whom she knew were living rough in a cave further up the hill. In the last few days, she had come to trust Giuseppe, but rumors abounded of more SS men dressed in the rough clothes of the partisans. Cara remained unsure as to whether the visitor she had encountered in the gardens, demanding thousands of lire from the villa, only to escape through the vineyards, had been SS or a partisan.

Tragically, a kindly farmer across the valley had agreed to help two begging partisans, only to discover that he had been duped by a pair of SS guards. Cara had blanched in horror at the story of how he had been dragged away, lined up against a tree on his own property, and shot mercilessly for betrayal. His seven-year-old son had discovered his father's body, and had been incoherent for days, shaking, and curled up in the fetal position in his bed. This had only exacerbated her broken heart over her own father, her loss. The seven-year-old boy was too young to do anything, but she wasn't.

Cara had marched into the commandant's office in the village when she had heard this awful story. He had told her firmly that the Nazis were prepared to be reasonable, but that if people were not prepared to treat them with the same respect in turn, and betrayed them, they would not tolerate it.

The sound of German bomber planes blowing up bridges south of the valley was a daily ritual, too, and the thud of bombs falling over the distant hills caused Cara and Alphonso to run upstairs to the top floor of the Villa Rosa, where they would see the rising of smoke over bridges.

Every now and then, Cara saw a falling Allied airplane, caught in the crossfire of anti-aircraft guns, and she was becoming used to silver parachutes falling from the sky. She couldn't begin to contemplate how Italy would ever recover.

Only one downed Allied pilot had come for food at the villa. Bettina had brought him into the kitchen and fed him, but warned him that he could not stay.

Cara had to prepare for the dangerous mission that she had promised to undertake for Raf the following day, but ever since the weekend the partisans had increased their vigilance, lining the main roads that led south from Florence and carrying out random attacks on passing cars, because they always belonged to fascists or Nazis. Nobody else could afford to keep a car or to buy petrol in Italy these days.

The Contessa's car sat in the garage. She had taken the train up to Florence with her lover. His gleaming German car was no longer parked in the driveway, as he had instructed one of his subordinates to drive it, clearly not worried about risking their life.

Cara dreaded the return of the elegant couple to the Villa Rosa.

That evening, Cara made her way down to the gardener's cottage, where the smell of bread being toasted on Alphonso's open fire was accompanied by the deep tang of roasting peppers in the oven. He would arrange these on the bread for a simple supper, and then he would follow this with the peaches that Bettina had bottled last summer in a sweet syrup flavored with honey from local bees.

She paused, her hand on the doorknob. "Alphonso?" she called.

Alphonso pulled the green door wide. "*Buonasera, signorina.*"

Cara was instantly enveloped with the sense of comfort that she always felt when she came into Alphonso's modest home. The waxed brick floors were swept until they were spotless, and the whitewashed walls were hung only with a simple cross over his single bed. His slippers were placed neatly on the floor.

"I am just preparing my evening meal," Alphonso said. "Will you join me?"

Cara shook her head, touched by his kindness. "Thank you, Alphonso. I have some tomatoes and bread to take down to the village. I have plenty." She reached out and placed a hand on his arm. "Please, you go ahead."

Alphonso walked over to the table and held out a chair.

Cara was thankful to sit down; it had been a long day. And when he lifted the bottle of wine, made by local winemakers from the grapes that Alphonso tended on the hillside, she nodded. The young man who had looked after the vineyards at the villa before the war had been killed in the North African campaign, and ever since then, Alphonso had made it his business to learn how to take care of and manage the vines.

A local winemaker still sent grape pickers out to harvest and, so far, had managed to send the bottles that were procured from the Villa Rosa grapes back to the Contessa, even though the Nazis had stolen as many bottles as they could from the winemakers in the last year.

"I could do with fortification—just a sip." She smiled at him, and he poured half a glass into the tumbler that sat in front of her. "Alphonso, I have something I need to ask you."

He paused, his bruschetta halfway to his mouth.

"I need to borrow the Contessa's bicycle tomorrow morning..."

CHAPTER 19

ANNIE

Annie walked with Luca down to the gardener's cottage. It was nestled behind the villa, beyond the rear courtyard and the overgrown vegetable garden that was tumbling with weeds. They passed a two-story stable, complete with stalls for a dozen horses. Annie peered into it.

"Someone must have been a keen rider," she said. She screwed up her nose. "I've always been terrified of horse riding; sitting up there, their ears twitching, not knowing what they're going to do next."

Luca turned to her. "You must come riding with me. There's nothing like going on a trek through the Tuscan valleys. I guarantee you will fall in love with riding out here."

Annie laughed. "You've got to be kidding me," she said. She grinned at him and shook her head. "I just tell you one of my deepest fears, and you say I should get over it?"

"Sorry," Luca said. He looked down at the ground, his hands in the pockets of his trousers. "I suppose when you love something as much as I do, you want to share it. I grew up with horses, and I love riding as much as I love tucking new plants into the soil and giving them a home."

"I understand. It's your passion, just as cooking is mine." She followed him past a stone garage with a faded wooden door. Beyond this, they came to a cottage set behind a picket fence. Luca held the white-painted gate open, and Annie stepped inside the garden, which had been set out with new plants, their green shoots looking healthy and well-tended in the freshly turned rich earth. There were new rose plants in each of the four sections of the garden, and lavender, already attracting bees. Salvias and hollyhocks were planted in the middle of the plots, and there were neat rows of box hedge lining the brick path. Again, this seemed curious. Why was he taking so much care tending to the garden around the house where he was staying for what could only be a short period of time?

"You've done an amazing job here," Annie said.

Luca indicated with his head. "Come inside." He led her to a green front door, with a smart round brass door knocker that was polished to a gleam. The front step had been swept, and two pots of daisies sat either side of the freshly painted door.

Inside, Annie looked around in appreciation. The contrast between the waxed brick floor, the whitewashed walls, the single bed tucked into the corner of the room with its antique white coverlet to the faded, decrepit grand beauty of the villa was disarming. There was something homely and charming about this simple cottage, a feeling that Sandro was clearly not planning to replicate at the villa.

Luca went over to the kitchen that lined one wall and, from the refrigerator, pulled out prosciutto, from the cupboard, some of the local flatbread, olive oil, and arugula, which he tossed with pecans and pears.

"Can I help?" Annie asked.

But Luca shook his head.

He set the table under the window that overlooked the new

cottage garden and brought over a bottle of local wine and two glasses. He reached forward and opened the dormer windows wide.

"Heaven," Annie said. She stretched her arms out and sat back in her seat while Luca held up the wine glass, and she nodded. "This all looks delicious," she said.

"Good." He offered her a plate of prosciutto and local flatbread.

They ate in companionable silence for a while, and then Luca put down his glass of wine. His expression was hard to define. "You know if there's anything I can do to help, you only have to ask me," he said.

Annie looked out at the garden, and all she could see was potential—potential for the villa and its own garden to be loved again. "It's an enigma, why Papa left me that letter," she murmured. "I simply have no leads."

After hearing Sandro's news about the affair that Evelina Messina had had with a Nazi, Annie had tossed and turned at night, feeling an inexplicable burst of shame. The acts of the previous generations were in no way the fault of the present ones, but Sandro's gloating about his own unsullied lineage only made her feel more at fault.

Monica and Paul had been in touch. They were both messaging her regularly, and she had had a brief conversation with Paul about the possible sale of Papa's house in Carmel-by-the-Sea. Neither he nor Monica wanted to live in the wooden house that Papa had designed and built, and while Annie had inherited the villa in Tuscany, Papa had gifted his house in California to his two eldest children. This was reasonable, and not something Annie was remotely interested in contesting, but as her own past became blurrier and blurrier by the minute, she felt she was losing her grip on anything worth fighting for.

Annie took in a deep breath. "Sandro tells me that Evelina Messina's wartime affair brought such infamy on the family that it turned them into pariahs in the district, and this was why his branch of the family avoided the Villa Rosa and Tuscany altogether. He was adamant that my claim is not only illegitimate, but reprehensible."

Luca reached out a hand across the table. "I'm sorry."

"Sandro's grandfather, Nicolas, was the Contessa's eldest son, but it seems he left the villa when the war broke out," Annie went on. "But there was a second son, Rafaeli. I don't know what happened to him... perhaps Evelina Messina was left living by herself, lonely with neither of her sons and this baby." Annie frowned. "That seems like a terribly sad outcome to me, but, looking at the state of the villa, it also feels like a realistic one. And then, there is me."

"There must be someone in the area who knows the story," Luca said. But his voice was shaky, and he was tapping the table nervously. "Archives? The library?"

But Annie shook her head. "The only way of finding out anything about Italian ancestry is to write to the local parishes, or the civil registry office, and there's no guarantee they will respond. They also only deal with those family members born in Italy."

"So many Italians migrated after the war," Luca said quietly. "What happened here was awful. Unbearable."

Annie nodded. "I've been doing some reading online about the history here during the war. I'm afraid I was ignorant." She gazed out the window at the serene garden again.

"We are all so aware of the D-Day landings, and the Nazi occupation of France, but it was brutal here. The Nazis occupied Tuscany... I don't know the ins and outs of what happened. I'd like to find out more as well, Annie."

"I need to find out whether what Sandro is saying is true. This afternoon, I'm going to search the Contessa's bedroom. All I can hope is that there will be some form of correspondence stashed away in a drawer in her bureau." Annie closed her eyes for a moment. Secret drawers in bureaus were not something that she wanted to search ever again.

Luca let out a shaky sigh.

"What is it?"

He stood up, gathered the plates from the table and moved across to the kitchen, loaded the dishwasher, then turned around to face her again. "Coffee?" he asked.

Annie nodded absently. "Thank you." But she watched him as he reached for a jar of coffee beans and busied himself for a time.

When he came back to sit down again, Annie leaned across the table and folded her arms.

"You look as if you have something to say."

Luca poured the dark brown, aromatic brew into two tiny espresso cups.

Annie gazed at the shots of coffee bravely. What she wouldn't give for a caffè latte... But when in Rome. She waited.

Luca shook his head and frowned. "I don't want to alarm you," he said.

Annie remained still.

"But the thing is," he continued, lifting his gaze to meet hers, "my mother is coming to visit me here, soon. I think... It would be good for you to meet her—if you would like to, that is."

"Oh?" Annie slumped with relief. She almost wanted to laugh aloud. "Well, I don't think we're going to alarm her," she quipped. "It's not as if we've jumped into some crazy relationship."

The sun beat a strong yellow shaft across the table, highlighting his hands. He brought them up and rested his head in them a moment. "No, we haven't done that," he said softly.

Annie toyed with her coffee cup.

"You see, my grandfather worked here throughout the war. His name was Alphonso, and he was the gardener at the Villa Rosa. I'm afraid he did tell my mother that the Contessa had an affair with a high-ranking Nazi, just as Sandro told you. I'm sorry, Annie."

Finally, when she was able to speak, she could only whisper. "Did your grandfather live in this very cottage on the estate?" That made sense. A little more sense... Why he was here. Was he on a family pilgrimage of his own?

Luca nodded. He leaned forward, resting his arms on the simple table. "My grandfather died years ago. I was only young. I hardly remember anything about him. My grandmother was years younger than him. All we know is that he left the Villa Rosa after the war, and I don't know why. I do wonder whether he left because of that liaison. My grandmother talked of it in hushed tones, and all I know is that she would shake her head and say that it was a very sad business. And my grandfather never spoke of it with me. But I couldn't resist coming here to work on the Villa Rosa. Somehow, it feels as if it's in my blood as well." He paused. "I didn't know whether I should tell you. I didn't want to complicate things. And I'm afraid my news doesn't help."

Luca looked down at her hand, and for a moment it felt as if he might reach across and place his hand on top of hers. But he didn't. She had questioned Sandro's story about her heritage being linked to the Nazis, but to hear it from Luca sent a punch right to her gut.

CHAPTER 20

CARA

Cara spent the night before her trip to Cortona at the villa. Alphonso had pumped up the tires on the Contessa's bicycle, and it was waiting safely in the garage behind the stables that used to resound with the whinnying of horses until they had been requisitioned for war.

People were more terrified than ever; German planes were dropping down more leaflets warning the people of Tuscany that if anyone was caught carrying out any resistance activities, they would pay the ultimate price with their lives.

At the same time, Allied planes were sweeping overhead and distributing leaflets telling the Tuscans to support the partisans, to blow up Nazi strongholds, to *resist, resist, resist*, because the Allies were on their way. But the local Nazis would not hesitate in carrying out fierce reprisals in their panic as their power diminished.

Bettina had asked one of the housemaids to make up a guest room on the first floor for Cara, and now, the villa felt dim and strangely quiet. Moonlight pooled across the wooden floorboards in the guest bedroom, and Cara leaned against the window, looking out at the empty courtyard at the rear of the house. She knew that Alphonso had taken to coming out of his cottage during the long nights to check that no one was raiding his walled vegetable garden, but there was no sign of him out there now.

Sleep was impossible, and she needed to be outside. The moonlit trees and flowers felt less lonely than the interior of the silent house.

Cara pushed the front door open, and stepped out onto the gravel driveway, slipping down the stairs from the top terrace. She stopped at the silvery olive grove, leaning against one of the old trees, closing her eyes and hoping to relax enough out here in the warm fragrant air so that she might be able to go back upstairs and fall asleep.

But her mind whirled with memories. She had walked into this garden on the very first day she had started working for the Contessa, her heart pounding, and her feet trapped in unaccustomed high-heeled shoes. She had been carrying a heavy leather diary and a stack of books on bookkeeping that Papa had bought for her to help her to do well at the job.

Raf had been working with Alphonso, helping him to clear a blockage in one of the fountains that was fed by the freshwater spring under the gardens, and he had looked up at her, shading his eyes against the sun. He had been wearing a pair of light-colored trousers and a white shirt held up by suspenders around his broad shoulders. He had seen her burdened with all her books and had dropped the shovel he was holding and had come down to help her. Raf had relieved her of the heavy books, and she had laughed about her high-heeled shoes, and he had walked alongside her slowly, keeping time with her before opening the green front door and letting her inside the old villa that at once both charmed and intimidated her.

One evening after she had finished work, they had walked

down to the village together. It was fall, and the air had turned chilly at the end of a crisp, blue-sky day that had been glorious with leaves dipped in carmine and pink, and he'd loaned her his jacket, placing it over her shoulders with delicate care. It was turning dark, and he had insisted on walking her right to her front door. There was an awkward silence while she stood with one hand on the door of the pensione that Raf's family owned, and that her father had run for over twenty years. Raf looked as if he was about to say something, but then he had shaken his head, wished her a good evening, and turned around to walk away. Papa had seen them through the front windows of home and had suggested that it looked as if Raf was fond of her.

Cara understood the boundaries of class that lay between them, and every time she saw him, every time she interacted with him, every time she thought of him and fought the growing attraction she felt toward him, the barrier of money and distinction hung between them.

But then, Raf had invited her to come and sit on the terrace one evening with a group of his friends after she had finished work. This was the crowd that was sent away to boarding school in England while Cara and her friends continued at the local village school until they began working on the Contessa's tenant farms or in the village.

Raf's good-looking, educated friends were sitting sipping local wine and laughing over some joke. But Raf had pulled out a chair for her, insisting that she join them, and she had felt less awkward after the first few minutes. After all, she was working as a professional and was dressed in a business outfit. She could be anyone, and Raf never mentioned the fact that she was the daughter of the innkeeper in the village at the bottom of the hill.

She had listened at first to their ideas. Ideas that seemed modern and exciting and were clearly borne out of expensive university educations, though at the time it seemed strange that these wealthy people needed to go to university to understand that the peasants in Italy and the villages had the same beating hearts that they did, and the same dreams.

And then, the war had intensified, and Raf had started walking her home in the evenings regularly, lingering in the village with her, and it had felt as if they could talk all night. Before long she had come to realize that he didn't share the same distance from reality as his friends did. He was a man who cared about his family, and the people in the village. Soon, he came to tell her that he also cared about her. He told Cara one evening that it was inevitable that he would have to go away. He asked her to go out with him for dinner before he left, at the most enchanting restaurant in Cortona, set into the hillside and overlooking the valley. Cara only walked past it when she was in town to go to the markets but had never imagined sitting out on the terrace in the moonlight, while candles twinkled on the tables and waiters floated about with appetizing dishes. Against her better judgment, she accepted his offer.

He had kissed her gently just outside the village gates after the dinner. It had felt as if they were made for each other, and Cara had looked up at him, and he had taken the little cross she wore around her neck between his thumb and forefinger and told her that he had fallen for her the first time he saw her tottering into the villa carrying a tower of books.

It had all seemed so magical, so wonderful, until she had overheard the Contessa condemning him for allowing Cara to think that there could ever be anything serious between her and Rafaeli. The Contessa knew that her son had been walking Cara home of an evening, but she had been appalled to think that her son would lead her on and take her out on a proper date. Raf had told her quietly that he did not want to do anything to hurt her, and that he feared this might happen if they continued seeing each other.

On the day Raf had left, his mother had also been icy cold toward Cara.

Raf had come downstairs in his military uniform, and Cara had sat frozen at his mother's desk, unsure of what to do—whether she had the right to say goodbye to him, although it was very clear where she stood with his mother. He hovered in the doorway with his kitbag and his jacket buttoned up to his neck.

His mother had appeared out of the living room and had taken his face in her hands, before pulling him into a close hug.

Cara had focused on her typing, eyes downcast, and she had not had a chance to say goodbye. But she had come to terms with this, over the years, and now the Villa Rosa faced out over the valley bathed in moonlight, sitting strong and firm, and the building looked safe and felt strong, just as she would be tomorrow when she would focus on the job she had to do. She would not let Papa down.

CHAPTER 21

ANNIE

Annie stood at the entrance to Evelina Messina's bedroom. The four-poster bed, hung with silk curtains and a matching counterpane, looked strange and pale in the sunlight. Dust gathered on the polished dressing table and covered the old glass perfume bottles with a fine, powdery coating.

Annie paused a moment in the light thrown in by the open shutters. It was as if the room was not used to being exposed in this way; the armoire and the modest bedside tables looked bigger than they had when the room had been cloaked in darkness this morning. As if admonishing her for disturbing the quiet.

The Contessa still seemed to be such a formidable presence. Annie felt as if she were intruding as she started with the top drawer in the dressing table, and she was, in a way, as she was going behind Sandro's back and searching his family home. But there were only a set of silver brushes, and some aging bottles of perfume—Coco Chanel, Christian Dior. The Contessa clearly had exquisite taste. Annie checked underneath the rose-covered drawer linings, but there was nothing. No hidden documents. And then, she opened the wardrobe that had lured her since the first day she had walked into this room. Luminous evening gowns hung in rows under white flowing wraps like elegant ghosts. Annie searched the pockets of negligees and countless pairs of silken pajamas. Fur coats, crisp business suits... the Contessa had been a superbly dressed woman. And a discreet one.

Finally, she closed the wardrobe doors, picked up the black-and-white photograph and, using the dusting cloth she had brought, gently wiped the glass frame to allow the Contessa's lovely face to regard her. Annie took the photograph over to the window to better study Evelina Messina's features, and to try to gain a deeper understanding of who she was, whether there was any resemblance to her. But the woman who looked out at her was enigmatic. Her eyes held a cool expression that Annie suspected very few people were able to understand.

Annie came out of the bedroom, her hands empty, and she made her way down the staircase to the first floor. She pulled her hair up into a messy bun, brushing her hands down her dusty jeans. Luca was still working, and Annie came to stand just above him, his revelation from earlier about his grandfather at the forefront of her mind.

"Any luck?" Luca asked. He crouched back and looked up at her.

"There's nothing in her bedroom. Not a scrap of information about anything untoward during the war."

Luca frowned. "I've emailed my mother, but I haven't heard back from her yet. I'm not sure how much more she knows about the Contessa's affair."

Annie peered at the great clump of ivy that Luca was trying to pull apart against the wall and walked down the rough stone steps to the level below.

"Look at this," he said.

They were peering down at what appeared to be a stone slide in a child's playground from long ago. But it cascaded into a deep hole that was dark and murky.

Annie looked up to the terrace above. There was a similar clump of ivy on the corresponding wall. "Luca, it's the fountain," she whispered. "A water garden that tumbles down the hill with a fountain on each level. Imagine if we could get it working again."

Luca's eyes crinkled with warmth.

"This is so exciting," Annie said.

"It is, but I'm sorry that you're not getting anywhere."

"I don't want to believe Sandro. More than anything, I want to prove him wrong. I feel like I want to exonerate my history."

"I think that's exactly what you should do. Annie... I've been meaning to ask you something. I hope you don't mind."

Annie waited.

"Would you like to go out for dinner with me?"

"Are you asking me out on a date? The granddaughter of a villain?"

"Yes," Luca said softly.

Annie held his gaze a moment and sent him a quiet smile. "Okay. Yes, I'd like that."

Luca looked at her thoughtfully, and then he reached into the back pocket of his shorts. He frowned at the slip of paper that he held in his hand. "I wasn't sure whether to give you this," he said. "But I went into the village last night for dinner, and I had a drink at the local bar."

"Yes?"

"I asked who might know about the history around here. It seems a lot of the locals are quite tight-lipped about what happened here during the war," he said. "Of course, they are open about the partisans." He sighed. "I heard an awful story about how a fourteen-year-old was shot just down the road from the Villa Rosa."

Annie brought her hand up to clutch at her necklace. Were the partisans fighting against her grandfather?

Luca handed the piece of paper across to her. "There is a bookshop in Cortona, and the woman who works there takes an interest in local history."

"Katarina Ricci." Annie read the name on the slip of paper. A dealer of antique books.

"There is a road that winds directly through the hills from the village to Cortona," Luca said. "And there is a pair of bicycles in the old garage behind the stables." He tilted his head to one side and regarded her. "If you'd like some company along the way, we could ride to Cortona together tomorrow. I thought perhaps a bicycle might be a good first step toward getting you on a horse?"

Annie chuckled. "So, you're suggesting we ride to Cortona, go visit this Signorina Katarina, and then..."

"We could stay for dinner?" Luca said. "And ride back as the sun goes down?"

Annie was quiet for a moment. The last thing she had planned when she came to Italy was developing feelings for someone. Her grief and confusion at the loss of Papa was still too raw and new. But surely this was harmless. Luca seemed like a lovely man, and she would never see him again once she went back to the States... *If* she went back. For the truth was, ever since Sandro had challenged her, the thought of going home to California had begun to feel more and more remote. Her business was running perfectly while she was here and she didn't miss home as she had expected to... Was it time for a real change at last?

"That would be nice," she whispered.

Luca smiled at her, and he turned his attention back to the deep, rich earth.

CHAPTER 22

CARA

Cara wheeled the Contessa's bicycle down the driveway of the villa, leaving the elegant front gates, and making her way onto the empty road that snaked around the hillside. Once she had cycled beyond the vineyards, she passed the neighboring house, but the gates were firmly locked with a secure padlock. The owners, an elderly British couple, had left Tuscany when Mussolini had entered the war alongside Hitler. The neighboring villa sat overlooking the deep green valley and the distant hills, waiting for life to begin again. The Contessa had promised the British couple that she would protect their home, and not allow it to be requisitioned for the war effort. She had succeeded.

A familiar seed of doubt unfurled in Cara's insides at the brazen risk she was taking today collecting explosives and at the fact that she was going to store them on Evelina Messina's land.

Her eyes switched back and forth as she pedaled along the narrow road that wove along the edge of the steep valley. Brambles and overgrown bushes lined the hillside to her left, while the slope that tumbled down to her right toward the village could hide anyone. The feeling of being watched was acute, and she took in a deep breath, her feet pressing heavily on the pedals of the old bike as if trying to heave it along faster, faster. All she could do was hope that it was only Raf's partisans who were hiding deep in the undergrowth in these parts, but even so, she could trust no one should she be stopped.

The road curved upwards, still following the hillside, and she came to a tiny village that sat achingly beautiful and time-less, and yet strangely still. No one was out, and she turned toward Cortona, passing by an ancient medieval church whose bells had not rung for over a year.

Her heart was hammering in her chest as the road turned back and left the empty hamlet behind. The narrow road became more isolated again. This other side of the hill looked out over a barren, rocky valley. The pale blue sky shimmered over sparse olive groves, and pale outcrops of rock that looked haunting.

Cara kept her eyes ahead now. There was still no one about. She passed a set of mysterious closed gates on her left, while to her right, the valley looked eerie and still. Cara frowned and kept pedaling straight ahead.

When she finally came to the old Etruscan wall that led to the medieval gates of Cortona, Cara swallowed hard. She had made it this far. No one had stopped her.

Two Nazis stood sentry at the old gates to Cortona. The medieval gates to the hilltop town were closed. Cara reached for her identity papers and wheeled her bicycle up to the two young German officers. She had put on a green dress decorated with polka dots and had left her long wavy dark hair flowing down her back. Her face was free of any makeup, and she hoped she looked like a young girl of sixteen.

"*Buongiorno*," she said, attempting a smile at the two young men. She had heard stories of women in France buttering up young German officers and tricking them into believing they were on their side.

But one of the Nazis simply held out his hand for her identity papers, and she handed them across, trying to look as nonchalant as she could.

"What is your business in Cortona?" the man who still held her papers asked.

"I am visiting a friend," Cara lied easily. "And I'm going to the markets."

"We hope you enjoy your visit to Cortona, just as you normally would. The Fuhrer welcomes you." The Nazi threw his arm out in a brief homage to Hitler, and Cara forced herself not to curl her lip with disdain.

"*Grazie,*" she said. And she wheeled her bicycle into the narrow streets of the old town.

Old men still sat in the doorways of the houses that lined the cobbled lanes. The churches in the town basked in the morning sun as they had for centuries, and the small shrines, built with their perfect semicircle arches, were still filled with local flowers. There was something about Italy that not even Nazis could put down.

Cara made her way through the lanes to the piazza, where the limited market was being set up under the watchful eyes of more Nazi guards. She pushed her bicycle through the labyrinth of narrow streets that led to the address Raf had given her. She had no trouble finding her way to Via Santa Margarita. Here, the patron saint of the falsely accused had lived among the friars of Cortona. She had carried out charitable works, devoting herself to caring for others, after the murder of her husband. Her stepmother and father had refused her admittance to their home.

Cara passed the shrine to Santa Margarita and came to a stop outside an old church, its faded blue door closed. The simple rectangular window was covered with rusty iron bars. She knocked on the faded, pale blue door and waited.

CHAPTER 23

ANNIE

Luca brought the two ancient yet lovingly restored bicycles out of the dusty garage.

"I'm guessing you restored these yourself?" Annie asked.

"Look at the craftsmanship. I hardly had to do a thing. Just a bit of oil on the chains, a polish, and new tires. They are not rusty, which is incredible."

"I'll take your word and trust that they work," Annie laughed. She reached out tentatively and held one of the old bike's handlebars. "I haven't ridden a bike since I was a kid and we used to go pounding around the streets in Carmel-by-the-Sea," she said. "That seems like another world, a lifetime ago."

"Once you learn to ride a bike, you never forget," Luca said. "That's what my dad always used to tell me."

"You are close to your parents?"

"Yes," Luca said softly. "But I'd like to know more about my granddad, Alphonso."

Annie wheeled the bicycle down the steep driveway to the

road that snaked around the hill to Cortona, staying quiet, and feeling intensely aware of the handsome man by her side.

Once they were cycling along the narrow road that wound its way beyond the Villa Rosa, with the steep descent into the valley on their right, Annie stayed focused on the road. To their left, the ancient, neglected, and overgrown vineyards that belonged to the Villa Rosa ran up the hillside, and soon they came to another set of elaborate iron gates. Annie glanced at them quickly, but Luca's voice broke into the serene summer air.

"That property belongs to a British family," he said. "They've owned it for decades. I've met them. They're keen for the Villa Rosa to be restored and want to have neighbors living next door to them permanently again."

Annie sensed him glancing across at her, but she kept her eyes straight ahead.

"Were the British family here during the war?" she asked. She was quite proud of the fact that her brain was still working out the mystery she was trying to solve, while her body was doing everything not to fall off the bicycle and tumble down the valley.

"The couple who own this villa say their grandparents went back to Britain for the duration. They spent summers here after the war, but only talked of their reclusive neighbor, the grand Contessa, who they said kept very much to herself." He sighed and there was a whisper in the trees, as if in sympathy. "They never mentioned a child."

The sun had risen high in the pale blue sky, and the pencil-like shade that the cypress trees threw onto the road was not enough to protect her face from the morning's heat. Annie dared not lift a hand to wipe her perspiring forehead.

"I had a message from Sandro this morning," Luca said. "I'll tell you more about that later on."

Annie remained silent, concentrating. If a car came at them, she would have to suddenly veer toward the hillside. The bends in the road were treacherous, and she kept her ears on alert for the sound of approaching traffic.

The road began a slight incline, and they came toward a hamlet set into the curve of the hill. There was an old church directly facing them, and a couple of houses. Here, Luca took a sharp turn left. They were traveling now along the back of the hill. The landscape to her right had fewer trees and looked more barren, though it was carpeted with grass. It was still lovely though, and a shiver ran up her spine.

"The Italian countryside makes me feel as if the past and the present are existing simultaneously," Annie said. "I always find it strange to think that the people who have gone before us are simply lost. And yet, it feels as if they never left."

Annie sensed Luca glancing across at her. They passed alongside an old medieval-looking wall, ten times the size of the drystone walls at Villa Rosa, and in much better condition. Above rose the old hilltop town of Cortona. Luca slowed his bike as they approached a car park to their right and dismounted. Annie stopped next to him and placed her foot firmly on the ground. There, she had made it. But there was no way she was letting Luca get her on a horse.

"We'll have to leave the bikes here. You can only walk in the old town."

A medieval gate was cut into the wall, and Annie followed Luca into Cortona, with its honey-colored stone buildings. Several tourists were already wandering around taking photographs and elderly men sat in doorways as they must have since medieval times, smoking and chatting with their neighbors. Washing hung overhead, from the windows of ancient apartments, while bougainvillea and roses tumbled in the sun. Annie wanted to stop and look in the window of every trattoria they passed. Menus sat enticingly in the windows or pasted to the front doors. She had come to realize that the cuisine of

Tuscany operated on variations of the same theme—simple roasted meats, pastas with rich ragus, and contornis of crisp fried potatoes, spinach cooked with olive oil and lemon juice, and fresh local peaches and cherries steeped in red wine.

Luca was following a map on his phone, leading her through the winding alleyways out into a piazza, where charming old buildings looked down upon the square.

"Would you like to have a look around?" Luca asked. "We don't have to go straight to see Katarina Ricci. We can spend some time here."

But Annie shook her head. "As tempting as it is, I'm not going to be able to relax until we've spoken to her." Although, the chances of Katarina Ricci knowing anything felt as slim as a reed blowing in the wind.

Luca led her out of the square and up a steep set of stone steps. There were apartments with window boxes filled with geraniums, and from inside the cheerful little homes Annie could hear voices and smell the scent of delicious food—garlic, tomatoes, and basil, lamb roasting for lunch, and olive oil cakes baking in centuries old wood-fired ovens.

At the top of the narrow alley, Luca came to a stop outside a sign swinging in the breeze. Antiquarian booksellers. Proprietor, K. Ricci. "Ready?"

Annie nodded. She took a deep breath and followed Luca inside.

CHAPTER 24

CARA

The carton containing the explosives was at the bottom of a picnic basket, and this was covered with a red checked cloth. The friar in the church in Cortona had placed a loaf of freshly baked bread, a jar of deep green olive oil, and the painted bowl that was supposed to be the gift for Evelina Messina in the basket as well.

"Please, travel safely, signorina," the priest said.

Cara found herself almost speechless at the gentle nobility of this elderly man, and when he took both her hands in his and pressed his bony fingers around hers, she could only thank him as she left the hushed monastery beside the old church. He had reminded her of her father.

There was something about the way the priest quietly prepared the basket, without fanfare, without fuss, but with the wisdom of a man who knew right from wrong. And that was what she had to remind herself to do as well. No matter how hard her heart was pounding at the thought of getting back to the villa safely, she had to focus on the fact that she was doing the right thing, for the right cause.

She placed the willow basket in front of the handlebars on the Contessa's bike. Were she unlucky enough to be questioned, she must not give anything away. She had heard stories of women braver and younger than her who had been caught and interrogated by the Nazis and who had held fast in their loyalty to the partisans, refusing to bow to pressure under the most horrific torture—nails being ripped out, being blinded, limbs broken, hair torn out... The *staffette* were heroines, and they were famous for not giving in. She must be as brave as they were.

She swung her right leg over the bicycle seat and started pedaling down the cobbled street. Cara rode toward the medieval gate that led out of Cortona, wishing she could turn around and disappear into the anonymity of the marketplace, a normal girl on a Saturday morning.

The two Nazis who had stood guard at the entrance to the old town had been replaced by two fresh and immaculate soldiers who looked no more than seventeen. Cara lowered her eyes as she approached them, kicking herself now for wearing the becoming polka dot dress. She should have dressed badly, disguising her curves, hiding them under a baggy shirt and an old pair of trousers, while piling her long dark hair back from her face. Now, she felt foolish at her plan to try to thwart the guards by looking young and fresh and innocent... or fair game.

And when she tried to look down, all she saw was her basket full of dynamite.

She stopped riding and hovered a moment in a shady part of the alley, while an elderly resident regarded her from her window in an apartment across the street. The woman's solid arms were folded on the open windowsill, and her gaze did not waver as she stared at Cara, clearly not caring whether she was being rude.

Cara slowly raised her head and met the woman's eyes. The elderly woman indicated for her to turn around. She made a swiveling movement with her hands that was clear—*Don't go this way. Go back out to Via Margarita, down through the valley, and avoid the Nazi guards.*

Cara stared at the woman. Could she trust her?

CHAPTER 25

ANNIE

Katerina Ricci's bookstore was dotted with table lamps, and Middle Eastern rugs covered the polished brick floor. Books were stacked on chestnut shelves and there was a hushed, almost reverent feeling inside, as if this place was somehow special and rare. A handful of visitors sat around in comfortable leather Chesterfield chairs, perusing leather-bound books with cracked spines, fine gold-leaf-edged paper, and titles embossed in gold.

In the back corner, a woman sat at an unimposing desk, with a yellow lamp in front of her. Her gray-haired head was bent over a large book. She looked to be in her seventies. A pair of glasses perched on her nose, hanging from a thin gold chain and she wore a kaftan in magnolia pink, edged with silver lining around the deep V-neck.

Annie came to a stop at the woman's desk. "Signora Ricci?" she said, keeping her voice low. It didn't seem right to talk loudly inside this quiet store.

The woman looked up, and slowly removed her glasses. "I

am Katerina Ricci. May I help you?" she asked in English.

Annie suddenly felt nervous, looking for Luca, but he had busied himself at a bookshelf, and had already pulled out an old leathery tome. It was probably about garden restoration, or hopeful well digging, or restoring old bicycles...

She turned back to Signora Ricci. "Signora," she started, "I am wondering if you have any information on a piece of local history that I'm trying to research."

Signora Ricci raised one brow. "Of course. We have many books on Cortona, and the local area," she said. "If you go into the back corner, that part of the shop is devoted to old books about the town and its history. My assistant is wandering around somewhere, with a name tag. He will help you." Signora Ricci returned her focus to the large book in front of her.

"I'm after something a little more specific," Annie said.

The older woman looked up again.

Annie swallowed. "The Villa Rosa," she said, and her words seemed to hover in the still, quiet, room.

The woman removed her glasses, lifted the chain over her head, and placed them down on the table in front of her. "What is it that interests you about the Villa Rosa?"

"I'm doing a research project for my PhD, into the Italian nobility during the war with a specific focus on the villas in Tuscany." Annie held the woman's gaze, the lies slipping as easily off her own tongue as those that she had been fed since she was young. "My understanding is that the villa has a partic- ularly interesting history, and as part of my thesis, I want to focus on the Contessa, on Evelina Messina. I have been told that she played a pivotal role here during the war."

"I'm afraid I don't know anything about the villa during the war. It was a long time ago."

Annie chewed on her lip.

"Are you familiar with the Villa Rosa?" the signora asked.

Slowly, Annie nodded her head. "Yes," she said, softly. "It is beautiful."

The signora eased herself out of her chair, and Annie wondered for a moment if she had been dismissed, but, to her surprise, Signora Ricci walked around the front of her desk and came to stand by her.

Annie noticed Luca looking up at her from across the room. She sent him a shrug in response to his questioning look.

"Is that your friend?" the signora asked, indicating Luca.

Annie nodded.

"What is your name, signorina?" she said, her voice low.

"Annie Reynolds. I am from California."

"Miss Reynolds, would you and your friend care to come with me? There is something that might help."

Annie sent Luca a hopeful look.

The signora called to the young man who was assisting another customer, telling him she was going out the back for a little while, and then she led Annie, with Luca right behind her, out through a dark wooden door. Annie followed her through a room filled with yet more books. Old tomes were stacked in shelves and tottered in piles on the floor. From here, they came to another room, and the atmosphere was strange and quiet and still. The space was filled with boxes, and a musty smell pervaded the room. But everywhere, boxes were stacked on the floor, and reached up to the ceiling, and on a quick count, Annie thought there were at least fifty.

"Oh my," she breathed.

"Every box in this room is filled with books from the Villa Rosa that were donated to us when the last owner, the Contessa whom you mentioned, died." Signora Ricci folded her arms and tucked her fingers into the silky kaftan.

Annie wanted to sink down on the floor in the middle of the room. Instead, she caught Luca's eye, and shook her head at him in disbelief. "They are all from the villa?"

Signora Ricci nodded. "Please," she indicated with her hand around the room. "Take your time, Miss Reynolds."

And with that, the bookshop owner turned and disappeared out of the room.

"Where do we start?" Annie whispered to Luca.

He looked at her and tilted his head to one side. In the dim interior of the musty roomful of books, he grinned. "At the beginning, Annie," he whispered.

CHAPTER 26

CARA

Cara took the elderly woman's signaling seriously, and avoided the two replacement Nazis, who were stationed at the medieval gates. She had not planned on traveling back to the villa via the other side of the hill out of Cortona. It was a longer route, and one she had not wanted to take, especially since it meant going through the main streets of three villages and traveling along busier roads with a basket of dynamite on the front of her bike. But despite the uneasiness that laced her insides, there were no cars in sight. The partisans' increasing attacks on passing vehicles meant that the Nazis and fascists had taken to traveling less.

Once she was out of Cortona, Cara freewheeled down the road that snaked through the back valley, wanting to get back to the villa as quickly as possible. The fact she had only managed to get a couple of hours' sleep was making her head buzz, and her eyes stung in the warm breeze. She knew she was riding too fast, but what kept her going was the thought of the summerhouse, sitting in the quiet villa gardens. She flew toward it like a beacon.

There was a crossroads at the bottom of the hill, and she turned left toward the first of the villages. The road was eerily silent, and she could already see the shape of the old stone church that was the centerpiece of the town. Overgrown bushes and trees tumbled along the side of the road, but beyond this stretched vineyards, green as crisp blades of grass. Every now and then, Cara glanced to her side to check that no one was lying in wait for her.

She rounded a curve in the road and came into full view of the village. She was in a wind tunnel. And she pedaled harder, standing up in her seat. Cara passed through without incident, but her heart was beating hard as she approached the second village. An SS truck was parked haphazardly outside the bar in the main street, and it looked like there was a kerfuffle on the sidewalk. A group of elderly men, five or six of them, was standing outside with their hands on their hips, while two Nazis spoke to them in officious tones.

Cara took in a shuddering breath. Her heart felt as if it would explode through her mouth, and her legs wanted to turn to jelly, but she forced herself to keep moving, to focus straight ahead. She sat up in the saddle and ignored the group outside the bar.

The Nazis did not even look at her as she cycled past. They were too busy berating the old men, who were gesticulating in the air.

Cara kept going, and soon the vineyards gave way to the narrow streets of her own little town at the bottom of the hill. Not far to go now.

She avoided the marketplace and, dismounting from the bike, walked it through the quietest lanes. She passed by the pensione, yearning to go inside, get into bed, and hide. As she wheeled the bike up her own alleyway, she felt eyes upon her. Cara was certain that she was being watched.

The eerie feeling did not go away as the tumble of caramel-colored buildings gave way to the steep road that followed the hillside up to the Villa Rosa, the valley suddenly spreading picturesquely off to her right.

She was certain she heard a noise in the undergrowth on the side of the road alongside her, but she spoke to herself sternly. It would be a fox or a badger. Nothing more.

But as she pushed the Contessa's bike up the steep road that led to the Villa Rosa, there were footsteps coming behind her, and a man's voice calling out for her to stop.

CHAPTER 27

ANNIE

Luca was systematic. He had placed all the boxes that he had searched over to one side, and even found a marker pen and had put a cross on those boxes, since he had found nothing of interest inside.

Annie wiped her hand over her forehead. It was stifling in the small room at the back of the bookstore and it smelled of musty cardboard. Every time she opened a box, she was hit with a whiff of stale damp paper.

The books that had come from the Villa Rosa were bound mostly in pale red and green hardcovers with their titles embossed in gold lettering, and while she had opened the first few boxes in wonder, chatting with Luca about each one, soon Annie had become overwhelmed, and had begun sorting as quickly as he was, looking at books, shaking the pages a little, placing them to the side, and then putting them all back in. She had no idea what they were looking for, and Signora Ricci had left them to it.

"Someone was a great reader," she said. "I only wish that

person had been less meticulous with throwing out anything of note, even a shopping list at this point would be helpful. A receipt from a car mechanic, or a cobbler who mended a leather shoe... I'm even looking back at all the farming records and business records from the Villa with a sense of nostalgia now."

Luca was sitting cross-legged on the floor, with a tower of books boxes tottering beside him. "Do you want to go and get some lunch? As much as I'm loving doing this, I think we need a break."

Annie picked up her phone and glanced at the time. It was midday, and the sun would be burning high and clear in the Tuscan sky. "I'd love to," she said.

At two o'clock precisely, they were back at their task after lunch. They had found an authentic-looking trattoria in one of the narrow backstreets of Cortona, preferring to avoid the tourist menus. Annie appreciated that Luca shared the same instincts as her, taking the time to scout around for a restaurant that was filled with locals, and that held no sounds of pinging microwaves, scents of reheated minestrone and rehashed lasagna.

They shared a salad of radicchio and walnuts, with local cheeses, olives, olive oil, prosciutto, marinated sweet peppers, and crusty local bread. Along with this, they both enjoyed a glass of one of the most delicate white wines that Annie had ever tasted. The owner of the restaurant had told them proudly that it came from his brother's vineyard in the valley, and he gave them the winery's card, asking them to tell his brother that he had sent them along. They agreed at once to go and visit the owner's brother, and the restaurant owner laid his hands on both of their shoulders, and told them to come back soon, because he loved to welcome strangers who appreciated his food. He told them they made a charming couple.

Annie now glanced across at Luca's handsome profile as he slid open the boxes with a Stanley knife he had bought in the town. In another life, Luca would have been lovely. But how could she contemplate a relationship when she didn't even know who she was?

The only sounds in the room were the soft thud of books and the flip of pages, as they both searched through farming manuals and cookbooks for loose envelopes or letters that might give anything away.

But the Contessa had been scrupulous. They found not one sheet of paper, not one stray item. Not a thing.

"It's hard to imagine what it must have been like living in the villa nearly a hundred years ago," Annie said. She traced her fingers over the embossed title of an old children's book, then opened it to have a look at the pictures inside. The plates were wrought so delicately, and she wondered if the book had belonged to Sandro's grandfather, the mysterious Nicolas Messina, or his even more elusive brother, Rafaeli. "Look at this," she said to Luca, "you know, much as Sandro concerns me, I think I should buy some of these old books for him, because they are his heritage. I don't know, perhaps one day if he has children, he might like to read these stories to them. I am not sure what Signora Ricci plans to do with them all, but it would be a shame for some of the more precious books to be sold on."

"They are probably completely inappropriate for children today," Luca said. "Particularly if they were written in the fascist era. But he might want them... Although I don't think Sandro is the sort to sit down and read a book." His eyes danced.

"You never know," Annie said. She ran a hand through her long blond ponytail. She had pulled it up away from her face to keep her neck cool.

"Annie."

Annie tore her eyes away from the enchanting illustrations

on the silky pages of another children's book. "Yes?" she murmured.

Luca was frowning over a large leather-bound book. Slowly, he was turning the pages, and he lifted his head and looked up at her.

He looked at her. "I've found... It's a diary," he whispered.

Annie's stomach started fluttering, but her brows knitted as she leaned over closer to Luca to have a look. Her hand brushed his, and they were so close that she could hear his every breath.

But as he turned the pages, his hand stilled.

Something was dreadfully wrong.

CHAPTER 28

CARA

Cara did not stop, or slow down, despite the sound of the voice calling from behind her. Instinctively, she sped up, pushing the Contessa's bicycle as fast as she could up the hill that led to the Villa Rosa. It was too steep for her to get back on to the bicycle. The gates of the villa were just around a bend. All she had to do was turn into them, and she would be safe. But the problem was, she could not see them from here and even if Alphonso was in the front garden of the villa, and there was no guarantee where he was working today, he could not see her. Still, she could hear rustling coming from the trees on the low side of the road.

If someone was tracking her through the forest that wound beneath the hillside road, she was on her own. Her breath hitched as she fumbled forward. When a figure appeared from the undergrowth, pushing aside the trees and blocking her in her tracks, Cara stifled her scream. Her pursuer must have sneaked through the bushes and caught up with her. Because the man who was blocking her way, his mouth turned down in a ruthless grimace, and his eyes blazing, was not a Nazi but none other than Cara's neighbor, the known fascist, Luigi Santino. She had always felt revulsion creeping over her when she encountered him. But his expression now truly frightened her.

He was marching toward her, his fist raised in the air, and his cheeks inflamed. His eyes were wild, and he was upon her, grabbing the handlebars of her bike. Cara stopped, her heart pulsing like a trapped bird against her ribcage, and the taste of her own fear burning in her mouth.

"What are you doing here?" she demanded of him in a voice that sounded far more confident than she felt. She held her ground and looked straight into the middle-aged man's beady eyes. His broad forehead was laced with sweat, and his usually red nose, threaded with purple veins, appeared bulbous, his nostrils moving visibly like those of an angry horse. His chest was heaving. One look at his face told her to run.

She started yanking his strong hands away from the handlebars, but he only shoved the bike back toward her, almost knocking it sideways, and it was all she could do to reach out and save the incriminating contents of her basket from spilling all over the road.

But in that split second that she reached out for the basket, he took advantage. He was beside her, behind her, he seemed to loom everywhere. He was a solid and powerfully built man, and when he reached out and grabbed her by the shoulder, Cara struggled to keep the bicycle upright with her free hand.

"Let go of me," she growled. She tried to tear herself away from him, but he pressed his fingers hard into the tight muscles in her thin shoulders, and she winced with pain.

"I've been waiting for a chance to catch up with you, bella signorina," he growled. "And now, we have the perfect opportunity. The road to ourselves."

Cara lifted her chin. "Go home to your wife, Signor

Santino. She would be appalled to know that you have accosted me like this."

"I would never allow my wife to be running around the countryside on her own. She is at home cooking for me, like all women should do." His eyes narrowed into two glassy slits. And slowly, he ran his tongue over his moist lips.

Something dark snaked through Cara's belly.

Signor Santino stepped closer. His face was on top of hers and she could smell the rank stench of strong alcohol and stale tobacco on his breath. Still, she clutched the bicycle, shielding it with her body, one hand on the seat and one on the handlebars to stop it from falling flat on the road. But the putrid fumes from Luigi Santino's mouth were overwhelming, and she tilted her head backwards. So many times, she had heard shouting coming from his neighboring apartment, had sat at home while crockery was smashed on the floor, and Luigi Santino yelled at his wife. Now, he was targeting her.

Several times, she had suggested to Papa that they do something. But he had shaken his head. He was not willing to confront Luigi Santino because he worked for the local butcher, who back before the Nazi invasion was providing black-market meat for him and Cara. Papa had looked at Cara and told her that they needed to be careful and to learn to pick their fights. She had no choice now.

Could she turn around and speed back down the valley?

Before she could get the bike turned around, it happened. Suddenly, Luigi was behind her. The bicycle had fallen flat on the road, and he had pinned her arm to her back. He held his other arm around her neck and twisted the arm behind her back until it was hard up against her body, and the muscles in her elbow almost screamed in pain.

The bike lay in full view in the middle of the road, the basket precariously balanced on its side, and the olive oil bottle smashed, the bread lying on the ground, and the box containing the Contessa's gift still wedged in the basket, along with the dynamite. If a car came up the road, it would run over the dynamite, and the whole lot would explode. She opened her mouth to scream but whip-fast he covered her mouth. He marched her forward like a prisoner; she was stumbling and helpless in his grasp as they neared the dense bushes on the side of the road, his breath rank in her ear, whispering foul words. In vain, she tried kicking at his shins and throwing her head back to hit his forehead, but he outweighed her so much that her efforts were futile, and all she could hear was the sound of his odious voice as her head bashed against his formidable chest. The stench of him was overwhelming. And when she tried to bite his hands, she almost buckled with nausea.

"I'll show you what happens to girls who don't obey the rules."

Cara still tried to flail with her pinioned arms, to kick with her legs, but soon, he had her face up against a tree. She threw her head back, trying to hit him in the face with the back of her head again, but he simply laughed at her, and reached down to rip the top of her dress. She let out a primal sob, but his hands were fondling her breasts.

"Stop," she managed.

But she broke down again as he lifted her dress. His meaty hands pawed her body, and he hit her hard on the head and everything turned black.

CHAPTER 29

ANNIE

Luca held up the book that he had found. "The date is 1944."

Annie bent over his shoulder and looked down at the old leather-bound diary. Her heart sank as she realized someone had taken great care to remove sections of the journal with scissors. In places, entire pages had carefully been cut out, leaving only a thin slip of paper near the spine of the book.

"I'm afraid all I can see are business ledgers, farming reports, dates for meetings with tenants and notes to tell the Contessa certain information from banks, and other business entities." Luca flipped through the pages of the book.

"It looks like it belonged to a secretary," Annie said.

Luca turned the old pages back carefully now, to the inside cover of the book. And there it was. Written in a neat, loopy rounded hand in sepia ink. *Cara Cartazzo. The Villa Rosa, May 1944.*

"Cara Cartazzo," Annie breathed. "It has a ring to it, don't you think?" She kneeled closer to Luca and traced over the name with her finger. "I wonder who she was..."

Just then, Luca's phone buzzed. "Sandro," he said.

Annie sighed and waited while he read the message. Her eyes grazed over the name of the young woman who had filled out this meticulous diary, only to have pages of it cut out for some reason. Annie only hoped it was not because of her.

What if Cara Cartazzo or her descendants were alive? Annie stood up and ran a quick Google search for Carla Cartazzo, Tuscany, 1944. Nothing came up. She opened the Italian ancestry site and ran a search through that.

The site took a few moments to load, and Annie went and stood by the closed window that looked out over the alleyway in Cortona. As if being near the only source of light in the room might help.

"Annie?"

Annie turned to face Luca. His lips were pressed together in a narrow line, and he frowned down at his phone.

"I'm afraid we will have to cancel our plan to stay in Cortona for dinner." He raked a hand through his hair. And he shook his head. "Sandro wants to meet me at the villa late this afternoon." He paused, as if waiting to decide whether she or not he should go on.

"Yes?" Annie said.

"He is bringing one of his business partners, a specialist in corporate retreats and conferences. Sandro wants him to repurpose the Villa Rosa, and he has flown him out to Italy."

Annie stayed still. She knew they had limited time to sort out the provenance of the Villa Rosa, but she had not bargained on Sandro pushing his agenda this way. She looked out the window, staring at the hard stone wall of the building opposite. "Then I will come with you," she said, her voice coming out surprisingly calm. "Because he cannot do this while the ownership of the property is in dispute.

"Don't worry," she added, seeing his look of concern. "My older brother is an attorney, and my older sister happens to be a realtor. We simply must politely ask him to delay and remind him that he has no right to make plans yet, and I think we need to intercept his meeting and tell him that it cannot proceed."

"I love your gumption," Luca said quietly.

She flashed a glance across toward him and couldn't help sending him a rueful smile. "Gumption?" She laughed. "Isn't that a word that hasn't been in use since about 1953?"

"It's a word I associate with Audrey Hepburn, and now... you."

Just then, Annie's phone lit up. Finally, her search was complete. "Oh, Luca," she whispered. She held her phone out to him. "Look at this."

CHAPTER 30

CARA

Cara opened her eyes. The first thing she saw was the sky, filtered through the trees that lined the road to the Villa Rosa. Her shoulders were bruised, and her breasts stung from where Luigi's hands had mauled her. Cara tried to ease herself up to her elbows, but when she did so, the back of her head ached with such a sudden throb that she collapsed back down again onto the rough ground.

Tears streaked down her cheeks. Slowly, she brought her hands up to do up the buttons on her dress. She would dress herself, and then go and retrieve what she could, but her mind was all over the place, as if playing a million different tunes, and she was not completely certain what had happened, nor, she realized in horror, how far Luigi Santino's attack had gone.

After a few moments, she heard a rustling sound in the trees nearby. "Oh, please, let him have gone away," she murmured. "*Santa Maria,* make him go away..." Cara stifled a sob. She had been working so hard, trying so hard to move through the grief she felt for Papa, and all she had wanted was to do something to help those who were risking their lives for this valley.

And yet, the forces of power in the world they lived in felt so formidable that it seemed anyone who wanted to do something to help those who are suffering had no hope. And nobody cared anymore whether you were vulnerable or unable to fight against those who wanted to torment you.

She brought her hand up to her mouth, and a trickle of blood ran down her fingers from where he had cut her lip. Or she had cut it on something sharp when she fell. She hardly knew.

When a shadow appeared over her, she closed her eyes, not being able to face Luigi Santino.

"*Cara mia?* Santa Maria!" Raf was down by her side, scooping her up in his arms, and instinctively, she reached up and curled her own arms around his neck, tucking her aching head into his firm chest and closing her eyes, feeling the salty tears running down her cheeks as he lifted her up.

"I'm sorry about the dynamite..." she managed.

"Don't you dare apologize," Raf growled.

Every footstep he took thumped through her entire body, and it was all she could do to manage the throbbing in her head as he carried her back toward the road.

She took in a shaking breath at the sound of her weak voice, and she closed her eyes again.

"Don't go to sleep, darling," he murmured. "You must stay awake. I'll take you to Bettina. Stay with me, sweetheart."

Blood still trickled from her lip, and her whole face hurt from where she had been pushed into the tree. "It was Signor Santino," she managed. "My own neighbor."

"I know who it was. I have dealt with him."

A sudden lurch of nausea roiled through her system, and she brought her hand to her stomach. "I'm sorry," she said. "I think I'm going to be sick."

Gently, Raf placed her down, and rested his hands under her sore shoulders. He held her hair back from her face, while she vomited all over the grass.

"The dynamite?" Her voice still sounded feeble, but having emptied the contents of her stomach, she felt a little clearer.

Raf stayed next to her, and with an extraordinarily gentle movement, he reached back and tucked a strand of her hair behind her ear. He handed her a handkerchief, and she took it, and wiped her mouth. On it were his initials embroidered beautifully.

"It's safe," he said. "You were absolutely brilliant."

She eased her head up and looked at the pearly blue sky. A throbbing pierced behind her right eye, and she staggered backwards.

"*Cara mia,* we need to get you to a darkened room. You must rest, and let Bettina take care of you. It's not going to be safe for you to live alone in the pensione after this."

Another wave of nausea roiled through her insides. "Did he..."

"No." Raf stood with his legs planted wide. "If he had, I would have murdered him. I got to you just as he hit you on the head. I was waiting by the summerhouse for you, but I heard a commotion and came straight away." Raf glanced around the clearing, and then he took her in his arms, and immediately, she felt safe.

CHAPTER 31

Alphonso was standing halfway up the driveway. As soon as Cara saw him, leaning on his rake in his old gardening clothes, she wanted to run up the hill toward him. The sight of his dear, familiar face was too much after the attack by Luigi Santino, and she almost broke down at the bottom of the hill.

But Raf still supported her and wheeled the bicycle. Her head throbbed, but not as badly as it had when she had tried to raise it earlier. Now, anger toward Luigi swelled inside her, and while she was immensely relieved Luigi had not managed to violate her, she hated to think what would have happened had Raf not been waiting for her to return.

"Signorina?" Alphonso had come down to stand beside them, his round face creased with worry.

"The signorina was attacked on the road that leads up from the village." Raf's voice was rough.

"Raf brought me back home..." Home. She made a face at the slip of her tongue.

"Are you all right, signorina?" Alphonso asked, his voice laced with panic.

Cara nodded. "I am," she managed. "He only knocked me around."

Alphonso visibly slumped with relief. The older man shot a glance at Raf.

"The signorina has a nasty bump to the back of her head," Raf said. "I thumped her attacker on the head. He was behind her, and they both fell backward. My execution was a little rough."

"Where is this man now?" Alphonso's tone was low and rough. "I presume he was a Nazi?"

"He is lying beneath the tree where he attempted to assault the signorina," Raf said evenly. "He will be there some time. I made sure of it. He will not be able to move. I am planning to go and... talk with him some more."

"There is nothing I would like more right now," Alphonso growled. "But as a priority, we need to get the signorina inside—"

"Yes," Raf said firmly, "so she can lie down, preferably in a cool, dark room with the shutters drawn, and she must rest for at least twenty-four hours, or until her headache subsides." He turned to Cara. "You have already been ill, although you may not remember."

The driveway spun and she was glad of his arm around her, keeping her from falling.

Alphonso glanced up at the house. And seeing this, Cara followed his gaze.

Parked right outside the front door of the villa was Bruno Klein's car.

The Contessa was back with her fascist lover. *Perfect.*

Cara glanced nervously at Alphonso. She had a basket of dynamite in her possession, and tonight it would have to be hidden in the Contessa's summerhouse while Evelina Messina was sleeping in the villa with a Nazi. And there was only one person who could do that. Her.

"Do not worry," Alphonso said. "The Contessa and her... friend have gone for a walk."

Cara almost sagged with relief.

Raf reached out and placed his hand on her arm a moment, and then he turned to Alphonso. "I will meet you opposite the villa gates once you have helped the signorina up to the house. Then, we will deal with our... friend."

Alphonso nodded grimly.

"Signor Messina?" Cara asked.

"*Si?*"

Cara closed her eyes and a wave of nausea swept over her again. "Thank you," she said.

Raf nodded at her and looked up the drive once more.

Gently, Alphonso took the bicycle from Raf, who disappeared down toward the road. "We will take you to Bettina, and she will clean you up, dress your wounds, and let you rest in one of the guest rooms." Alphonso expertly maneuvered the bicycle while he held an arm around her, propping her up as they walked toward the villa.

"I went to the markets in Cortona," she said, looking at Alphonso meaningfully. "But I also have a gift in the basket that is delicate, and I was wondering, would you help me transfer it into the villa?" She would have to get it to the summerhouse once she had recovered, and it would be best to do that under the cloak of darkness, tonight.

His eyes clashed with hers, and she held his gaze, entreating him to understand. The basket was heavy, and she could not manage to carry it herself now. Were she to drop it... "No one must know about the surprise."

Alphonso focused straight ahead and looked thoughtful. Finally, he gave a little nod.

"*Grazie*, Alphonso," Cara whispered, and a swell of emotion burst inside her. Thank goodness for friends, and for the humanity that always seemed to surface, even in the face of cruelty of the worst kind.

Cara lay quietly all afternoon. Light filtered gently through the closed wooden shutters into the guest room where Bettina had left her to rest. She had not been able to eat all day, but had managed to sip water, and a stone jug sat by her bed with a full glass. Touchingly, Alphonso had brought her a single pink rose in a vase from the rose garden, and he had carefully placed her basket in one of the big wardrobes. She had asked him to remove the small gift from Raf to the Contessa and to take it to her. This, she hoped, would soothe the Contessa's ruffled feathers if she found out inadvertently that Raf had been at the villa and hadn't even come to greet her. The Contessa must be deeply disturbed by the fact that both her sons seemed to have abandoned her. Raf had all but disappeared from his mother's life, and the Contessa was throwing herself into the arms of a Nazi, when the tide seemed finally to have turned and the Allies were advancing.

What a mess.

With the bedroom door cracked open, Cara had heard Bettina and Alphonso saying that the Germans had set fire to several farms locally, in reprisal for what they called *increased partisan activity* in the valley. Cara had lain, feeling useless, while they had discussed whether it was safe to remain at the Villa Rosa. She had heard them talking about ideas that seemed fantastical—hiding out in a cave in the nearby forest or building a bunker—but their conversation had trailed off, and Cara had no idea what was in store next.

As she dozed, she heard planes swooping over the valley and then fell asleep at last.

.   .   .

Cara rolled over onto her side and tried to ease herself up. Her head still ached but did not pound so painfully, and she was grateful that Raf had suggested she rest. Light, the pure clear light of Tuscany, would have blinded her, and instead while she rested, the dark allowed her headache to ease. She sipped her water and lay back down again.

When would she see Raf again? She had felt that old magic when he had held her in his arms. And who was going to be carrying out the attack on the Nazi anti-aircraft battery outside Cortona tomorrow? Please, don't let it be Raf.

Cara closed her eyes and turned away from the filtered light that was coming through the shutters into the cool room.

She still had one more mission to complete.

CHAPTER 32

ANNIE

Annie and Luca wheeled their bicycles back into the stable of the Villa Rosa. Sandro's Italian car was parked outside the villa, and he stood waiting with a well-dressed middle-aged man in a business suit. Annie disliked Sandro's companion on sight. His' beady eyes appraised her, and his nose was red and laced with purple veins. She knew she should not judge him harshly for his appearance, but she couldn't help it. The fact that Sandro was determined to prove his ownership was understandable, but it also seemed he was willing to play dirty to get his way.

She left the old bike next to the one Luca had been riding and turned to him.

"Feeling okay?" he asked.

Annie nodded. "But I can't help..." She closed her eyes. "I can't help wishing... that something would turn up to resolve this." The only piece of information she had found in her search for Cara Cartazzo was the name of the secretary's parents, which had been listed on the ancestry site. It seemed that her father, Lino Cartazzo, had died in the summer of 1944. But

Annie had no information about where he had come from, or who Cara's family were. Nothing beyond the fact that she was an only child, and that her mother, Loretta, had died years before. "I have this feeling that it was the Contessa who cut the pages out of the diary, and she did so to hide any evidence of her relationship with a Nazi... And the child she had. The child appears to have been completely wiped out. And that is what Sandro wants to do with me."

Luca was close to her. "Hey," he said. "We've only just begun."

"You know, it's strange. I never knew Cara Cartazzo, but I wish I had had the chance. Her notes were meticulous, and her handwriting... It was lovely."

They had spoken to the bookstore owner, but she had not known anything more about the diary. She had told them that they were welcome to take it with them and had refused to accept any money for it.

"We have to keep going," Luca said. "We won't give up."

Annie looked at him. "Are you sure?" she asked. "I worry that you're putting your own work for Sandro at risk," she said, "getting involved in my search. You don't have to continue. But I do," she added.

"My grandfather was here too," Luca said. "Something drove him away from Italy." He folded his arms and surveyed the empty stable. "And I don't think that Sandro particularly cares what his gardener does, to be honest."

"I do," Annie said. And then checked herself.

Luca caught her eye. But Sandro appeared at the door to the garage, and Annie stood tall. It was one thing to let her guard down in the stables, but she would not do so in front of him.

"Come and meet James, and we will talk," Sandro said. His tone was surprisingly gentle, and Annie glanced at him in surprise.

She walked with Luca out toward the bright Tuscan late

afternoon, shadows falling from the cypress trees onto the gravel driveway, and weeds sprouting around her feet.

"Annie, and Luca," Sandro said expansively. "Meet James Sheffield, from London."

Luca moved forward and shook the middle-aged man's outstretched hand. Annie hovered, inexplicably feeling alarmed and upset by his presence.

"Hello," she said shortly, but she did not hold out her hand.

"I wasn't expecting you to be here," James Sheffield said. He sniffed, and looked out over the gardens as if appraising them.

Annie folded her arms. Her instincts had been right. There was something about him that she instantly did not like one bit.

"You are going back to the village now?" James Sheffield asked, looking pointedly at Annie. "Are you staying in the *pensione*?" He managed to make the last word sound dirty.

"No. I'll stay, as this is my villa."

She met Sandro's eyes.

"You can stay if you like," he said, sounding perfectly affable.

"I don't need an invitation," she said.

"What a superb view," James said, turning to Sandro. "I must say, we're going to be only targeting top-end corporations and wealthy families, because they'll love the exclusivity. High-end actors, rock stars, et cetera, who will fall in love with this place at the drop of a hat. You want to target the absolute best. And only blue-ribbon corporations. You've got your reputation to consider. Only the right people for the right place. It's about attracting their money." James dictated a note to himself on his phone.

Having sat through James Sheffield's spiel for the last half hour, Annie leaned forward, her hands folded on the table that

Sandro had set up on the terrace for the purposes of this business meeting. Luca had offered to leave, but Annie had invited him to stay. And so, he had.

She looked at Sandro, a sudden idea coming to mind. "Your great-grandfather left Italy for America at the outset of the war, no, Sandro?"

He sat back, clasping his hands behind his head, his elbows wide. He said nothing.

"Might that not have been the beginning of all the problems the Villa Rosa has faced?" she asked. "We need to find out why the villa passed out of your family's hands into mine. And I say, we set a reasonable time frame for me to find out the truth."

"For goodness' sake," James Sheffield said.

"I can't enter into a gentleman's agreement with someone who is trying to steal my heritage," Sandro said.

Annie looked up at the old façade of the house. The peach-and honey-colored paint was faded in the sun. Back in the day, young girls would have been preparing for their supper before heading for their bedrooms upstairs, the French doors flung open to the balcony, and the sweet scents of the Tuscan air drifting in from outside. Somewhere along the line, had one of her ancestors been one of those girls? "Give me a month, and I will sort it out," she said. She sensed Luca taking in a sharp breath right next to her. But she needed a time frame, and if they were going to reach an agreement, both she and Sandro had to play fair. "In the meantime, Luca can continue his very good work getting the water in the gardens back up and running, but we will hold off on any further planning until the ownership is decided."

"I can't wait a month," Sandro said.

"Yes, you can." Annie sat up taller in her seat. This felt good. She had never had much agency in her own family. She realized now that she had always allowed Monica and Paul to make the important decisions. Perhaps, things needed to change. She could look at the situation with the villa as a problem or an opportunity, and looking at it as an opportunity might give her the chance to make a new start.

CHAPTER 33

CARA

Later that evening, footsteps came toward the bedroom. Cara tensed, still haunted by the fear that hung over her after the assault.

"Cara?" The Contessa's lilting voice broke into her thoughts as she opened the door and came toward her.

"Contessa," Cara whispered. She tried to sit up, but the Contessa was at her side and, with surprisingly gentle hands, helped her to lie back down on the bed.

Cara closed her eyes, and the Contessa's hand softly stroked her forehead. "My dear," she whispered. "I am so sorry for what happened to you. And I feel responsible. This should never have happened outside my home. It disgusts me."

"It seems ironic to have been attacked by my own neighbor."

Evelina Messina lowered her voice. "Alphonso has dealt with the dreadful man. He has taken him to the Carabinieri and has supplied a full report of the incident."

It will be interesting to see if the Carabinieri do anything.

"Alphonso tells me he witnessed part of the attack and thumped the man on the head."

Alphonso...? Cara's eyes opened, and she shook her head. But the Contessa had moved away to lean on the windowsill. She closed the curtains, and turned around, folding her arms. Clearly, the Contessa did not know that Raf had been here.

"Cara, I do not trust that the Carabinieri will bring that odious Signor Santino to justice. And I am worried about you going home to live next door to him." The Contessa came over and patted Cara awkwardly on the knee. "I want you to stay here with us until things settle down." The sound of aircraft whined like a swarm of wasps somewhere in the distance over the valley.

"You want me to live in the villa?"

"It will be too dangerous for you to go home," the Contessa said. She rubbed her hands down her skirt. "This way, we can work more closely together, and keep an eye on everything as we move toward the next stage in this war."

And this way, you can make sure your secretary is not working for the partisans.

Cara opened her mouth to say something, but her cut lip swelled with pain.

"Good," the Contessa said. "I will appreciate having you here all the time. I hope you will be comfortable in the Villa Rosa?"

Cara floundered about for something to say. To be honest, she was floored. And it was hard to know what game the Contessa was playing, or whether she genuinely worried for Cara's safety. But either way, it felt churlish to turn the invitation down. And if the Contessa did suspect her of doing anything for the resistance, then so be it. It would not stop her. It must not stop her. Raf might be hesitant to tell his own mother the truth about himself, but she had always had an

honest relationship with Papa. And she had made him a promise. Come what may.

"I will send Bettina later to see if you can manage some
food. Some minestrone, perhaps, and bread. You will need to
gather your strength. Goodnight, Cara. Please rest until you feel
able to return to work."

Little did the Contessa know what that work was.

CHAPTER 34

ANNIE

Luca had suggested holding a picnic for the villagers in the gardens to celebrate the discovery of the fountains, and Annie had convinced Sandro to agree based on their uneasy truce. James had returned to England, and this had allowed Annie to feel a little more comfortable with Sandro here. She was also proud of the fact that she had stood up for herself, and for the villa.

A group of villagers were gathered under the olive trees. Long trestle tables with pretty flowers in glass jars, proper china and wine glasses were set out on the lawn. Adults of all ages— from the elderly to those in their early twenties—were standing around with glasses of spumante, and several wine bottles sat on the checked tablecloth ready for lunch. Children ran through the terraced gardens, nestling in secret hiding places, their laughter ringing through the air. And the Villa Rosa sat at the top of the hill like a benign old friend, looking down at the unaccustomed party in her gardens.

Annie had worked alongside Luca these past few days, fully

unearthing the hidden fountains that would showcase the water from the underground spring. It had been light relief, helping Luca get the fountains going again. She had enjoyed spending time in the old gardens, working alongside Luca. But being there only made the Villa Rosa feel more like home, and yet, she had discovered nothing about her ancestry. With only a week to go before her agreement with Sandro lapsed, there seemed no way of discovering who she really was. The villagers had shaken their heads and changed the topic when she had asked them if they knew anything about what had happened here during the war. No one wanted to talk about those dark days, and Annie was beginning to wonder whether she really did want to find out the truth herself.

She had spent this morning in the kitchen of one of the local families, helping to prepare some of the region's specialties— salads freshly picked from villagers' gardens, white bean soup, flan of eggplant with tomato sauce, egg pasta with zucchini and squash blossoms, roast lamb, and duck breast in a sauce of grape must vinegar. It had been wonderful to enjoy cooking these dishes, and for a moment, she missed home, and the way she, Lucy and Lauren had worked together, cooked together, just like these people in Tuscany were doing.

She stood next to Ernesto, the owner of the village café, while the sun shone down on them through the trees, slanting beams of warming light on them.

"It is my great pleasure to restore the fountains to life again at the Villa Rosa." Sandro stood in front of the small crowd that had gathered. He was dressed as if straight out of a boutique in Rome or Florence, his rumpled tanned linen suit and shiny leather shoes accessorized as always with his Wayfarers, while his hair was styled to sit on his shoulders. "I only hope that soon I shall be able to share another announcement with you about the future of my family's home."

Annie smoothed down the green polka-dot sundress she

had chosen, and then fought the urge to undo the top button, which suddenly felt constricting around her neck. She had bought it in Florence, and it made her feel that bit more Italian, but now, with Sandro standing here so confidently making an unexpected speech, there seemed no chance she had any claim to the villa at all.

Sandro continued: "My plans for the future of the Villa Rosa are exciting, and I want it to be a showcase for the entire valley. I will share my vision with you as soon as I can, and I want you all to become involved and profit from this wonderful opportunity."

She moved over to stand next to Sandro. "The future of the Villa Rosa is not clear," she said, surprising even herself, not least because her Italian was so limited. She looked up at Luca where he stood above them on the top terrace.

Next to her, Sandro let out an audible groan.

But Annie lifted her chin. "When my father died, he left me a note saying that I had inherited the Villa Rosa. The local notary has confirmed this, and I intend to restore the villa and turn it into the family home that it once was. As a passionate cook and chef, I believe that my birth family came from this valley too, and my search has brought me back here to you. My commitment is to restore the walled vegetable garden, to bring the vineyards back to life, to welcome you, the villagers, up here to sit on the terrace with me and enjoy a glass of wine. I don't know, perhaps I will run a small cooking school, and teach cooking, because as a chef that is something I have long wanted to do."

She paused and scanned the crowd. A couple of middle-aged men stood with their arms folded, and skeptical looks on their faces.

Annie cleared her throat. "But I will not turn the villa into a conference center, which is the other proposal on the table, crowding this road and my neighbors with more tourist buses. I love the Villa Rosa, and I want it to be my home and part of this community in a new way, while honoring local traditions and respecting the heritage of the house."

There was a full moment of silence among the crowd, and Sandro muttered something indiscernible that almost sounded like a threat. But then Luca, taking advantage of the quiet confusion in the crowd, turned on the new tap that he had installed up near the old well, and the joyous sound of water running down the multiple fountains through the mouths of the gargoyles on each level, from terrace to terrace, seemed to bring the old villa back to the first stages of life.

Everyone clapped and held up their glasses. Annie felt the unwelcome touch of Sandro's hand restraining her arm. She had no interest in listening to him right now, in this moment of triumph for the villa, for the community. She pulled away from Sandro, ignoring him, and walked to the bottom of the stone steps. Luca made his way down the terraces, until he came down to the olive groves, where he was surrounded by local villagers, clapping him on the back, and congratulating him.

The wine was poured, and people began piling their plates with the crisp green salads and local cuisine. Annie and Luca chatted companionably, watching the water dance in the fountains. She stilled as a flash of color caught her eye and a taxi pulled into the bottom of the driveway.

The back door of the car opened, and a woman dressed in a cool black linen dress, with a string of pearls around her neck, stepped out, and then went to the trunk of the car and collected an expensive-looking designer suitcase on wheels. Her chestnut hair fell to her shoulders in thick, lustrous waves. She scanned the crowd, and her aqua-blue eyed gaze landed on Luca.

"There he is," she said clearly, turning to the driver, who had helped her with her luggage.

"*Arrivederci, signora,*" the driver said, and he climbed back into the car, turned on the engine, and left.

Luca went straight over to the expensively dressed woman and enfolded her in an embrace. He led her into the garden, chatting with her animatedly, and the woman looked up at him with complete admiration in her eyes.

This must be his mother. Annie swallowed the ache inside her that reminded her that she had no mother of her own. At this point, she had no idea who her mother was, nor whether she was still alive. But Luca's mother had a real connection to the villa. Would she be able to help?

CHAPTER 35

CARA

Cara lay on her side in the bed in the guest room, her eyes trained on the wardrobe where Raf's ammunition was hidden. Grief was hitting her like a tumultuous wave after the Contessa's visit. She missed her father more than ever. It had been Papa who had always taken care of her when she was ill. Cara had woken with a lump in her throat, remembering him appearing at her door with a mug of warmed juice made from local lemons and honey when she was poorly; his presence alone had always cheered her up. Once, she didn't know when, she had sat up too quickly at the sound of male footsteps coming into visit her, only to find Alphonso standing in the doorway, his hat in his hand, his dark eyes full of sympathy and concern. A dear, kind man, but still she felt so sad.

All evening, Allied warplanes had roared overhead on their way north, where they were still bombing German trains and military storehouses. Cara frowned at the closed wardrobe. Part of her wished that the local partisans would allow the professionally trained Allied pilots to bomb the ammunition storage

facility and potential bunker that Raf and his friends were planning on attacking with dynamite outside Cortona, while she
also wished she could hurl a grenade at the thing herself. A
couple of times in the last hour, she had stood up and tiptoed to
the door in preparation to take the dynamite to the summerhouse, but the sound of Bruno Klein's booming voice still
droned on and on in the living room, along with the tinkle of the
Contessa's replies. Annie's stomach tensed.

A small, swift-flying group of fighters swooped right over
the villa, and Cara sat up slowly in her bed, swinging her feet
over the side and placing them down on the floor. If the Allied
fighter planes kept up their attacks all night, and began
sweeping down and machine-gunning any German vehicles on
the roads and bombing Nazi lorries, and if those attacks were
carried out nearby in the valley, then the Contessa would order
everyone down to the cellars. Cara could not afford to wait. The
planes would at least cover the sound of her footsteps.

She padded across the room in her slip, and stopped at the
chair where she had draped her ripped cotton dress. A fresh red
dress was laid out for her. And there was a note pinned to it.

*Please, take this. I am so sorry for what happened today on
my property. I was mortified. Evelina.*

Cara tiptoed across the room with the dress folded over her
arm. She laid down on the bed a moment, her head pounding.
The sound of bombs falling in the distance only served to
remind her that she had to get moving.

The house was otherwise quiet.

Cara pulled on the dress, and crept over to the wardrobe,
opening it as quietly as she could. She removed the wicker
basket that still held the sticks of dynamite. If she was stopped,
she would simply say she was going home to the pensione.

But when she came to the kitchen, holding her basket, Cara
stopped at the sight of a figure before her.

CHAPTER 36

ANNIE

Annie stood by herself on the edge of the picnic, while Luca took his mother to get some food. When Sandro came to stand beside her, she turned to him in surprise.

"Annie. I have been thinking. All this angst between us is not healthy. I do not want things to be hostile between us," he murmured. "Why should we be enemies?"

"The Villa Rosa is a home, not a building," Annie said, keeping her tone as even as possible. "It deserves a better fate than the one you have planned."

"You think I do not care about the villa?" He indicated the villagers enjoying the gardens. "Look how happy the local people are. They would not be here if it were not for me. And they would not be here if it were not for my family."

Annie glanced out at the olive grove. Little girls in white dresses ran around and squealed in delight. This was the happiest she had ever seen the villa since she arrived.

"There is a long tradition in my family of looking after the villagers and the local farmers. My plans will bring industry and jobs to the valley. Young people can come and work at the villa."

"It is not all about business," Annie said. "To turn the Villa Rosa into a function center will tear the heart and soul out of this beautiful old home. And the valley is a world-renowned tourist destination already. Things have changed since the pre-war days, and it seems to me that the villagers and farmers are doing well without your patronization. They are running their own businesses, producing olive oil, wines, running exquisite restaurants. Your family have been gone a long time."

Sandro's honey-colored eyes warmed. "I know you love to cook. I know that you run a successful catering business back in San Francisco. Work for me... Or rather, work with me."

Annie took a step back.

"You can refurbish the kitchen gardens," Sandro went on, his voice silky smooth. "Back in the day, there were gardeners and cooks who worked together to grow all the fruit and vegetables that the villa needed. Chickens laid fresh eggs every day. You can do exactly what you want to do here, without the pressure of ownership. I know you have fallen for Tuscany. I can tell. Why not let me worry about the financials, so that you can be entirely focused on being creative? You could write a cookbook. Working for me, the sky would be the limit."

"I don't need you to follow my dreams, Sandro."

"No, but I can make your dreams come true. For so many years I have wanted to make my home in Italy," he said. "It is not my battle, but my grandfather's battle, that has alienated my branch of the family from Italy."

Annie sighed. "Yes, but—"

"I grew up imagining still, green hills, olive groves and vineyards while staring at the gray skies of London. I should have been surrounded by the land that is in my blood all my life. The first time I came back here, I felt at home," he murmured.

"As did I."

Perhaps there was some grain of truth in his feelings and his words. People could be so complex, and right now, trying to fully understand Sandro, the Contessa, this family, felt as impossible as trying to grasp the history of this villa that she needed to unravel to get to the truth.

She felt as if she were unwrapping the layers of an impossible gift.

"I know that James can come across as somewhat threatening," Sandro said. "But under his financial management, we will all benefit. If you come on board, it will be much easier for you."

Annie pressed her lips together tightly. For one wild moment, she felt the presence of her papa looking over her. Papa had always told her how his father, Annie's grandad Bernard, had encouraged Papa to be an architect, to design and build homes for people where they could live and make memories with their loved ones. What was more important than that? It was all she was trying to do here. She had grown up knowing the importance of home, and she felt as if Sandro was threatening to take her future home away. Somewhere deep inside her, Papa's assurance to her that she owned the Villa Rosa beat like a flailing chick trying to make its way out of the nest.

"You are alone here," Sandro continued. "As a woman in Tuscany, the local builders will take terrible advantage of you."

"That is the most—"

"With James' and my backing, they won't dare to play any tricks. We have contacts in the trade, and will send the finest craftsmen, the best artisans to restore the villa to her former glory. I want to bring people together. Not separate them. Separation was what happened to my family during the war. I want to put things right once and for all."

Sandro was magnetic. He was a stunning man, with a stunning capability to convince. He was also the last man on earth she should ever trust.

"Annie, you want family. You want to find out where you belong."

She focused on his rose gold signet ring gleaming on the little finger of his right hand.

"I am offering you family. Come and meet my father with me in London. Let him tell you how much the villa means to us. To lose it would be impossible. The Villa Rosa beats in the Messina family's blood."

Just then, Ernesto, the owner of the café in the village, approached them, and on his arm, an elderly woman who looked to be well into her nineties stood dressed in traditional black. Ernesto nodded at Sandro deferentially. "Excuse me, Signor Messina," he said. "But my mother traveled from Rome today to be here because the Villa Rosa means a great deal to her. My mama grew up in the village. And she worked at the Villa Rosa during the Second World War."

Annie transferred her gaze to the elderly woman leaning on Ernesto's arm. She was tiny, but her blue eyes were bright, and her hair was tied back in a neat and severe bun. Her hand trembled but was pressed firmly onto her son's skin.

"My name is Bettina Passarella," the old woman enunciated in a clear voice. "I know every speck of earth in that vegetable patch. I know the best place to rise dough in the villa kitchen, and exactly how long the yeast needs to be left to prove. I can still cook every Tuscan specialty. And some of my most wonderful memories are of sitting outside in the back courtyard in the twilight, while the Contessa Evelina enjoyed her coffee after dinner. I remember her husband, Arturo. I remember better times."

Annie glanced across at Sandro, but his expression was hard to read.

Bettina lifted her chin. Her voice was tremulous. "I was the cook at the Villa Rosa for Evelina Messina during the war." She turned her gaze toward Annie. "And I know the truth."

CHAPTER 37

CARA

Bettina stood in the doorway to the kitchen, a shawl wrapped around her shoulders. She spoke formally. "Bruno Klein has informed us all that a unit of German anti-aircraft artillery is to be stationed at the villa. They are on their way." The cook eyed Cara's basket warily.

"Don't ask," Cara whispered to the young cook, her friend. She clutched her basket, holding it close, her chest feeling light, and her pulse racing.

Bettina closed the door to the hallway behind her. "I won't ask any questions, Cara, but whatever you are doing, you need to make it quick. We are to be taken over, and they are demanding all the beds in the house. Their trucks will be parked in the driveway before the sun is up, and already the Contessa is planning where they will all sleep."

Cara stared at the closed kitchen door.

"The Contessa insists that we must not take any risks, that we must not in any way help the partisans. We are to lie down

after all this time, and let the Nazis simply walk into the house."
She eyed Cara's basket.

Cara watched in alarm as Bettina went and stood by the
back door, checking it was locked. Would Bettina not let her
leave?

"The Contessa says they will want to wash in the laundry,
that she will be dealing with naked young Nazis in the bath-
house and that they will take over the entire villa. The Contessa
and Alphonso have been digging holes in the garden during the
evening to bury any items that they want to keep, as this division has the reputation of being light-fingered, rude, and especially brutal toward young women. The Contessa says that they
will take what they want... Cara. I think you should leave the
villa."

"I will go immediately, and you?" She would leave the
basket in the summerhouse on the way. In truth, it had given
her a welcome excuse to get away from here.

"I am to stay." Bettina lifted her head, her blue eyes
catching Cara's dark gaze. The cook reached into a kitchen
drawer and pulled out the only piece of evidence that Cara had
ever worked at the Villa Rosa. It was the business diary that she
kept with little notes and entries for the Contessa as to the bills
she had paid, and meetings she had organized. "I was going to
bring this up to your room in the morning. Take it with you and
keep it hidden away. You don't want anyone knowing you
worked closely with the Contessa... after."

Cara reached out and took it, her hand brushing against the
other girl's. "Bettina—"

"Alphonso has said that he will guard me with his life,"
Bettina said, lifting her chin. "The Contessa insists that I must
stay to cook, and yet, the two remaining housemaids are going to
flee at the crack of dawn."

"So, this is it," Cara whispered. She placed her basket and

her diary down for one precious second and pulled Bettina into a hug.

"Cara... Where will you go?"

Cara moved toward the door. "I have no idea."

Bettina stood clasping her hands in the kitchen. "I will always remember you. I hope we get to meet again."

"Me too." Cara swallowed hard. She sent Bettina a searing look, unable to shake the feeling that this was a final goodbye. With one last smile for Bettina, Cara turned the doorknob and left the Villa Rosa.

Cara was about to step into the driveway from the summerhouse, the dynamite deposited safely, when headlights beamed into her face. A slow rumble of trucks was coming up the driveway. In a quick flash, Cara slipped back into the shadows of the olive grove, only to see what she had feared: a cavalcade of dark German lorries making their steady way up the gravel drive, their tires throwing up pale dust.

Cara crouched down behind a tree, while heavy boots landed on the gravel after the first truck pulled up by the front door. Cara winced at the sight of a man spitting on the ground. A hearty laugh, clap on the back. From what she could see, these men were not the polished Nazis she was used to. Their uniforms were in disarray, their hair unkempt. These were Göring's men. The men they dreaded.

She glanced at the villa, silent in the moonlight. The valley was about to become the front line, the part of Italy that was going to make world news.

Another truck pulled up in the driveway, and loud, arrogant voices speaking in German filled the air.

Cara turned and ran.

CHAPTER 38

ANNIE

Ernesto led Annie toward a table set with a white cloth in the olive grove. She followed the café owner whose mother, Signora Bettina, walked alongside him, her back ramrod straight, her hand resting on her son's arm. The sun streamed through the branches of the trees, and the blue-green leaves shifted slightly in the afternoon breeze. Ernesto helped his mother into a white plastic chair, before pulling out a chair for Annie and insisting she sit down in pride of place next to Bettina. Sandro sat down opposite her, and fiddled with the signet ring he wore.

"I was fourteen years old when I came to work at the Villa Rosa," Bettina said.

Ernesto poured white wine into crystal glasses, and offered everyone pieces of *torta della nonna*. Annie accepted a slice and let the lemon-scented custard linger on her tongue, while the sweet pastry melted in her mouth.

"I believed that I was old enough to be in possession of all my faculties back then, and I believe that I am still in possession of them now." Bettina lifted her chin and moved stiffly in her seat. She accepted a slice of the tart from her son and nodded at it briefly, although a practiced frown appeared on her forehead, and Annie couldn't help smiling in recognition of a fellow cook appraising a dish she knew well.

Ernesto placed a hand on his mother's arm. "No one is questioning that, Mama," he said.

Bettina swung around to look up at him and made a clucking sound. "But you asked me a question, Ernesto, and told me that I must only answer it if I was clear. And I am clear. The Contessa Evelina Messina had an affair with a Nazi during the war," she said. "I witnessed it. I was here. And she was pregnant with his baby."

Annie placed her fork down on the white china plate and glanced across at Sandro, but he had stood up, and was leaning heavily against the back of his chair.

"I was head cook at the villa by the time I was eighteen," the elderly woman went on. "I lived in the same house as the Contessa Evelina Messina and her Nazi lover for a time. A terrible time. I prefer not to remember it. What happened here was unthinkable. It was a disgrace. I could not abide it. So, I left." Bettina sat up, rigid. She crossed her arms over her chest.

Sandro stared downward. His face was unreadable.

But Annie focused intently on the elderly woman who had been here during those tumultuous years and who may be able to understand her past. "Was a child born?"

The old woman's face assumed a complex expression. And she licked her dry lips. "Si."

Sandro raised his head and looked at Bettina intently. "This is not something that I want broadcast," he said. "It is time to move on and leave this to rest. That is what I'm fighting so hard to do." He sent a pleading glance toward Annie.

The elderly lady turned her steady blue-eyed gaze toward Annie. "But now, you have arrived."

"Sandro, surely you wish to know if this is my lineage, to disgrace me once and for all?"

Annie tipped her head back. The blue sky was endless and clear. Too clear for a murky story such as this, but she had to know. "Obviously, Signora Bettina, I was hoping that you would be able to tell me something different."

The old woman scowled. "It was a disgrace. I could not abide it. So, I left."

Annie glanced across the garden to where Luca and his mother were talking. "Do you know the name of the child? The baby?" she added.

"The baby's name was Loretta."

Annie glanced over to where Luca was standing with his mother and a group of villagers.

Bettina sat up straight. "Her name was Loretta Messina."

Was this Loretta her mother? If so, Loretta had never wanted her either.

CHAPTER 39

CARA

"Cara mia."

Cara froze right outside the gates of the villa.

A convoy of bombers swooped overhead, and a shell exploded not far away, on the road to the village. One of the Nazi generals in the villa grounds was getting angry, and he started barking orders to his men.

"Quickly, Cara," Raf whispered. "Please, you must come with me."

Cara hesitated.

"Do you trust me?" he asked.

Cara glanced about. "Of course, Raf," she sighed, frustration biting at her insides. It broke Cara's heart to turn her back on Alphonso and Bettina, who had become family since Papa had died, but what choice did she have.

"Quickly, I know exactly where to hide." Raf reached out for her hand, and took her basket with his other hand, and she ran alongside him under cover of the trees that lined the road. He led her down into the forest. "There are underground tunnels that have connected the Villa Rosa to the village since medieval times." He glanced back in the direction of the villa, and then reached down to open a trapdoor buried under a pile of leaves. "Find your footing. There is a ladder," Raf said.

Cara glanced down into the pitch-black below. She hesitated, but Raf indicated for her to go underground. She eased herself down into the labyrinth, her heart beating in her mouth. When Raf followed her and closed the door, she was in total darkness. She carefully reached for the treads, and froze at the bottom of the rudimentary stairs, her senses adjusting to the damp air in the tunnel that connected the villa to the village at the bottom of the hill. She could hear Raf moving, hear his breathing in the musty quiet. He struck a match, and lit an old-fashioned lantern, holding it up and highlighting their new surroundings.

The tunnel was about six feet tall and three feet wide, and Cara looked down to see that she was standing on a stone floor. Someone had carved their initials in the walls. Cara turned to Raf in alarm. "Was this used as some sort of prison?" she said, wrapping her arms around herself.

Raf shook his head. "It was simply a convenient way for the inhabitants of the villa to reach the village and vice versa if undercover methods were required. We used to come down here as children." His expression darkened. "Nicolas and I."

Cara yearned to say something about his brother. About the family member he had lost. Raf hardly spoke of their relationship, and yet, Cara was certain that he was torn by his older brother's departure and must be struggling to cope with him not being around. Sometimes, she wondered if Nicolas might have given his younger brother more guidance when it came to their mother.

The sound of dripping water, somewhere deep into the tunnel, was not reassuring, but the stonework on the floors, walls and overhead was masterfully wrought.

Raf led her further in, before stopping where the tunnel curved deeper into the hill, and Cara frowned at the sight of a rough straw mattress, a blanket, a crate turned upside down, upon which there was a loaf of bread, a pitcher of water and a peach from the orchards.

She looked at Raf, her eyes holding all the questions that would sound too obvious to ask.

"Alphonso helped me drag this down here," he said, indicating the mattress, while indicating to his own arm. "And Bettina has been supplying me with stores," he said, looking down at the food.

Cara looked down longingly at the straw mattress, and yawned uncontrollably, her body feeling so very heavy after the last two days.

"Cara," he said. And she winced at the way he no longer called her Cara mia, only to chide herself- why was she worried about that? "Rest. Sleep. I will guard you."

It was impossible to think beyond the next few hours, about what was going to happen next. Cara almost fell onto the simple bed of straw. It felt like heaven, and for the first time since she had been attacked she closed her eyes, feeling truly safe.

Cara woke hours later, and the headache that had plagued her since yesterday was gone. There was something about the dim interior of the tunnel that was soothing.

Raf sat in the light of the kerosene lamp, reading.

"Bettina raided the library as well?" Cara said, propping herself up on one elbow.

Raf looked up at her. "*The Count of Monte Cristo,*" he said.

Cara raked a hand through her tumble of dark hair. It had fallen into a mass of unruly waves, and she would do anything to be able to run a brush through it, to clean her teeth. To wash. She felt like one of the partisans—dirty, rough. The basket containing the dynamite was stored neatly next to Raf, and he had pulled Cara's business diary out and placed it by her bed along with her pen.

She sat up on the bed of straw, crossing her legs and stretching her arms in the air.

Raf went to the makeshift crate that was being used for a table, and broke a chunk of bread, poured some water into a glass, and handed her the peach. "Please take these and enjoy them," he said. "You need to build up your strength."

"And you?"

"Oh, I had a feast this morning," he said, grinning at her. "Insalata, pasta ragu, roast lamb, and torta della nonna."

"We could write out a menu," she said. She picked up a pen and grinned at him. "What do you think? Cara and Raf's summer menu for lost souls?" The last thing she wanted to talk about was the mission that Raf was about to carry out. Not yet. She reached for the diary and began to write.

"I didn't realize that you like to write."

Cara broke off a piece of bread. It tasted sweet and delicious on her tongue. She began to write out a wonderful menu.

"There. I have written down your precise wishes."

"Delicious," he declared.

Cara smiled at him and finished half of the peach, and solemnly handed the other half across to Raf. "This is yours," she whispered.

He took the other half. "Will you write your secrets in there?" he asked, looking at the journal.

Cara was quiet a moment. "I think it would be nice to write something more personal. Perhaps it would help me to process everything that has happened... it's been a long journey, Raf."

Raf took in a deep breath. "You know, what is getting me through this are my memories. Memories of my grandparents' villa outside Venice. We used to spend our summers there. It belonged to my mother's family."

"It is special to you?"

"I think it was the place where my father, Arturo felt truly relaxed." But then Raf shook his head. "Cara, can I show you something?"

"Of course."

"Look at these," Raf pulled out a series of sheets of artist paper from underneath the rudimentary mattress. She drew closer. He held a whole series of small paintings.

Raf pulled out the first painting. It was an abstract, deep blue, and sunny yellow, and what looked like cornfields blowing in the breeze. Cara looked at the painting for a few moments, and she was certain she could discern the shape of a solitary figure standing on the small canvas.

"These were my father's. He wanted to be an artist, to travel, to see the world, but he had inherited the Villa Rosa, and all the farms and estates that went with it. I know how privileged he was, but there was always a yearning in his eyes. My mother was... brought in by his parents as an appropriate bride to marry him, and she came from a wealthy aristocratic family in Venice. He had no choice, Cara. He had to stay here at the villa. But that whole time I knew him, he was a dreamer who wanted to paint. My mother took over the reins and saved our family home. She not only gave the Messina family two sons but encouraged my father to embrace what he could here, to get to know the people and the community, and to make something of the role that he had. She encouraged him, and gradually, he developed the confidence to run the Messina estates. It was natural for her to take over when he died."

Cara listened in silence.

"In time, he came to love his role, he came to respect and admire the people and their hard work in the valley. He and my mother complemented each other. She gave him time to paint..." Raf looked at all the neatly gathered paintings. "And he in turn designed an epitaph to them both on the villa gate and on the staircase in the great entrance hall, entwining their initials in the villa for perpetuity. Together they were the foundation of this house and my family." Raf's face clouded.

Cara's heart went out to him. And now, what had war done to their family? To his mother?

Raf handed Cara the little painting, and she drank it in, reveling in the simple colors while he spoke. "When my father was in his mid-forties, he changed... Dramatically. He could see the way Europe was going, and he and my mother started arguing. My father took up with a local girl in the village, and he broke my mother's heart. The morning after a particularly vicious round of fighting between them, he stepped outside the villa to go for a walk and collapsed and died."

"I am so sorry," Cara whispered. She had no idea about what was going on behind closed doors. Did anyone, ever?

"My mother couldn't bear to see his paintings in the house. She hid them. I think she honestly felt that she had supported him, and encouraged him to be himself, only to have him let her down. And then, my elder brother turned against her. Everything went wrong in our family. Cara...you must understand that I still feel..." He turned to face her; his handsome face torn with grief. "I cannot break her heart again."

Instead, you will break mine. But the words sounded selfish...

"She has been lost ever since that day he died, and I think another part of her died when Nicolas left. I don't think she ever got over the grief. She is lost, Cara. This affair with Bruno Klein is so unlike her. I cannot hurt her anymore."

Cara was silent. She looked out at the moonlit garden. "Grief can be... so hard."

Gently, he took the painting out of her hands and placed it back down on the bench. He took her hands in his and looked into her eyes. "Darling, I don't want to bring you into this mess."

Cara wiped a tear away. "And what is it that *you* want?" she whispered. "Apart from everybody else. Your brother, your mother, the partisans. What do you want? Tell me?"

He sent her a sad smile and looked down at his father's little painting. A figure standing alone, no matter how enticing the landscape, at odds with himself.

She turned away.

"Not to cause anyone else to suffer, Cara. You have suffered too," he said, his voice extraordinarily soft. "I don't want to add to that. And I don't want to see our lives are going up in flames. My family is in a bad way."

There was a silence. And in the distance, the thud of falling bombs. The whistle, and then the crash.

Raf leaned against the tile wall.

"Were you close to your father, Raf?"

Raf clasped his hands between his knees and stared down at the ground. "I was in awe of him. I idolized him; you know? But I think I was always just the youngest son. My mother, my father, and Nicolas had such distinct personalities and problems. But I care about them. And I am terribly worried about my mother."

Cara took in a shaking breath. "I know what it is to wish that someone would love you enough to prioritize you. And I know what it is to wish that you could have one more day with someone who did." She swallowed a lump in her throat.

"Cara. I'm..." But his voice trailed off.

Above them, there was only the forest, and war... and down here, the ashes of something that she had secretly hoped might come full circle, even when Raf had left so suddenly, even in the face of his mother's disdain.

Raf's face flickered in the lamplight, but he seemed lost in his own thoughts. And even though he was right here, he felt more lost to her than ever. Caught up in the entanglement of his family, his fierce loyalties. How to survive.

Cara reached for the journal. Against the rhythmic sound of dripping water, she began to write. Everything.

She paused after a while and placed her pen down. Raf had fallen asleep where he was sitting, and she went over to him, and placed a blanket over his shoulders.

Someday, would he fall in love with someone who meant more to him than her? It was impossible to imagine ever loving someone as much as she did him, but she knew that he, too, had made his choice.

Cara looked down at his sleeping profile. She turned away, and slid back down on the mattress, and a single tear trailed down her cheek.

CHAPTER 40

ANNIE

Annie had excused herself from the table under the olive groves, but her thoughts were spiraling out of control and she could not stop them. She was the product of the Contessa's shame. Her mother had been Loretta Messina? Whoever that was. She was sickened by her heritage, and by the awful connotations of what it meant.

The people at this party would not be living here freely if it were not for those who fought against her grandparents! Imagine what it must have been like growing up here for the child, Loretta; imagine how the people must have ostracized her. No wonder she was nowhere in sight and had not wanted to raise the next generation. She would have been haunted by a past she hardly understood. Annie swiped a tear away. She took a deep breath, knowing that she must work through this logically, but now, all she wanted to do was panic, or run away.

The powerful secret Papa had kept from her had only crippled her grief for him. He had avoided telling her because he understood that the truth would be impossible to bear. She would keep the secret. She even understood Sandro's shame.

The old line of primogeniture still ran strong. Sandro was the deserving owner of the villa. She had no place here, and no right to lay claim to any dreams of her own. What was she going to do? Stay here and be a cook for Sandro?

She pulled out her phone and sent a message to Monica. *I'm coming home. My home is in San Francisco, and as far as I'm concerned, you and Paul are my family. xx*

Annie pushed away the dark thought that curled inside her, reminding her that Paul was married and had children, that Monica was married and wanted to have a child. That she was the solo unmarried aunt. Perhaps it was the best way to be. She shouldn't have children. The line that came down from the Contessa and her Nazi lover should end with her.

Three dots appeared on the screen, and Annie scoured them, her eyes raking over the little movements as if her life depended upon them. But then Monica stopped writing.

Annie frowned and started typing again. *I just want to come home. I'm never going to find out anything. It's too hard. I miss San Francisco, and I miss you and Paul. And I want to cuddle Portia!!*

She scrolled through her photos of her darling cat. Animals were less treacherous than people. She would go home and live with her little cat, Portia. Portia was all she needed. She didn't need another family, a family tainted by the past.

Annie pushed aside her churning thoughts. The water might be flowing again at the Villa Rosa, but the only water she wanted to fly over was the expanse of the Atlantic Ocean, never to return.

Twenty minutes later, she had said goodbye to Ernesto, Bettina, Sandro, and Luca and his mother, Emilia, whom he had introduced, and she was packing in her room at the pensione. Annie would just leave Italy without telling them, as the shame she felt was overwhelming now that she knew of her origins without doubt. She did not want to hear anything more from Luca's mother about the Villa Rosa's past. There was nothing more to be said. She went to the wardrobe where she had hung the summer dresses she had bought in Florence. She would donate them to charity when she arrived home.

Annie pulled her suitcase out from under the bed and placed it on the white counterpane, folding the dresses and placing them inside. She emptied the drawers, cleared the bathroom, checked under the bed, under the pillows, and scanned the floor. Finally, Annie unlocked the safe and pulled out her passport and her credit cards. She tucked the keys to her apartment in San Francisco inside her bag. Then she picked up her phone and searched for flights to LA. There was no point in lingering. She would move forward with her life without anybody knowing the dirty little secret that she would take to her grave. At least, she would not have to leave a note to her descendants like her father had done.

There was a flight leaving Florence at 10.30 p.m.; that would do. She would hire a car at LAX and drive back up the coast to San Francisco.

Annie sent a message to Lucy and Lauren to let them know she was coming home, and they replied immediately, telling her that was great. Telling her they hoped she'd had a restful time.

Annie scanned the apartment in the pensione that she had fallen in love with the moment she had stepped inside. And then her eyes alighted on one thing that remained. Cara Cartazzo's diary sat on the table in front of the open window. Its leather-bound, worn exterior suited the old room so well that Annie had forgotten it was there, pages cut out, her words snipped away for good.

Annie needed to get moving. It was time to leave. The diary should either be left at the Villa Rosa as a record for Sandro, or perhaps destroyed.

At the last minute, Annie picked up the diary, placed it in her handbag, and towed her suitcase out the front door.

CHAPTER 41

Visitors were taking photographs by the fountain in the middle of the piazza, and young locals sat about on the benches that were dotted around the square. A violinist had started playing near the tables that were set up for the evening at Ernesto's café, and a group of Italians chatted with one of his waiters, who was holding a bottle of local Tuscan wine.

Annie sighed at the twilight scene, wishing she could stay, having felt such a connection to this place, but everything was now tainted. All she could do was understand Sandro's desire to keep the past hidden and to stake his claim over the villa. She gripped the handle of her suitcase firmly, and turned away toward the bus that would take her on the first leg of her journey home.

But when she felt someone brushing her arm, she turned around. And then her hand froze on the handle of her suitcase. She was standing face to face with Luca and his mom, Emilia.

"I'm sorry to interrupt you, Annie." The woman looked down and took in Annie's suitcase. She raised her eyes again and frowned. A delicate line appeared between her finely arched eyebrows, which were the same hue as her chestnut hair.

"But there are some things that I would love to talk about with you. Have you got a few moments to grab a coffee with us? Sandro has just told us what Bettina said, and I wanted to talk to you."

Emilia busied herself, getting a waiter to help find a table and then sitting down.

"Have you got time to talk to us?" Luca spoke softly, glancing at her suitcase. "Please, come, and sit down. You are among friends here, Annie, you have a friend in me."

Annie swallowed hard. Italy was playing with her emotions and all she wanted to do was escape. "Sure, Luca, but it does seem that there's nothing that can be done any more. Sandro is going to take over the running of the villa, and I just don't want to know any more—"

Luca held out a hand and rubbed her arm. "Please. Hear my mum out?"

Annie sighed and followed Luca to where his mother had found them a table at the far end of the café.

Emilia rested her hands on the table. "My son tells me how much the villa means to you, and what wonderful plans you have for its future. He says it would be a tragedy if you left." She sent Luca a smile.

"I have decided to let go of this," Annie whispered. "I don't belong at the villa. I need to let it go."

Emilia reached out and placed her hand on Annie's arm. "So, you are going home?"

Annie nodded. "Yes," she said, not looking at Luca.

"Can I ask you one question? Promise to answer me honestly."

Annie waited. She took in a shaking breath, and bit down hard on her bottom lip. Three espressos arrived, and Luca toyed with his cup. She was horribly aware of him, but a big part of her wanted to get up and walk away. Just sitting here, knowing what she had come from, was heartbreaking. The thought of

Portia, her little home in San Francisco, her pot plants and her kitchen filled with herbs was all she wanted right now.

"It must be impossible to have your family history so tainted with stories that may or may not be true."

I think we know they are true now.

"And I understand that being here in Italy, surrounded by happy families, must be challenging when you have just lost someone so dear to you." Emilia lowered her voice, and her eyes were full of sympathy.

Annie turned away from the woman, unable to swallow the lump that formed in her throat.

"But can you tell me one thing?" Emilia went on. "Can you tell me what it is that you love about the Villa Rosa? Why you fought so hard for it, even though there was a risk you weren't the owner?"

"It felt like home the moment I stepped into the garden, Emilia."

Emilia leaned forward and took Annie's hand. "My father's name was Alphonso Bianchi," Emilia said. "I always sensed that he, too, must have felt a strong connection to the place where he lived and grew up as a child, but it was as if he had cut Italy out of his memory. You know?"

Annie nodded. She was cutting her past out of her memory too. Wasn't that a good thing?

"But that left me with this yearning to know what it was that happened in the villa to make him want to walk away from a place that meant everything to him. He grew up here, you know? He had lived in the valley all his life. You see, you are not alone. I have history here, and I know absolutely nothing about it either. I was so glad when Luca accepted the assignment at the villa. I thought it was fate. My father was a gardener, Luca is a landscape designer. And then, when he told me he had met you, and when he told me that instantly he felt a connection to you, and that you had inherited the villa but didn't know why, I dared to hope that things might have gone full circle. I dared to hope that the reason my father decided to move away from the village that had been home to his family for generations might be found at last. Through you."

Annie glanced across at Luca. But he was looking at his mom.

Emilia gently let go of Annie's hand. "You don't want to get involved in this. I understand, Annie."

Annie reached out for her suitcase, but her hand was shaking. "I can't in all honesty stay here and try to fight for something that absolutely does not and should not belong to me."

"I wanted to let you know that you are not alone, Annie. I am in the same boat, not knowing what happened here, and if there is any way I can help, or work alongside you to help figure this out, then I'd love to."

Annie was quiet. *If only.*

Emilia sighed. "Around here," she said, "it would have been a bloodbath. Farmhouses burned to the ground, the villas bombed... bridges destroyed, mines everywhere. The Nazis burned and looted as they left."

"Yes. Exactly." *Which is why I have no place here.*

A young waiter brought out dishes of local olives, crisp flatbread, and prosciutto to the table next to them. Annie allowed herself a wistful smile. The food, the love of living your life. These were the memories of Tuscany that she would take with her. Like Emilia's father, Alphonso Bianchi, she would beat down the tragic part of her past.

Annie looked back at Emilia.

"I adored my father. But I want to know who he really was. What he kept hidden. What happened to make him leave his old life. He never came back to see his elderly parents, and so I never knew my grandparents, or my cousins or my uncles. Now, they are spread all over the world, and it is too late." A tear fell down Emilia's cheek, and she gathered herself. "It was all lost. My extended family..."

Annie looked away.

"I feel that it is now or never," Emilia continued, "it seems that you and I have been given one chance to find out what happened. Please, Annie, let's work together and discover what happened to drive my father away from the valley he loved all his life, and to leave you in the position you find yourself in today, not knowing who you really are. If it seems difficult to do this for yourself, think of your future children."

Annie took in a sharp breath. She had never imagined herself with children. And while Monica always said this was because she felt that she would never find someone as wonderful as Papa, that argument seemed to have ebbed away in recent weeks and been replaced with something much more sinister.

Annie stared down at the white tablecloth and her empty espresso cup.

"There was often a faraway expression in my father's eyes, and all his life he buried himself in his work. I'm sure he regretted not coming home to Italy. I just don't want to regret not finding out what happened. You know?" Emilia said.

Annie was quiet. Burying herself away, avoiding this terrible story, what choice did she have other than to accept it? And what good could possibly come out of staying here now?

"Don't you think regrets can be some of the worst things to have to bear?" Luca asked softly. Annie turned sharply to him. "Luca—"

"What if we could find her? What if she knows what happened here during the war? What if she knows something about my father?" Emilia smiled but her eyes were welling up.

Annie looked away, anywhere but at Luca and Emilia. *Regrets are some of the worst things to have to bear.* Did Papa ever regret not opening up to her? What had he been thinking all those months when he sat, uncommunicative, staring out the window to the sea? She would never know now.

"If you want to find out what really happened, then Luca and I will do so alongside you."

Annie rested her head in her hands.

"Please, keep trying. Keep trying to find out why your father left you that note."

Annie stood up. She could not look at Luca. The bus to Florence pulled up on the other side of the piazza. "I'm sorry, but I am going to have to let this go. I don't deserve the villa. The atrocities in that war... and the idea that my grandparents played a part in such unbearable cruelty? I can't bear this. I won't be coming back. I am clearly the last person the Villa Rosa and this village need."

"Annie..." Luca's voice cut into her heart. "Why settle with not knowing who you are? Why not fight for the life you deserve?" His voice cracked. "Why not fight for the *love* you deserve and for your home in this valley, which is as much a part of your heritage as it is a part of mine—fight for what you want to do."

She placed a few euros down for her coffee, shook her head, and walked toward the bus.

CHAPTER 42

CARA

Every breath Cara took in was infused with the tunnel's musty air, and the only sound that broke the incessant dripping of water was the crash of random shells exploding above. Cara leaned against the brick wall while Raf slept. She had counted out the intervals between the explosions as if she were timing thunder and lightning. Her wristwatch beat the hours continuously, and she knew that now, the villa would be cloaked in the darkest part of the night before the break of dawn.

Raf was still sleeping, but Cara had avoided looking at him. She needed to move on from her troubling emotions if she was going to be a good partisan in the coming days. If war did one thing, it would be to force her out of her own head and her own heart, because she must focus on helping the people in the valley where she had lived all her life.

She was young, she was healthy. And many of the local citizens did not have such advantages on their side.

When Raf opened his eyes, stretching, she stood up and

went to the small, upturned crate to pour him a glass of water, and to break a piece of bread from the new loaf that Alphonso or Bettina must have delivered while they were sleeping.

"Thank you, Cara," he murmured. "How are you?" His voice cracked, and she turned away from the ache in his eyes that mirrored hers.

She folded her hands, staring down at the basket of dynamite that Raf had placed further into the tunnel. "When we go up today, I want another task, so that I can contribute properly. Let me prove to the partisans that I can complete a mission without failure."

"You feel bad because you were attacked by a thug?"

"Of course not. As I said, I am only grateful to you. When are we going up?" She looked at the closed trapdoor. The urge to do something, to be able to take action that would get her somewhere felt overwhelming, and all she wanted to do was get out into the fresh air. It felt claustrophobic in here. With him.

"Bella?" he said softly.

Cara shook her head at his use of the name he used to call her all those years ago. She could not bear the confusion, sometimes, Bella, sometimes Cara. She would always love him, but they needed to walk on one clear path and accept they could not be together. "Cara." She turned to him, and an agonizing dart pierced her insides. "We need to move forward," she whispered. "And we must work together. Please. Call me Cara."

Raf placed the piece of bread back down on his trouser leg and bowed his head. "Darling... Cara." He raised his head and swallowed. And while he spoke, he stared up at the ceiling of the damp tunnel. "It is far more dangerous than it was a week ago, two weeks ago. Messages are coming through from the Allies telling citizens not to take shelter in the forests, but to get underground." He turned to her again, and his eyes scorched against hers. "Nobody knows about these tunnels. It is too dangerous up there..."

"I am not seeking safety and I'm not asking you to shelter me," Cara whispered.

"I want you to be safe, so much..."

But Cara stood up and went to the trapdoor. "We need to go, before those buffoons at the villa wake again, and the road and surrounding areas is overrun with them."

Raf threw himself back on the old mattress and folded his hands behind his head. He stared at the roof of the tunnel, his expression inscrutable.

Cara remained stock-still.

Finally, he sat up and reached for the rough partisan's jacket that lay strewn across the end of the bed. "I hate this. You have no idea how much I detest this entire situation."

Cara stared at him. He picked up the basket of ammunition and indicated for her to follow him outside.

The sun was rising over the hills in the distance and bathing the sky in a warm pink glow. It was going to be a glorious day. One that should be for picnics in the gardens of the Villa Rosa, as used to happen before the war. A day for lying on a blanket under a tree in the sunshine, and for staring up at the cloudless blue sky.

In the green coolness, everything was silent, except for the sound of the waking birds. Clearly, it was too early for Göring's infamous men to be wandering around. But the looming menace was there in the very air she breathed.

Raf was quiet as they crept through the forest below the villa. He constantly turned around to check that she was following him, taking up his pattern of ducking behind trees, and dashing out with his head down to the next leafy shelter. The light was still dim and pearly.

Cara came to a stop beside him underneath an old linden tree at the edge of a clearing.

For a moment, he reached out as if to take her hand, but then pulled it back. "We are nearly at the partisans' cave."

It had been the right time for them to move. Soon, the sun would throw luminous shafts onto the forest floor. She followed him around the clearing, until they came to the next bank of thick trees. Here, the land rose steeply up the hill, and Raf stopped opposite a boulder. There was a slight indentation at its base.

He looked at her, and she could see the worry in his eyes.

But Cara simply nodded. If she couldn't be with the man she loved, she would do everything she could to help protect the things they both cared about. He had saved her life. And in the coming days, she wanted to be near him. She wanted to go through this last stand for the valley with him by her side.

Cara walked with Raf to the edge of the cave. The moment they started approaching the narrow opening in front of them, a young man appeared in the classic regalia of the partisans, his shirt half hanging out of his trousers, which were stained with days' worth of dirt.

The man, who looked to be in his thirties, took the basket from Raf and turned his gaze to Cara, a frown line appearing between his blue eyes. His lips curled downward, in the mass of his sandy beard.

Cara stood next to Raf and held her ground.

"Pietro," Raf said. "This is Cara. She is capable and will be with us in the coming days."

Pietro shrugged and stepped aside at the entrance of the underground cave, but the look he sent Raf was laced with doubt. "Bringing a woman here? It is your responsibility."

"And it is one that I take extremely seriously," Raf said.

Inside the cave two men slept on the ground with their backs to the entrance, their stocky bodies and gray hair betraying their advanced age.

The younger man whom Raf had called Pietro snuck back into one of the corners, placed the ammunition down and sat with his legs crossed, watching Raf, as if following his every move.

Cara hovered. There were no beds made of straw, there were not even food stores. How were these people going to take on the Nazis?

She turned to Raf. "Where are they getting their food from?"

"Our mutual friends," Raf whispered, his eyes flicking to Pietro.

Alphonso. Bettina. That's what they had been doing.

"We need to make sure that those friends are kept safe at all costs," Cara murmured.

"I have men watching the villa," Raf said. "Guarding them..."

Cara's eyes flickered toward Pietro. Bettina and Alphonso were living in a pit of snakes.

Raf sat down on the dirt near Pietro, and Cara tucked her dress around herself and did the same thing, joining the two men in a circle of three. Raf spoke softly, glancing briefly at the two sleeping older men. "We know that the Nazi storage facility will be expanded into a fully-fledged barricade and will be the main German defense against the Allied liberation of Cortona, and it is vital we destroy it immediately. We have the ammunition, thanks to Cara, and now, there is no time to lose."

"But there are more than fifty men stationed at the storage facility and around the new base at any one time. Armored vehicles, and tanks," Pietro said.

Raf continued in a low voice. "Nevertheless, we must destroy it, but the Nazis have lined all the roads in this area with landmines, and the ammunition is too heavy to carry such a long distance. And I won't risk it. I won't risk that with the local men. My plan is to seize one of the German trucks in the village, and I want to do that today. If we must kill the driver to get the truck, we will." Raf glanced across at Cara. "It is a risk we have to take."

Cara stood up, wrapping her arms around her waist, and shaking her head at Raf, even though Pietro was clearly sneering at her. "You cannot do that, Raf."

"What sort of stupidity is it to bring a woman here?" Pietro snarled. "Even if she is your girlfriend."

Cara ignored him. "You steal a German truck and murder the driver, and the Germans will execute innocents... You want to protect the village? There must be another way."

Raf was silent.

"The people trust you," she said.

Pietro scoffed, but Raf was watching her.

"I hate this as much as you do, Cara, but our tenant farmers are starving, livestock is being stolen, crops stolen. And with Göring's men in the vicinity, it is only going to get worse. It is an awful choice to have to make, but I am going to send scores of men to guard the village while we steal the truck."

"The partisans cannot yet outrun the Nazis. Once the Allies are here and we can join forces with them, yes. But they are not here yet." Cara shook her head and looked down at him.

And when they do arrive, and when they are nearby, there is going to be a bloodbath and the Nazis will be even more brutal toward us all...

Raf clasped his hands between his knees and looked down at the ground. "There is no other way to carry out the mission."

Cara crouched down next to him. Gently, she lifted his chin to face her. "I am a *staffetta*. I will go back to the villa tonight and collect the bicycle, take the explosives to where you need them for the mission, and if I am stopped, I will say that I am going to town to pick up essential medicines for a sick child. It is the safest way."

"No," Raf insisted. "No."

But Cara touched his good arm, her fingers gripping the hard muscle for a moment, and staying there. "Yes."

CHAPTER 43

ANNIE

Annie handed her luggage to the porter. He loaded her suitcase into the storage area under the bus. Out of the corner of her eye, she saw Emilia and Luca leaving the café, and walking out of the piazza. They were going back to the villa. *Her villa?* Now, she would never know.

Annie stared at her suitcase, packed away neatly with the other suitcases in the bus. A middle-aged couple arrived next to her, arguing, and handing their bags to the porter. Once he put their luggage in front of Annie's, hers would be buried, and her time in Italy would be over for good.

Why not fight for the life you deserve? Why settle? Why not fight for the love you deserve? Luca's words burned in her heart.

Annie took in a shaking breath. Her throat hurt when she swallowed, and horribly, her chin began to wobble. She did not know whether her likely real mother, Loretta Messina, was alive or dead. What if Annie died herself, never knowing? If Loretta was alive, did she think of Annie, and would it not heal her to meet her lost daughter as well? And what of love? Could she not find love back in the States? Did she want love? Or would she continue on her own, even though the rug had been pulled from under her feet not once but twice since Papa died?

Annie had lost her adoptive mother, Valerie, when she was so very young, and she barely remembered having a mother of her own. As an adult, she had always struggled when she saw how important her friends' mothers were to them. Several times, she had turned down offers of being a bridesmaid, because she could not bear the fact that weddings highlighted the bond between mothers and daughters. There were rites of passage that she could never experience without a mother of her own.

She thought she had become used to it. She thought she had accepted that she would spend the rest of her life without a mother's love. All those times when her friends at school had flown into their mothers' arms at the school gates. Then, when they were teenagers, fighting with their mothers as they figured out who they were and flailed around trying to grow into a woman. Annie had known none of this. Did she truly know who she was?

No.

Somehow, not knowing who she was felt entwined with her inability to put herself front and center, to have the confidence to state her claim in the world, whatever that may be. Was Luca right? Should she stay and find out, so she could move forward knowing the truth, and if that truth meant she had something to fight for, what then?

She looked down at her phone. Laughter rang out from the piazza where people were enjoying their lives. She turned back to take one last glance at Luca and Emilia, a myriad of feelings coursing through her insides.

Annie took a step forward and spoke in clear, confident tones to the porter. "I won't be leaving the valley. Please, take my suitcases out of the bus."

The man wiped a hand over his brow. It was hot beneath the Italian sun, and he glanced back at his neatly packed luggage. "Are you certain, signorina?" he asked. "Because I will not be packing again if you change your mind."

Annie nodded. "More certain than I have ever been in my life."

CHAPTER 44

CARA

"Cara," Raf murmured. "I have terrible thoughts of what I would do should anything happen to you today," he said, his voice so low and yet so clear that she closed her eyes.

"You know," she said, her voice echoing in the cave, "when I carried out my last mission... I was motivated by anger." She opened her eyes wide and looked up at Raf, and he searched her face. "It was anger that fueled me and urged me to push forward and avenge my papa's death. But now, anger has left me. And I have realized that, when my father died, he somehow gave me the strength that I used to place in him. I'm not scared, Raf. I'll deliver the dynamite for you, and let's do our part to free Cortona and the valley for good."

"Cara, when this is all over—"

But she reached up and placed a hand on his lips. "Raf, it is impossible. Your mother."

He grimaced. "My mother is making stupid decisions. I cannot control them."

Pietro was loading up the bicycle at the entrance to the cave for Cara's second journey as a *staffette*.

Raf softly enfolded Cara's hand in his own. His eyes held hers, and he was so close... But then Pietro was wheeling the bicycle, the dynamite wrapped in a brown paper bag in the basket, out to the clearing.

Raf ran a hand through his hair. "Once you have delivered the dynamite, I wish you would stay in Cortona, and seek shelter in the cellars with the villagers. I can put you in touch with one of my friends."

"Raf—I'm not doing that." But she stared at the parcel in the bicycle's basket. The parcel looked exactly like a wrapped bomb.

Five minutes later, Cara was out on the road that led to Cortona, keeping right in the middle due to the landmines. She took the quietest, narrowest roads that she could. The fields on either side were strewn with wheat stalks that had been scattered as if a bride had tossed her dying bouquets.

Cara rode past her village, which felt tainted after Luigi's attack. She averted her eyes from the tumble of honey-colored old buildings and kept her eyes firmly on the road.

It was Saturday, but there was no bustle of visitors going in and out the village gates. The place was quiet, for nobody dared to set up a market stall now that Göring's men were in the vicinity, and the farmers had nothing to bring into the village this week. The air of desolation that hung over the old valley was unsettling, and overhead, the skies were still leaden and heavy, like a storm was brewing.

The sun shot defiant yellow shafts through the bulging gray clouds, and Cara cycled on, thanking goodness that she was a local, and she knew exactly where to meet Raf's contacts and where to deliver her load.

The residents were all huddled away in their houses, either

in the village, or on their farms, and the strange light on the yellow fields only served to increase the tension in the air that nature needed to break.

When a Nazi lorry came straight toward her, she pulled over as safely as she could, leaving just enough room for him to pass. She placed her foot down on the ground delicately, holding her breath in case, heaven help her, she were to step on a mine.

The truck came to a halt beside her. It had a cross painted on its side. It was the German doctor who had been in the village with the local commandant for over a year.

"*Buongiorno, signorina,*" the German doctor said, nodding his head formally.

"*Buongiorno,*" Cara said, as confidently as she could, and hiding her surprise that the Nazi was speaking Italian. She focused on the man's face, determinedly avoiding glancing at the package in the basket of her bicycle.

"*Signorina,*" the middle-aged doctor went on, "you should not be out. We are advising that all women hide in the safest place possible throughout the coming days." He lowered his voice: "The Allied invaders are showing no mercy to Italian women as they pass through the conquered towns. There were reports of multiple rapes in other Tuscan villages when they were liberated. Find a safe house in Cortona and barricade yourself inside with several other people."

Cara held his gaze so that, in turn, he would not look down at her incriminating load. "Thank you, sir."

The man nodded at her, and released the handbrake, accelerating off. The sound of the engine rumbling into the distance was the only noise to break the eerie silence.

Cara gripped the handlebars of the Contessa's bicycle. There was only one way forward, no matter what happened now. Her home and the people she had loved and known all her life were what she was fighting for.

CHAPTER 45

ANNIE

All Annie had wanted to do since she ran up to Luca and Emilia as they left the village square and called to them that she was staying was to get into the old farmhouse kitchen at the back of the Villa Rosa, where Ernesto's mother Bettina had once held sway all those years ago, and clean it out, stock the pantry with olive oils, local wines, and her own homemade pasta. She wanted to grow herbs in terracotta pots on the windowsills, throw the French doors wide open to the back terrace, and sit outside with her morning coffee in the sun, but all they were allowed to do was work the garden until the ownership of the villa was sorted out, and at this point she had no reason to believe it wouldn't go in Sandro's favor.

The sun was starting to set over the valley, and Annie frowned at her paltry efforts in one section of the terraced garden.

"I've hardly made any inroads," she said, looking at the tangled mounds of ivy that still choked the old wooden pergola that had once been strewn with tiny pink roses. "It seems that it will never end."

Today, she and Luca had spent an hour digging out the roots of one ivy plant alone.

"We will get there," he said softly.

She looked away, biting her lip. Her eyes, head, everything ached. She was having trouble sleeping. Tossing and turning at night, she worried about what she was doing, whether she should have simply gone home.

Emilia had spoken to every business owner in the village, to the notary, the librarian, and the old men who sat in the village square, but no one knew what had happened to Loretta Messina or remembered her birth from so long ago.

Annie had accompanied Emilia for the first few days on these hopeless rounds of enquiry, but Emilia, sensing Annie's despair, had suggested she take today off to rest.

But there was no rest. Being idle only caused her thoughts to spiral. And when Luca had offered to keep her company, she had willingly accepted, and had refused his suggestion of a day out exploring Tuscany, instead preferring to dig away at the garden that so desperately needed restoration, to be allowed to breathe.

"Sandro is bringing another builder in to give him a quote this evening," Luca said. "I didn't want to worry you." His eyes held that deep, understanding expression that she had come to respect in him.

Annie looked around the dear, tired gardens. She hated the idea of them becoming some corporate networking space, but what right did she have over them? Even if she was a Messina, her lineage was tainted by Nazi blood. "Let's get out of here for a little while?" she said.

No matter what the outcome of the search in Italy might be, one thing was certain: Papa would want her to live her life. And surely living was the answer once you had worked your way through grief.

"Should we go out for dinner?" Luca asked, sounding a little tentative. "I know a wonderful restaurant in Cortona. It looks over the valley, and at night, the terrace is all lit up."

Annie smiled at him. "You know," she said softly, "I'd love that."

CHAPTER 46

CARA

A unit of six Allied bombing aircraft flew low over Cortona. Shells whistled through the air, landing on the road, and Cara tucked her head down and pushed the bicycle onward. Finally, she arrived at the abandoned barn where she was to deposit her load, and as the earth shook with the roar of aircraft flying low overhead, Cara pushed open the heavy door.

And then, as she pulled the ammunition out of the basket, easing the hidden trapdoor in the floor open, and hiding the dynamite where Raf had told her to, the rain that had threatened to fall beat down upon the roof, torrential, thundering, as if nature were fighting back.

Cara slid down the wall and sat, leaning her head against it. Her hands were clasped in front of her, her heart beating hard, and she stared at nothing.

When the barn door heaved open an hour later and Raf appeared, Cara stood up and went over to him.

"Thank you," he said simply.

She scoured his face, and he looked down at the ground, fine lines forming on his forehead.

"My heart was in my mouth the entire time you were on the road."

"It was fine. I had no problems. No one suspects a girl like me."

Raf lifted his head, and his hand trailed out to her. "If anything had happened to you..." He shook his head and turned away.

To Cara's horror, his shoulders were shaking.

"Let me come with you and hurl hand grenades at the Nazi barricade."

Overhead, another bank of aircraft flew low in the air. The sound of anti-aircraft gunfire rattled in the distance, and the thud of bombs rang through the valley.

"The local farmers are being stubborn. They will not leave their homes," Raf said.

Cara exhaled, slow and long.

"Both the Nazis and the Allies are warning everybody to seek shelter immediately." Raf sank his head in his hands. "It is going to be a nightmare—food, water. Electricity. All are gradually losing their supplies as the days roll on, and the Germans remain here so stubbornly."

"The water and electricity have been cut off in the valley?" Cara asked.

Raf nodded.

"Then I will round up the villagers and the farmers and tell them to go to Cortona. There is an old bookshop that my father used to favor, at the top of the via Medici. There is a strong basement, and I am certain that the owners will provide sanctuary."

She looked at Raf resolutely, and his eyes lingered on hers.

"I want you to take refuge as well," he whispered. "The partisans, the army, even the darned Nazis are advising all

Italian civilians to seek shelter for the next few days. Especially women."

Cara stood resolutely opposite him.

"If you could save my family's farmers from the Nazi's departing wrath, I don't know how I could ever thank you. I don't know how my mother could ever thank you. I only wish she would."

A silence hung between them.

"I will take the bicycle and spread the word," Cara said. "I will direct all your farmers and the villagers and their families to hide in Cortona." But then she shook her head. "But after that, I will come and join you, add to the efforts to liberate the town. I'm not hiding underground while you fight to save our homes. And I will pray for you as you complete the mission to blow up the barricade." She held a hand to her heart. "Please. Come back... safely."

Raf stood by the entrance to the barn, his chest heaving, and his dark eyes burning into her soul. Cara went over to him. She pulled him into a rough hug. But even as she did so, one last question burned in her mind.

"Your mother?" she whispered, looking up at Raf. "We are moving all the farmers into Cortona, but there is no guarantee that the Villa Rosa will be safe." Her eyes searched his face, and he sighed heavily. "Where is Bruno Klein, and is the Contessa in the villa alone?"

Slowly, he reached out and traced his thumb across her lips. "Darling, I don't know... I just know that I need to fight for these people. I can't control what she does, who she is. The choices she makes. All I know is that I do not want her attitudes, or my fear, to stop us being together anymore."

He reached out and was holding her hand. These were words which she had longed to hear, but which he only said now when so much was on the line...

"Stay safe, Raf," she whispered. "That is all we can do at the moment."

"And you." He pulled her close, and she felt his hand stroking the back of her head gently.

And it was as if at the same time she felt like she had come home, she now had everything to lose.

The storms had given way to blinding sunshine, and Cara knocked on the front door of a farmhouse. The farmer's wife answered, holding her tiny baby to her chest as Cara explained the need to leave. But her elderly father was implacable.

He thrust his chin out. "This is my livelihood. I cannot abandon it."

His daughter sent him a worried glance. "But Papa, we must. You are defenseless. In a war zone..." she whispered.

Cara stayed quiet and let the reality of the words hit home.

"The instructions are clear. And there is no time." She addressed the daughter.

But the woman's father still stood, shaking his head. Cara had learned something during these weeks, these months, these years. And that was, that obstinacy got one nowhere. That to survive in this world, in this war, a person must not be resistant to change. He would have to leave his home behind to protect himself and his family.

The old farmer gazed out over his fields. Like so many other farmers in the area, he had lost crops, livestock, and the stores that his daughter had carefully prepared so that they could survive had been raided, looted, stolen. They had been left to starve by the Nazis.

But in the set of his eyes, Cara could see what she had been fighting against with every one of these brave locals. There was one thing they would not give up. There was one thing that these local men refused to hand to anyone. It was their dignity.

"I will not leave my farm," he muttered. He folded his arms. "I will die defending it. If I don't stay, my whole life's work will be destroyed. I know that. I am not a fool."

Cara closed her eyes. What she was about to say was the last thing she wanted to say, but deeply ingrained in these people's hearts was still a sense of loyalty to the old systems that had been operating in these parts for hundreds of years. Even if the current incumbent at the Villa Rosa was living in a way that no one in these parts understood. The Contessa's name would still pull rank.

"Signor Rafaeli Messina has ordered it," she said, lifting her chin. "And his mother insists. I am afraid you have no choice. You must come with me, now."

Cara glanced around the old farmhouse kitchen, which had been entirely unchanged since the last fires of war had roared over this valley.

"Come," she said firmly.

The old man stared at the floor, his hands balled into fists, but finally, he nodded.

And when he raised his head, Cara gasped at the sight of a single solitary tear rolling down the old man's cheek.

CHAPTER 47

Cara had managed to convince nearly all the local farming families and many of the inhabitants of the tiny, unprotected village to abandon their homes and seek refuge in the basement of the bookshop in Cortona. She had told them that it was a matter of life and death, and that instructions were to keep away from the forests, keep away from the farms, and to hide in the old town that was built for just this purpose with protective walls and a gate centuries ago. By all accounts, she had heard that the mission the partisans had carried out on the stronghold outside Cortona had been a success. She had nearly collapsed with relief when she learned that the storage facility was blown up, and the road to the town was now clear for the Allies to liberate Tuscany. But still, Cara worried about deliberate reprisals, and the tension in the valley was palpable. The Nazis were still terrorizing the local population and stealing livestock and crops.

Despite reports that the Allies would be in the valley within days, even hours, the progress north felt achingly slow. Still, the Germans held out even as the Allies liberated the towns of Tuscany one by one. After two days of pleading with farmers and their families, Cara had relocated more than sixty people—mostly women, children, and the elderly—to safety, and had organized food drops to be brought to them twice a day.

She had become accustomed to feeling a sense of relief as she opened the trapdoor at the bookstore and ushered people down the precarious ladder, from elderly women dressed in traditional black who ran their fingers through rosary beads, their voices mellifluous, to small children who were either terribly serious, with their heads bowed, or delighting in making up fantastical games.

Thunder had rolled over the valley for forty-eight hours, bringing torrential rain and then searing sunshine.

Overhead, aircraft swooped, and shells whistled and thumped on the ground. Sometimes, entire buildings shook as Cara held hands and ran people up to safety, windows smashing in buildings nearby because of the force of explosions.

Papa's friend Signora Ricci, the bookstore owner, had provided blankets as the temperature dropped overnight. And the kindly woman had brought down a selection of old books for people to read. Cara had left her journal in the woman's hands, knowing that at least it would be safe. But before she had given Signora Ricci the journal, Cara had cut out the pages on which she had written about her feelings for Raf, her grief for Papa, her hatred of Luigi Santino. If she did not survive in these coming days, no one would know what was truly in her heart.

Whenever she opened the trapdoor that led down to the basement, a pale gleam of yellow light shone into the cellar's dim interior, and the inhabitants of the basement simply looked upwards at her, nobody arguing or fighting to beat anyone else to some of the meager rations that the partisans delivered to them twice a day. Milk was reserved for the children and the elderly, and most of the healthy adults survived on bread, water, and fruit. The Red Cross were dropping food parcels that contained dried beef, which allowed the breastfeeding mothers and the elderly a little protein.

Cara eased a baby boy down to his mother on the ladder. The young woman had told Cara, her face pale, how her older children were waking to nightmares in the early hours of the morning. And every child whose hand Cara had held while accompanying them up through the hilltop town yearned to see their father. But none of the fathers were here. They were fighting, and many of them would never come home to see their children again.

She watched the mother and her baby find a place in the cool dark basement, and she moved away from the safe harbor. Her head down, she walked through the empty streets of Cortona toward the address Raf had given her for the partisans.

Ten minutes later, she stood in one of the Messina family's bare apartments in a narrow street in the town. Pietro had led her in silently, nodding at her, finally, with respect.

The two middle-aged partisans whom Cara had seen sleeping in the cave in the forest now sat with furrowed brows at the wooden table in the middle of the room. Standing with his back to the wall, looking out the window, was Raf.

He swung around the moment Cara entered the room.

Cara paused, uncertain at the way he was looking at her.

Raf's face was pale, and dark shadows bruised the skin under his eyes. His black hair had grown a little since he had been home, and a shadow of stubble covered his chin.

"What is it?" she asked, knowing her voice sounded sharp, but unable to contain the concern she felt at the sight of him.

By all accounts, the Allies were well on their way and British troops were expected to advance into the valley at any moment. The targeted bombing missions were continuing, and everything was in place. So, what could be wrong?

"There is one last major Nazi stronghold in the area," one of the middle-aged men said. "Our order is to disarm and attack it this afternoon prior to the Allies' arrival."

Cara glanced anxiously at Raf, but he turned away again, and she looked instead toward the two partisans sitting at the table, but they remained stony-faced, staring at the patterns in the wood as if it held any answers...

And a horrible realization dawned over her, just as the partisan confirmed it.

"The Villa Rosa," the man said, his words resonating in the strange silence in the room. "The orders from the Allies who are working with the partisans in the area are to show no mercy. The villa is a Nazi stronghold, and if Rafaeli's mother is caught, she is to be taken as a prisoner of war, alongside her lover and the staff."

Alphonso. Bettina. Raf's mother.

Cara walked over to Raf and she turned him to face her, pulling his shaking body into a close hug. There was nothing she could say. Raf would not defy the order if it came from the partisan movement. But if there was any way to save Alphonso and Bettina she would fight until her last breath.

Dusk was about to fall over the forest at the edge of the Villa Rosa. The birds were singing their last songs for the day, and a slight breeze rustled the trees as if the surrounding forest was humming a lament.

Cara stood with Raf. He had once more tried to stop her from coming, but she had told him firmly that the Villa Rosa meant almost as much to her as it did to him. All around, bands of burly partisans hovered, ready to fight. From where she was standing, Cara could see Nazi trucks still parked in the court-yard, just as they had been when she had left. She turned toward Raf, opening her mouth to say the words she had struggled to find all day. But he was staring straight ahead, his expression inscrutable, his eyes trained on his home, where his mother and her Nazi lover were awaiting their fate.

"You are certain you can cope with this?" she whispered.

A myriad of expressions passed across his face, and he stared down at the ground that had nurtured him, and silently, he nodded.

All they were waiting for was the signal, and then the bloodbath would begin.

When the call came—the imitation of birdsong from the depths of the forest—the partisans began to move. And as Cara stepped forward, her heart hammering in her chest, she reached out and took Raf's hand for a fleeting moment.

Then, everything was a blur. The rough partisan army surged forward and descended on the courtyard of the Villa Rosa and the air burst with war cries. Cara ran forward; her instructions were clear. She focused on them like a mantra in her mind. Into the villa, take any Nazi documents from the offices that she knew so well.

She put her head down, and ran across the back courtyard, her hand slipping from Raf's as the sound of gunfire ricocheted through the usually quiet gardens. She kept her eyes trained on the kitchen door, and prayed as hard as she could that Bettina had left the villa, had found shelter, that Alphonso would not try to be brave.

The back door handle gave with a twist of her fingers, and she was standing in the empty kitchen. Outside, shouts and gunshots exploded through the air. A truck rumbled to life. German voices hurled instructions. Jackboots pounded on the gravel, and Cara shuddered, suddenly turning cold. The partisans' plan was to target the Nazis who were guarding the transport and slaughter any Germans that stood in their way.

Footsteps thundered down the main staircase of the villa, and alarmed German voices rang through the air, snarling, swearing, shouting. Cara slipped behind the kitchen door as a flurry of soldiers ran out into the courtyard.

Her chest heaving, she waited until they had all passed, and then, when the kitchen was silent and empty again, she ducked down and flew toward the office, running through the room into the next room, which had been Arturo's sitting room, and then to the narrow room at the end of the house that had once been a stable.

Cara's eyes widened at the deception that had gone on in this very room, at the sight of a wooden desk sitting underneath the bare light bulb. Papers peppered with German handwriting and diagrams were sitting on the table. The Germans had been meticulous.

They must have caught them in the middle of a planning session. But the diversion outside was working, and there was more shouting, and screaming, and gunfire, and the sound of trucks rumbling to life. Cara sent up a heartfelt prayer for Raf, as two young partisans appeared next to her, and she started loading files and documents into their arms.

Thank goodness she had left her diary with Signora Ricci at the bookstore.

"Is this everything?" one of them asked her.

Cara surveyed the room and nodded.

"Go, while you can." she ordered the two young men.

They put their heads down and disappeared. Cara turned the light off in the storage room, and crept back out through Arturo's living room, through the study, where the Contessa's desk was exactly as she had left it, and into the entrance hall, where she came to a shuddering stop.

Opposite her, standing on the lowest step of her own staircase, stood the Contessa, holding a small gun.

"Cara," the Contessa said. Her voice was only faintly brittle, but it still held that unmistakable air of authority. Outside, gunfire rattled on the driveway. Smoke poured through the open front door.

Cara stared at the handgun. The older woman did not move, and her gaze was steely, hard, cold.

She raised the gun and pointed it at Cara. "I'm sorry it has come to this," the Contessa said. Cara's heart almost came to a stop. Was this what things had come to? Raf's mother was willing to kill her own secretary to fight for whatever it was that had driven her to have an affair with a Nazi? It was impossible to understand the Contessa. She had always been enigmatic, aloof, and clearly superior to everyone else. But the fact that she had taken things to this level, knowing... she *must* know how Cara felt about Raf, and how he felt about Cara, was so heartbreaking, and yet, it stood between them like a barrier made of steel.

"Put your hands in the air." It was a German voice. A voice she had imagined, yet dreaded, and had never wanted to hear again.

Bruno Klein stood on the staircase behind the Contessa.

"Ah, the little secretary. So loyal," he jeered. "Or, perhaps, not."

Cara lifted her chin, and she stared at him.

"Finish her off, Evelina," Bruno Klein ordered.

But the Contessa stayed rigid, her face white, and her hand steady.

Cara took in a shaking breath.

"Better still, bring her back to Germany with us," he said. "When we get back to Berlin, she can work for us. She can help with our baby."

Cara's gaze locked with the Contessa's. *Baby?* She was going to bring the child of a Nazi into the family? Cara could not move and yet her stomach caved.

Bruno Klein stepped down the grand staircase of the Villa Rosa, as if he was master of all he surveyed.

And he stood in the entrance hall, turning to Cara. "For every Nazi killed, ten Italians will die. But I am a merciful man. I will let you live a little longer. And then we shall see what will be in store for you once we get to Germany. The Fuhrer does not take kindly to disloyal staff, and neither do I."

Bile coursed up through Cara's chest. Her heart was frozen, a block of ice, and she had imprinted her nails into the palms of her hands. But she could only stare at the Contessa. How could she bear a child for this man? Cara's heart went out to Raf. How would he cope? What should she tell him? If she ever saw him again... the camps in Germany, slavery to this awful couple. The scenarios whirled in her head.

The Contessa still stood with her gun pointed at Cara, and her eyes flicked to Bruno and back again.

"Take this one prisoner, Evelina, if you wish. But she will watch while we execute the traitors who dare to defy us today. Perhaps she has a lover among the partisans. I'm sure she'll enjoy watching him die."

With the practiced ease of a criminal, Bruno pulled out a gun from his suit jacket, and ushered Cara out.

Outside was carnage. Cara's hand flew to her mouth at the sight of Alphonso, his arms pinned behind his back, being hauled off to one of the Nazi trucks. All through the gardens, partisans battled with Göring's rough Nazis, while others pushed past them, into the villa's open front door. Cara closed her eyes as she heard the sound of shattering glass. They would wreck it. In the moment that the Contessa and Bruno swiveled around in consternation at the sounds from inside the old house, she took the opportunity and ran to where they were loading Alphonso into the truck. She stared in horror at the sight of Bettina already sitting on the hard wooden benches. Ready to be transported to Germany or murdered in cold blood.

A Nazi smirked at her. "You know the rules. Ten Italians for every Nazi killed. The execution will take place in Cortona this afternoon."

There was a gunshot. And the Nazi slumped to the ground. A clean bullet through his forehead.

Cara yelled at Alphonso and Bettina. "Get out. Run!"

And after a split second, where they both stared down in horror at the body splayed in front of them, they stood up, grabbed the maids, and ran.

Where was Raf?

Ducking from tree to tree in the garden, her heart in her mouth, Cara's eyes roamed to the summerhouse. Raf was backed into the corner with his mother's lover, Bruno Klein. The Nazi had a gun pointed at Raf and, from where she stood, Cara could see the evil etched on the older man's face.

"No!" she cried.

She hurled herself forward, head down, and grabbed a loose stone from the drystone wall that led to the next terrace. Picking it up and holding it high overhead, she threw the rock at the back of Bruno Klein's head, and it hit the target, felling the Nazi immediately.

For one long second, Cara stared at the fallen German, but then Raf was in her arms, and she felt his shuddering body, and she heard the tears and sobs. She held him while the last of the Nazi vehicles rumbled up the driveway and on to the road.

"They have gone," Raf whispered. And in the still silence that followed, several men and two young women appeared at the bottom of the driveway. They had driven the Nazis out of the Villa Rosa for good, although at a heartrending cost.

The garden was a bloodbath. Bodies lay strewn on the driveway, both partisans and Nazis.

Raf sank to his knees, his arms tight around Cara, burying his head in her shoulder and sobbing. The partisans who remained came to stand near them and stood silently.

"Where is the Contessa?" Cara said, her voice surprisingly even as she spoke to the small group of remaining men.

"I am here."

Cara looked up, her head jerking to the terrace above, and there she stood dressed in pale blue silk, her hair exquisite, her hands by her side, and in one of them, she held her gun, slack at her side.

Slowly, Raf raised his head and met his mother's gaze.

"My son," she said, her voice only the whisper of a murmur. "Rafaeli..."

Boots crunched on the driveway.

She turned with all the partisans, and they raised their guns and pointed them at the Contessa. And next to her, Raf stood up.

"Put down your weapons," Raf whispered, but his voice resonated louder than any Nazi bark. "They have come."

In the driveway of the Villa Rosa, framed by the wrought-iron gates, there stood two soldiers in British army uniform just as the sun sank over the green valley below.

CHAPTER 48

Cara and Raf walked to Cortona in the early hours before dawn broke, with the young British soldiers who had appeared at the villa, and several of their fellow countrymen. The Nazis had disappeared, and Alphonso had stayed at the villa, clearing bodies into makeshift graves in the forest, and stoically ignoring the Contessa, who had retreated into her bedroom and locked the door after an altercation with Raf, but Bettina had run. She had walked out of the villa with the band of departing partisans, hugged Cara and told her that she could not work for the Contessa any longer.

Cortona was liberated quickly, and easily, as the British division simply walked into the town now the way was clear. Raf and his band of partisans had played an important role in paving the way for the Allies to liberate the town on the hilltop, and the Nazi barricade lay in ruins nearby.

Finally, Cara opened the trapdoor at Signora Ricci's bookstore. It was a full few seconds before anyone moved. And then slowly, like the rumbling of thunder, a cheer rippled around the room. People were standing up, hugging each other, and the children were jumping about excitedly, even if they did not understand what this meant. One day they would. The valley was liberated. The Allies were here. For their little part of Italy, it was over. And now, they were free to go home. People started gathering their belongings, still staring at each other in amazement and hugging each other as if they were family who had been reunited after years spent apart.

The young British soldier who had accompanied Cara held out his hand, and helped people up the ladder. "We have cordoned off the area where a shell landed right outside the trapdoor and marked out a safe path to the street," he said.

"Thank you," Cara whispered to him as she made her way out.

The foundations of Cortona had held strong. Partisans embraced each other in the streets, citizens cheered, and someone had already hoisted the British flag from a balcony.

Cara felt herself wrapped in Raf's arms. There was cheering, and people crying, yelling out all the frustrations that they had held in for so many years.

"Darling?" he murmured. "I love you. I don't want anything to keep us apart anymore. I'm never going to let anything stop me being with you, sweetheart," he whispered, and he leaned down, searching her face.

She knew what he was asking, and she nodded, and kissed him. No matter what, come what may, she adored him.

He squeezed her hand. "I have spoken with my mother and told her that I love you. I've told her that I can't live without you."

Cara wanted to say something about the knowledge that burned in her heart, but the farmers and their families whom she had led to safety in the cellar were embracing her, and suddenly, she was being held aloft. She held Raf's hand, and people were emerging into the morning light from the hole in the ground near the bookseller's.

Raf looked up at Cara, and he reached up for her, and lifted her gently down to the ground. "Marry me," he said, his voice cracking, and tears pouring freely down his cheeks.

The crowd turned quiet, and then, a whisper spread among them. "Raf Messina," the citizens murmured. "*Il Conte!*"

But all Cara could see was the man whom she had always loved. She did not care that he was the Contessa's son; it did not matter whether he was from the illustrious Messina family, or from a peasant's house in the village... And he was not to blame for his mother's actions, no matter what the future held. She loved him. And love, in the end, was the most important thing there was. The love that she had for Papa would continue in her heart for the rest of her life. She would never lose it, and she knew that the love she held for Raf would always burn inside her just as it had since the day she had first laid eyes on him.

"Cara, I adore you. All I could think of throughout these past terrible times was you. When I was fighting, I held you close in my heart. And when we resisted, the thought of you kept me going. I want to spend the rest of my life with you. I would love, if you will have me, to bring the Villa Rosa back to life again with you."

Cara searched his face. Life was short, and if she got this right, then everything else would fall into place. Silently, after what seemed like an age, she nodded, and then she threw her arms around him.

The farming families whom she had brought to safety broke into a roar, and all around her she felt the warmth of her community, and the love of these people whose light and bravery would never grow dim.

And yet, as she stood encircled in Raf's arms, one image still played over and over in her mind. The Contessa, pointing a gun at her. "*She can come help with our baby...*"

CHAPTER 49

ANNIE

The sky was bathed in dusky pink. Waiters glided around the terrace that overlooked the serene valley, and the birds had finished their songs for the day. There were strings of fairy lights and soft chatter, and enticing aromas coming from the kitchen of the restaurant.

Annie turned to Luca. "You know, sitting here, I could pretend that Sandro didn't exist, that I lived in the villa, that it was my home. That I got to sit outside in the burgeoning Tuscan moonlight with you, every evening." She lowered her eyes, catching her breath at the words that had slipped out from somewhere deep inside.

"I could get used to Tuscany too," Luca whispered.

Annie chewed on her lip, sensing his eyes on her.

Luca toyed with his glass of prosecco. A bowl of olives and breadsticks sat next to a single yellow rosebud in a crystal vase.

"You know, I prefer yellow roses to red roses," Annie said.

"Red is for passion." He attempted a smile.

"Yellow," Annie said, "is for the sun."

Luca's hand drew toward her, and then stopped.

There was a loud bark of laughter from the other side of the terrace, and a waiter was leading an elegant, elderly woman with an upright back and her hair swept away from her beautiful face to a table. The waiter stopped, clearly indicating that the woman take one of the front tables that overlooked the valley, but she laid a hand on his arm, and shook her head. Determinedly, the elderly woman made her way to a quiet, secluded table right at the back of the terrace.

Annie couldn't take her eyes off the scene, because something inside her had started to unfurl, and suddenly, everything began to make sense.

CHAPTER 50

CARA

Cara stood in the olive grove at the Villa Rosa, the simple white dress that she had prepared for her wedding day falling to her ankles and flowing softly down the slim contours of her body. The Nazis had stripped the pale oyster silk curtains from the Contessa's bedroom and left them on the floor; Raf had decided that one of them would make a perfect wedding dress.

Cara had worked tirelessly along with Raf and Alphonso to help the local farmers tidy up after the Nazis had left rubbish strewn everywhere; the remains of dinner on dining-room tables, dirty dishes, rotting food, filthy floors, beds soiled, swastikas painted on walls, treasured ornaments scattered underfoot, glasses smashed, and baths lined with rings of dirt.

Every day, the villagers and farmers still trudged up the hill to the villa, relying on water from the old pump that came from the underground spring to survive. It had become a morning ritual to stand by the pump and fill their buckets.

There had already been two deaths from typhoid in the valley, and Raf was beside himself with worry that if the water was not turned on again, soon disease would spread, and the loss of life could be palpable. Every day, he went into Cortona, working with the new, hastily established local government being set up along democratic lines. Raf had accepted a position as one of the leaders and spent his evenings in the Contessa's office, talking with the group of local men who had been nominated alongside him.

Now, Raf stood at the open door to the summerhouse, an elderly priest from the village next to him. He was wearing a simple white shirt and black trousers. His face was neatly shaven, and his eyes melted with warmth when Cara threaded her way through the olive groves and stood at the beginning of the makeshift aisle.

She turned and looked up at the man who had agreed to walk her down the aisle in replacement of her father. Alphonso. She squeezed his hand.

Ahead of her stood groups of villagers and farmers, families who had walked up the hill for the wedding, having known Cara and Raf since they were children.

Cara walked toward the man she had always loved.

They had stayed up late every night, talking about how he felt working alongside the locals, looking after them, representing them.

Cara looked up at the loyal friend who had walked her down the aisle. "Thank you for everything, Alphonso," she whispered.

He smiled down at her. "It is my pleasure, Cara," he said, his voice soft, right back to her. And he placed her hand in Raf's.

That evening, there was dancing on the terrace. Cara had set candles out on the long bridal table, and the wedding guests had enjoyed what was almost a feast at the tables that Alphonso had set out on the terrace. The local farmers whom Cara had helped to safety during the liberation of Cortona had insisted on bringing up whatever crops they had left. And one of them had appeared, grinning, with a brace of chickens that he had managed to hide in a coop. A group of locals had cooked in the villa kitchens and had served the chickens with cream, spinach, and peppers, the cream from the Contessa's few cows that had survived on one of her tenant farms.

Cara danced slowly with Raf, her arms entwined around him, and her cheek resting on his shoulder. The day had been perfect, and although they both had people missing, they had each other.

One of the villagers had brought his violin and was playing a steady waltz. But when Raf pulled back, and hesitated a moment, Cara stilled. Opposite her, the Contessa stood dressed demurely in a pale green silk dress.

They had worked tirelessly these past weeks, skirting around each other, the Contessa remaining silent about what had transpired between them on the day Cortona was liberated. There had been no mention of Bruno Klein.

Raf had been reserved with his mother at first, but then, in recent weeks, he had seemed more open and relaxed around her, and Cara had not mentioned the fact that the Contessa had pointed a gun in her face, nor had she repeated anything about a child or seen the Contessa's slim figure showing signs of a growing bump.

Now that the wedding ceremony was over, she knew that she had been so swept up in the romance of being in love that she had avoided facing the difficult situation with the woman who was now her mother-in-law.

Raf melted away into the crowd of guests, and in the flickering candlelight, the Contessa appeared even more beautiful than usual.

"Thank you," the Contessa murmured. "Thank you for loving my son."

Cara inclined her head. "It is not very difficult."

The Contessa clasped her hands together and held Cara's gaze. But her expression was so earnest and her eyes so wide with honesty that Cara took a step backwards.

"There is something I need to tell you."

Cara waited.

"I had not been able to tell you until now," the Contessa went on. She took in a breath and glanced around the terrace at the happy locals. "Bruno Klein was taken prisoner by the Allies recently, and now I am free to tell you the truth. I was not collaborating with the Nazis," the Contessa said.

Cara froze and she frowned.

"I have been spying for the Allies, relaying information about the Nazis' top-ranking officials based in Florence, in an effort to provide more information about fascism to the British government." The Contessa shook her head. "I am not proud of the way I behaved on the day Cortona was liberated, but I had no choice. Had Klein suspected that I held any feelings of loyalty to you, he would have murdered us all."

Cara's hand floated to her mouth, and she looked about for a chair, her knees suddenly weakening. She wanted to sink to the ground.

"The war is not over yet, Cara," the Contessa went on. "I have not been able to reveal what I have been doing until now, because Bruno was in Florence until it was liberated." She lowered her eyes, and her dark eyelashes swept over her translucent cheeks. "I had to wait until the mission was complete."

"But he said you were pregnant?"

"Unfortunately, the only way I could keep him away from me during those last weeks was to tell him I was expecting his child. I'm afraid he had an inflated sense of protectiveness toward family, and so, I fabricated a pregnancy and feigned ill

health to protect myself from his attentions. You understand..."
The Contessa's mouth worked, and to Cara's horror, the older
woman's eyes misted over. "It seems I am far too good an actress
for my own good, and I am truly sorry for the heartbreak that I
have caused to you and Raf. But as for a baby, no. I am not as
foolish as that."

Cara stared at her employer, her mother-in-law, and a wave
of respect, and sympathy and downright awe swept over her for
this brave woman who had borne what no woman should ever
have to bear. Impulsively, she reached out and threw her arms
around the Contessa. Who cared about Mussolini's class
distinction? Who cared about what everybody thought she had
done? The truth was more important. For the first time in what
felt like forever, the Contessa had opened to her as an equal.
They had both been fighting for their people, in the only way
they knew how. "I am sorry for what you went through," Cara
said, meaning it.

The Contessa stepped back and held Cara at arm's length.
"I am truly sorry for what this war cost you as well, Cara. And I
want you to know that you are part of my family now. But we
will never forget your proud tradition, and the immense bravery
of your father in standing up for his neighbors."

Cara nodded. Papa would've loved being here today. All of
it. But she was certain that he was watching over them. She was
certain that he knew.

CHAPTER 51

Spring sunshine filtered into the bedroom, and Raf had left a miniature rosebud on his pillow, just as he had every day since they had been married. Cara gathered the tiny flower and placed it in the vase next to her bed. He had promised her that he would do this every morning for the rest of their lives. Raf was spoiling her, bringing her up breakfast of freshly baked bread when she woke well after him every day, and there was always a little pot of homemade preserves.

Last night, they had stayed up late celebrating. Milan had been liberated at last, Mussolini captured, and Italy was free after more than twenty years of living under a fascist regime. Together, she, Raf, the Contessa, and Alphonso followed the progress of the liberating Allied army and the partisans, listening to the radio, reading the sporadic newspapers that the Contessa managed to get, as Florence and then the northern cities were finally released from Nazi rule.

Cara stretched back on her pillows, her lips forming a contented smile. The movements in her womb fluttered like a butterfly, adding to her joy. Her baby was due in the late summer, and already she was imagining welcoming a child into a world that now felt full of possibilities again. A world that was completely different from the one they had been living in the year before.

Cara slid out of bed and moved across the room to the dressing table. She picked up one of the silver-backed brushes that Raf had given her as a wedding gift. They had belonged to his grandmother, and he had assured her that his beloved nonna would have adored her. The Contessa had hidden them in a box at the back of the garden from the Nazis and had carefully brought them out after Raf proposed.

Cara ran the brush through her long dark hair, smiling at the fact that the color was blooming again in her cheeks. She wandered over to her wardrobe, wrapping her simple cotton dressing gown around her waist.

And then it happened.

An explosion rocketed through the room. It was close enough to rattle the windows, leaving the entire building shaking to its foundations.

Cara rushed out into the hallway in her white dressing gown, almost falling down the stairs that led to the first floor. Alphonso was in the entrance hall, and she flew with him down to the villa's gates.

A landmine had exploded on the road opposite the villa's driveway.

And Raf lay right next to it. On the road beside him, freshly picked flowers were scattered everywhere. Blood trickled from his mouth, and his eyes were open and glazed. There was a huge crater in the road, right in the spot where Luigi Santino had attacked Cara.

Raf was not moving.

Cara rushed toward him. "*Mio amato*," she tried to shout, but her voice was hoarse, and came out as a whimper.

He did not respond.

"*Mio amato? Please,*" she whispered, and sobbing, she cradled Raf's body.

Cara felt a soft pair of arms embracing her. The Contessa was here, right with her. Cara reached up and took Raf's mother's hand.

CHAPTER 52

ANNIE

Annie made her way across the terrace. Couples chatted at tables decorated with candles, and in the distance, the woman Annie had recognized instantly, was sitting down, while a waiter held out her chair.

Annie came to a stop by the woman's table. "Ms. Ricci?"

Katarina Ricci stopped what she was saying and glanced at the waiter, as if she was hoping that he would rescue her.

But he stood back like a true professional, a white napkin folded over his arm.

"Ms. Ricci, please. Will you come and join us at our table?" Annie said, hurriedly. She rushed out the words before the waiter walked away. She appealed to him. "Could you pull up another chair for the signora with us?"

Katarina Ricci seemed not to know where to look. She fluttered her hands about in the air, her large eyes looking at the waiter in alarm.

And there it was, again. Annie's hand curled around her

phone in her pocket. She held it like a talisman, like a link to the past that had seemed so elusive until now.

"No," she murmured. "Please. I only came for a quiet meal. I have no need for a table front and center of the restaurant. I am perfectly happy back here."

But you are missing out on so much, hiding away.

Signora Ricci reached for her napkin and began unfolding it and placing it on her lap. "A glass of prosecco please," she said to the waiter.

"Of course," he said politely. "But I am happy to set an extra place at the table overlooking the valley if you would both be happy for me to do so," he said.

Annie looked at him and nodded.

Katarina Ricci continued playing with her serviette, shaking it about, and glancing around, her eyes running here and there like quickfire.

Annie leaned down next to the older woman's chair. She reached into her handbag and pulled out the old leather-bound diary that had once belonged to Cara Cartazzo and placed it carefully on the table in front of Signora Ricci.

Katarina Ricci cleared her throat and poured a glass of water from the bottle on the table.

"Please, Ms. Ricci. Will you come and talk to me some more?"

"I don't know anything," the older woman said. But her eyes danced over the leather-bound volume, and she drew the water to her lips, only to put it back down. Her hands interlaced the napkin around and around until it was tied in knots.

Gently, her own hands shaking, Annie leaned forward and took the napkin out of Katarina's hands. "Please, I mean no harm."

The waiter was back again with a sophisticated couple. "This is the last table we have," the waiter said, looking pointedly at Annie and Katarina.

The couple hovered behind him, clearly not used to being relegated to having to wait for anything. The man looked at his watch, and the woman sighed.

"Kindly tell us whether you would like to share a table upfront?" the waiter asked Katarina. "It is up to you. There is no pressure."

Katarina Ricci looked heavenwards. She muttered something and pushed back her chair.

Annie led the older woman through the restaurant as if she were in a dream. What she was going to say, she had no idea. But she slipped into her chair and leaned close to Luca.

Luca simply stared at Katarina Ricci and frowned.

Annie laid Cara Cartazzo's diary on the table like a talisman. "Half the pages are torn out," she said. "And this has been stored in your bookstore for decades."

The waiter brought Katarina Ricci a glass of prosecco. She stared at it, then picked it up and took a long sip.

"This diary is from the time of the liberation of Cortona in July 1944." Annie leaned forward and lowered her voice. "Ms. Ricci, Luca's mother also has ties to the Villa Rosa. Her father was the gardener at the villa during the war. Over the past few days, she has been trying to research more about this and she learned from Ernesto in the village café that scores of local farmers sought refuge in the basement under your bookstore during the war. Are you the daughter of the owner of the bookstore?" Annie asked.

Katarina toyed with the stem of her glass. "No. I married her son, Nino. Eventually." She lifted her chin. "But his mother was there during the liberation. She helped save many people in the valley, along with—"

Annie pulled out her phone. She flicked through her photographs to the one she had taken of the photo of Evelina Messina that was in the upstairs bedroom in the Villa Rosa.

"Ms. Ricci, forgive me, but tonight you are all dressed up, and the resemblance is remarkable…"

Annie bit on her lip, her chin was wobbling. It had all come down to this. A photograph of a mysterious Contessa, and a diary with the pages ripped out of it. Two women, from an era so momentous that even her generation was still struggling to understand.

Katarina Ricci turned, her eyes huge and expressive, toward Annie. "Before I married Nino Ricci, my name was Loretta Katarina Messina—and my darling, I knew who you were the instant you walked into my store."

Annie felt Luca's hand landing on top of hers. She choked up.

"My mother was the Contessa Evelina Messina's secretary, Cara Cartazzo. And that is her diary. She tore out the missing pages. She and my grandmother Evelina Messina raised me after my father, Rafaeli, was killed by a landmine in the fall of 1944. I am sorry. So very sorry." Katarina Ricci's hand shook as she placed her glass back down.

Annie took in a shaking breath. She sat back in her chair, unable to focus, for the green valley in front of her was all a blur.

"My grandmother was devastated after losing her youngest son, Annie. He was the only family she had left, and she became a recluse after the war. I am afraid that my mother, Cara, became a recluse too, grief-stricken in the aftermath of losing my father, Rafaeli. My mother rarely left the villa's grounds at all. So, rumors abounded about whose child I was, and my grandmother would not acknowledge them. She simply said they were beneath her. She was quite stubborn, and absolutely refused to address the gossip."

"I see," Annie breathed.

Katarina lowered her eyes. "But I am sad to tell you that those rumors affected me so badly that I felt I never fitted in here. Families were always circumspect about me, and when I was a teenager, my peers taunted me as well. I think it was because I was so blond, so like my grandmother, and nothing at all like my mother, Cara, to look at. I always felt as if I was in the wrong place, that I was undeserving... That if my mother had not been expecting me, my father might never have gone out to pick wildflowers for her, while she rested in the mornings in bed."

Katarina pulled a tissue out of her bag and blew her nose.

Annie caught Luca's eye. *At least we know now...*

"My mother remained in the Villa Rosa, and the Contessa Evelina, her mother-in-law, insisted that they raise me together. They did so quietly. You see, my grandmother refused to talk of the war after she lost both her sons. But I had to live with those rumors. All my life. I couldn't put you through it."

Annie nodded. She could not think of any words.

"I am sorry. But it was a tragic time. It was after my father's awful death that the gardener, Alphonso, left the Villa Rosa because he had always adored my father and he could not bear to never see him again. My mother, Cara, always spoke so highly of him." Katarina smiled bravely at Luca.

Just then, Emilia slipped into a chair next to Katarina. Annie glanced across at Luca, and he held up his phone. He had messaged his mother to come from her hotel nearby.

Annie could not move...

"Throughout the war, my grandmother, the Contessa, had been working for the Allies as a spy," Katarina went on. "The British government wanted her to gather information about the true nature, goals, ideals, and tenets of fascism in Italy, and on the activities of the Germans occupying Italy. So, she agreed to have an affair with a top-ranking Nazi to extract the information the Allies needed from him. Everything Bruno Klein told her, she reported to the British. But... there were rumors that she fell pregnant to him. Awful rumors, that she had a child."

"Sandro's grandfather, Nicolas, left Italy due to conflict with his mother about her fascism," Annie said. "Sandro is adamant that he is the true owner of the villa, and that it should be passed down from the Contessa Evelina's eldest son Nicolas, who is Sandro's ancestor."

Katarina shook her head. "That is the most appealing narrative for Sandro, my darling," she said. "But the truth is, it was Nicolas who had the fascist opinions, not his mother the Contessa. She argued with *him*. And he left."

Annie sank further back in her chair.

"Annie, I am so very sorry for the impact this has had on you. I only wanted you to be away from this, to have a free childhood. Not tainted by this war." Katerina wiped a stray tear from her cheek. "But I have messed it up. I hope you did have a happy childhood, Annie?"

Annie moved her hand away from Luca's, floundering. "I... Why didn't you tell me who you were the moment I walked into the bookstore?"

Katarina pressed a palm over her lips. "It was too much... I'm sorry." She took in a couple of hitching breaths.

"So, Nicolas had the fascist views, not the Contessa?" Emilia asked, her tone gentle.

Annie sat back in her seat, glad of Emilia's diversion.

Katarina nodded, her chin trembling. "Nicolas fell out with his mother at the outset of the war and moved to Venice, where the Contessa's family owned a palazzo on the Grand Canal. After the war he became a successful businessman in America and never contacted his mother again. Not even after my father was killed... I think Nicolas perpetuated the rumors that his mother had given birth to a Nazi's baby to justify his abandoning her."

Annie raised her hand to cover her mouth in horror. She felt torn. Torn by the fact that the woman sitting opposite her had never contacted her, and the fact that she could be the mother that Annie had never had.

"Sandro is not the heir to the villa," Katarina said. She lifted her chin and spoke with great dignity. "You are the heir to the villa, Annie. The Contessa made me her heir. But," she shook her head sadly, "I am happier in my late husband's bookshop. You see, I adored him, even though I did not meet him until I was in my late fifties."

"So, the bookshop owner, Signor Ricci, is not Annie's father?" Emilia said. "Forgive me, I came into the conversation a little late."

"When my grandmother died, I was devastated," Katarina said. "I was extremely close to her and had lived at the villa all my life. I decided to travel after the Contessa's death because I needed to get away from Italy. I needed to get away from the dreadful rumors that still surrounded her after she died." Katarina shook her head.

"Sometimes, distance is the only way to cope," Emilia said.

Annie sat quietly, suddenly overwhelmed with fatigue.

Katarina nodded. "I went to California, and sought work in a bookstore in San Francisco for a few months. There was a lovely customer who used to come in often to buy books on architecture."

Annie's hands stilled, and her heart began to race again.

Katarina wiped her eyes, and her voice wobbled. "Oscar Reynolds was a charming and gentle man, and I loved him very much. He was an architect."

"*Papa*," Annie whispered. *Papa.*

Katarina nodded, and she took in a deep breath and went on. "Oscar's wife, Valerie, was diagnosed with terminal cancer. He was devastated and heartbroken, as was I due to the loss of my grandmother. We were both grieving, and we started spending time together." Katarina lowered her eyes. "I am afraid things got a little out of hand, and when I found out I was pregnant..." She shook her head. "I was in no state to raise a child. I was in my mid-forties, and I simply felt that I would give a child a boring and dull life. I did not feel worthy of being a mother. And the Messina family did not need any more scandals. So, I returned to Italy after I gave birth to you and, with my mother Cara, lived on in the Villa Rosa, until she moved to a retirement community in Florence... My mother loved the villa more than me. It always felt like her and the Contessa's home. Not mine. After my mother left, the Villa Rosa did not feel the same to me. I couldn't live there, so I left it to you. I wrote to Oscar and told him. It was the least I could do."

Annie brought her hand up to rest against her throat. All this time she had thought she had lost her mother, Valerie, when there was another mother, her birth mother, back here in Italy. Maybe she would never understand why Katarina had not reached out to her, and maybe she would never truly understand the complexities of the Second World War. She certainly found Nicolas hard to comprehend, and Sandro, but now, would the Villa Rosa truly have a chance to come back to life again, to come to a new life that was even better than what was here before the war?

"Perhaps it was because my grandmother had let the rumor that I was her child, born out of her affair with a Nazi, sweep through the village, without contradicting it... when she died, and her strong protection of me ended, I felt alone in this identity... So, I went and worked in the bookshop in Cortona, fell in love with its owner—in a different way than I had loved Oscar—and I never lived in the villa again. I locked it up and left it alone. Wondering, perhaps, whether you might return."

Annie was silent. The way she had felt when Papa died had astounded her. It *had* felt impossible that she had not been his daughter. And she knew now that she was. And that the Contessa was her great-grandmother. The woman who had bravely been a spy for the Allies and refused to acknowledge the rumors that must've swirled around her for the rest of her life. Rumors that had been fueled by her own son, Nicolas, her grandson, and great-grandson Sandro!

"I can tell you that my mother, Cara, adored your father Alphonso," Katarina Ricci said to Emilia. "She said he was marvelous."

"So, he must have been close to your parents, Cara and Rafaeli. Perhaps he viewed them in a fatherly way. He was always a darling," Emilia said.

Annie felt Luca's presence strong and sure next to her, and she sensed the trust that her grandmother, Cara, had felt for his grandfather, Alphonso, also a gardener. The warmth of Emilia and Katarina completed this little circle around her, and now, she did not feel alone at all. There was still so much to work through, but knowing the truth was a strong start.

Katarina reached out and placed a hand on Annie's shoulder. "The villa is yours. I will talk to Sandro and tell him the truth. It is time. I know that. You don't have Nazi blood, Annie. Far from it. And I am only delighted that Alphonso's grandson has come back again after all these years."

"Welcome home, both of you," Emilia said. "Annie, and Luca."

Annie turned to Luca, and her heart warmed at the kindness in his eyes, and there was something else there too. And she knew what it was. After all this time, it was hope. The valley spread, sleeping and peaceful below, and the fairy lights twinkled on the terrace.

Luca reached out under the stars and placed his hand in hers.

A LETTER FROM ELLA CAREY

Dear reader,

I want to say a huge thank you for choosing to read *An Italian Secret*. If you did enjoy it and want to keep up to date with all my latest releases, just sign up at the following link. Your email address will never be shared, and you can unsubscribe at any time.

www.bookouture.com/ella-carey

An Italian Secret is my twelfth novel. I feel like things have come full circle—a dozen books, a dozen stories. This book is reminiscent of my first novel, *Paris Time Capsule,* which is also set around an old, abandoned building. I have long been fascinated by enchanting old houses. As soon as I walk into them, I am imagining what might've happened there in the past. All those people, and all their stories...

I remember the first time that I had this feeling. I was eight years old, and we were touring an old house in New Zealand. The tour guide asked if anyone would like to play the grand piano, which was called Olveston. My father pointed to me, and I played a Slavic march. I remember it to this day!

But there is another connection that is deeply personal to this book for me. Recently, I had the opportunity to read my father's Second World War diaries. As many of you will know from reading *The Paris Maid,* my father was an RAAF pilot in the Second World War who dropped parachutists over France. His diaries have been with another family interstate, and when I was visiting recently, I finally had the chance to start reading them. But they come with a twist... several pages and paragraphs have very neatly been cut out with scissors, and I'm not sure who did this. My mother? I think it might have been. I wonder if these people knew what sort of books I would write! But he was a talented writer, and his descriptions of London are quite wonderful. I am looking forward to reading more of his work. I have been sharing pictures of these diaries on my Ella Carey Facebook page, and you are very welcome to have a look at them if you would like to.

I hope you loved *An Italian Secret* and if you did, I would be very grateful if you could write a review. I'd love to hear what you think, and it makes such a difference helping new readers to discover one of my books for the first time.

I love hearing from my readers—you can get in touch on my Facebook page, through Twitter, Goodreads, or my website.

Thanks,

Ella x

www.ellacarey.com

 facebook.com/ellacareyauthor
twitter.com/Ella_Carey

ACKNOWLEDGMENTS

My deepest thanks to my editor, Maisie Lawrence, for your hard work and dedication to bringing this book to life. Thank you for talking the story through with me, for your brilliant editorial suggestions, and for your overall guidance in my novels. Thank you to everyone at Bookouture, especially my copy editor, Jade Craddock, proofreader, Anne O'Brien, and to Sarah Hardy for doing such a wonderful job with publicity for the book. Thanks to Debbie Clement for the gorgeous cover design, and thanks to the marketing team, especially Melanie Price and to Mandy Kullar for coordinating the copy editing, proofreading and final files. Thanks to my family and friends, especially to one of my oldest friends, Kelli Jones. This one is for you. Thank you to my readers, and to the bloggers and reviewers for your time spent reading and reviewing my work. I am enormously appreciative, and value you very much.

Made in the USA
Middletown, DE
27 December 2023